ONE DAY WITH YOU

SHARI LOW

Boldwood

First published in Great Britain in 2023 by Boldwood Books Ltd.

A CIP catalogue record for this book is available from the British Library.

Paperback ISBN 978-1-80426-867-4

Large Print ISBN 978-1-80426-863-6

Hardback ISBN 978-1-80426-862-9

Ebook ISBN 978-1-80426-860-5

Kindle ISBN 978-1-80426-861-2

Audio CD ISBN 978-1-80426-868-1

MP3 CD ISBN 978-1-80426-865-0

Digital audio download ISBN 978-1-80426-859-9

Boldwood Books Ltd
23 Bowerdean Street
London SW6 3TN
www.boldwoodbooks.com

To Caroline Ridding, the best editor and friend a writer could have.
To Jade Craddock and Rose Fox, who go above and beyond to turn my words into books.
And to John and our brood, who are, as always, everything. xx

ON THIS DAY WE MEET…

Tress Walker, 42 – interior designer, originally from Newcastle, Tress was working in Glasgow on the day she met her husband, Max. Now pregnant with their first, much-wanted child.

Max Walker, 35 – finance director at Bralatech, raised in Weirbridge and has now returned to live there with his wife, Tress.

Noah Clark, 35 – paediatrician at Glasgow Central Hospital, Max's best mate since childhood, just celebrated his eleventh wedding anniversary with his wife, Anya.

Anya Clark, 34 – sales director at Bralatech, daughter of an American dad and Scottish mum. She met Noah and Max on her first day at Glasgow University and has been with Noah ever since.

Nancy Jenkins, 66 – widowed after losing her husband of over 40 years, Peter, to cancer. School dinner lady, head of Neighbourhood Watch, force of nature.

Eddie Mackie, 66 – Nancy's teenage boyfriend.

Val Murray, 66 – Nancy's friend since they met at Weirbridge Primary School a million years ago. Married to Don, the love of her life, and heartbroken that her wonderful man has dementia.

Big Angie, 50 – another of Nancy's friends and neighbours, a bus driver and fond of sharing her menopause woes with the world.

Johnny Roberts, 66 – an old school pal of Val and Nancy.

Dr Cheska Ayton, 35 – head of A&E at Glasgow Central Hospital and Noah's friend since medical school.

Dr Richard Campbell, 44 – head of ICU at Glasgow Central.

Georgina and Colin Walker, both 66 – Max's free-spirited parents, who live in Cyprus and love a good time.

9 FEBRUARY 2023

8-10 A.M.

1

TRESS

The two furrowed stress lines between her husband's brows made Tress smile. If he carried on like this, Max Walker was going to have aged ten years before their baby was born.

He dropped his overnight case on the hall floor and reached for her, his voice matching the anxiety on his gorgeous face. 'Damn, I don't want to leave you. It's such crap timing. I'll be back tomorrow night, though, so keep that little guy safe and warm in there and tell him to take it easy.'

The beeping horn of the taxi outside forced a pause before she could reply. Out of habit, Tress's hand rested on the space-hopper-like curve of her belly. 'Stop worrying. We've still got three weeks to go, and if he's anything like me, he'll be late because he's floating around in there having a chill time to himself.'

It still gave her a thrill to say 'he'. They'd thought about waiting until the birth to find out the sex of the baby, but only for about five minutes before dismissing the idea. Max was desperate to know because he couldn't bear the suspense, and the interior designer in Tress wanted a heads up so she could start dreaming about the perfect nursery. 'Now go. Have fun. Stop fretting. Be brilliant. Then come home tomorrow night and feel up your wife,' she teased, stretching over her bump to kiss him on the lips.

His hand came up to her neck, cupping it, his thumb gently rubbing her cheek. 'Do you have any idea how much I love you, Tress Walker?' he murmured, his face still so close she could smell the lingering minty aroma of his toothpaste.

'Enough to get me knocked up and saddle yourself to me until the end of time.'

He grinned as he kissed her again. 'Exactly. It was your romantic outlook and sweet tender words of love that got me.'

Another beep from outside.

A giggle caught in her throat as she nudged him away. 'Yeah, well, doesn't sound like your taxi driver is feeling the love, so move your impressively tight arse so he'll stop pressing that bloody horn. Nancy next door will take him out with a swift right hook if he carries on with that.'

She wasn't wrong. There was a reason there had been no crime in the street since Nancy Jenkins became the head of Neighbourhood Watch for this area of Weirbridge. Originally a quaint village just outside Glasgow, it had now grown to the size of a small town, and with that came the occasional crime. Nancy, who was the most big-hearted sweetheart of a woman, unless she was crossed, knew everyone in the village, so, even though she officially qualified for a pension, a bus pass, and a quiet life, she'd volunteered to protect the streets. Even the local scumballs were terrified of the woman who once caught a thief trying to break into her house and threatened to puncture his kidneys with her knitting needles if she ever saw him again. He was relieved when the police took him into custody.

Another beep.

'Max stuck his head out of the open front door and shouted, 'Okay, okay.'

Tress's heart melted at the sight of his still-furrowed brow. The conference couldn't have come at a worse time. As the head of finance for a relatively new tech start-up, he usually worked from their Glasgow office, only travelling to the head office in London once or twice a month. Today, there was an extra journey south for their annual conference, but they'd already agreed this would be his last trip before the baby was born.

Tress still marvelled that such a sexy guy could have such an unsexy job. Craziest thing was, for someone who could nail a part-time gig as a catalogue model, Max had absolutely no cocky self-awareness or raging ego at all. His genuine niceness and easy laugh had been the first things she'd noticed about him – after his kind eyes and libido-swirling smile – when she'd literally bumped into him in Greggs in Glasgow city centre a few years before. She'd been up in Scotland sourcing tweed for the corporate interior design company she worked for and had popped out of their supplier's city-centre office for a quick walk around George Square, then nipped into the baker's for a bite to eat. It was the worst cliché ever. They'd both reached for a tuna crunch baguette at exactly the same time, and then did that whole, 'You have it,' 'No, you have it,' for at least a minute, before she finally conceded to his chivalry. She got the tuna crunch baguette and the guy at the same time. Meeting the love of her life, marrying him within a year and moving to Scotland hadn't been on her life-bingo card, but here she was, and she hadn't regretted it for a single second.

Her shoulder rested on the door frame as she watched him go down the path, throwing a wave and blowing her a kiss as he climbed into the Skoda Estate for the fifteen-minute ride to Glasgow airport. The taxi took off down the street and she sighed as she made her way back through to the kitchen, then picked up her mobile phone to call her husband's stunt double.

Nancy answered on the first ring. 'Is the baby coming?'

'That's the first thing you've said every time you've answered the phone for the last three months. No, he's not coming.'

'Oh, thank goodness.' There was genuine relief in Nancy's voice as she went on, 'I've just got my perm lotion on and if I have to wash it out now, I'll end up looking like I've had an electrical accident while I was changing the plug on my Dyson charger. Did I mention I've got a new Dyson?' she said, in her very best faux-posh voice.

'Only once or twice. Or every time I've spoken to you since you got it,' Tress ribbed her.

Tress could picture the scene in Nancy's kitchen, in the next cottage along the road, and it reminded her so much of the kitchen activities in the house in Newcastle that she'd grown up in. They'd moved to the brand-new housing estate there when Tress was a toddler, along with a wave of other families who'd been high on the council waiting lists, and her mum, Julie, had lived there until she'd passed away a few years before. She'd had the same neighbours all her life, families who'd all raised their children together, mothers who'd become friends and support systems through ups, downs, divorces, remarriages, tears, celebrations, pain, happiness, loss and love. Many of them were single mums like Julie, most of them had at least one job, sometimes two or three, and they'd all pitched in to help each other out. It wasn't perfect, but Tress was grateful for every one of those women. They'd helped raise her, made her childhood as happy as possible, and they'd cared for her mum right up until breast cancer had taken her at the far too young age of fifty-five.

Nancy had a band of friends who were just like that. In fact, Tress was 100 per cent certain that Nancy's pal, Angie, would be sitting at her kitchen table right now, handing perming rod papers to her other pal, Val, who would be winding the rods into Nancy's salt-and-pepper locks. Nancy could never replace her mum, but she'd taken Tress under her wing when she'd moved here, and Tress was beyond grateful for her care, her laughs and her ferocious love of hand-made baby clothes.

'I was just telling Val and Angie that I've been stress knitting my heart out this last few weeks. I hope we're in for a shite summer, because this baby already has fourteen cardigans, twenty-two hats and enough mittens to survive a childhood in Siberia.'

A cackle of laughter made a muscle in Tress's side twinge, and she winced.

'What? What was that?' Nancy demanded.

'Nothing!' Tress insisted.

'There was something. Your breathing changed.'

'Nancy, your skills are wasted in the school canteen. Is it too late for you to become a police interrogator?'

'Probably not, but I'd miss the caramel cake. Anyway, love, are you sure you're okay?'

'I'm fine. I was just phoning to say that's Max away to the airport, so you're in charge.'

Nancy didn't even attempt to hide her disapproval. 'Still can't believe he's leaving you at a time like this.'

'It'll be fine! I've still got three weeks to go and he's only going away until tomorrow night. I'll be okay.'

'I know, but that doesn't mean I won't spend the rest of the day moaning about that handsome big lump of yours to Val and Angie.'

'I wouldn't expect anything less...'

'Although Angie says if you ever tire of him, she'll take him off your hands.'

That made Tress smile again. Angie was a fifty-year-old bus driver, who took no nonsense from anyone and went everywhere with two hand fans, complaining to anyone that would listen about 'the change'. She'd chew mild-mannered Max up and spit him out before lunchtime.

'Tell her thanks for the offer, but I'll hang on to him for now.'

'Sorry, Angie, she's keeping him.' Nancy informed one of her nominated hairstylists, before returning to Tress. 'Anyway, call me every two hours and don't you dare do anything strenuous. I've got my night out tonight, but I'll check on you before I go. And then tomorrow, I'll bring some lunch over for you and we can Netflix and chill as you young ones say.'

'Nancy, that means something different from what you're thinking...'

Nancy wasn't listening. 'Val was saying there's a new film on there with that Piers Brosnan. Och, I wouldn't throw him out of bed for leaving crumbs with his Garibaldis, let me tell you.'

Tress could hear the laughter in the background. 'You lot are incorrigible. I'm hanging up now in case my child can hear through the womb and is being corrupted as we speak. Thanks, Nancy.'

'Any time, pet. See you later. And don't forget to tell me how lovely my perm is. Extra points if you say I look like that Madonna lass. We're about the same age, and I reckon underneath all those fillers and her leather knickers we're dead ringers. Cheerio.'

With that little deadpan of conversational wisdom, she was gone, leaving Tress amused as always. After her mum had died, there had been times when Tress thought she'd never have that feeling of belonging again. Julie was an only child, and so was Tress, so with no other family, it really had been just the two of them. Meeting Max had changed that. She was hundreds of miles from where she grew up, but now she had a husband, his friends had welcomed her with open arms, and the women in this village had befriended her. This was Max's world, but it really felt like it was hers now too.

Tress dropped her phone on the kitchen table, then made a cup of tea. Plenty of milk. No sugar. It was barely 8 a.m., but she'd been awake for an hour and already she felt exhausted. Knackered but happy pretty much summed up her whole pregnancy. She took her 'I'm Not Pregnant, I Just Ate All The Pies' mug – a gift from Nancy, naturally – through to the desk she'd set up in the conservatory, looking out onto the back garden. Room designs were spread all over the vintage mahogany desktop – her favourite find from a day of second-hand furniture shopping in the charity shops on Weirbridge high street.

Max hadn't minded in the least that she had wanted to put her own stamp on the place. He'd bought this house off his parents for a knockdown price when they'd retired to Cyprus a few months before she'd met him. The timing was perfect. He'd moved back from a flat in Glasgow's city centre to the house he'd lived in as a kid, and Tress had quit her job to move from Newcastle to Scotland.

When she'd arrived in Weirbridge, Max had carried on working, while Tress, with her creative talent for interior design, had focused on the house, transforming the ordinary three-bedroom detached cottage into a gorgeous, open-plan barn-style conversion. Tress had done loads of the work herself: wallpapering, tiling, painting, ripping out the kitchen and bathrooms, re-upholstering and renovating gorgeous old pieces of furniture she found in antique warehouses and second-hand shops. If she didn't know how to do it, she learned. She'd even done manual labour with the builder as he opened up the ceilings, knocking down walls, laying walnut floors throughout and exposing the original brickwork. The end result was gorgeous. Sometimes she still couldn't believe that she lived here. Or that, inspired by the gorgeous home she'd created, and years of experience working in design for corporate workplaces and hotel chains, she'd left the company she worked for back on the Day of The Tuna Baguette Tussle, and had now set up her own interior design business.

She'd kicked off with one client, but word of mouth had helped it grow year by year and she now had a solid client base and enough jobs booked in to keep her busy for the next few months. She specialised in creative solutions on modest budgets and did everything, from new window treatments to full house designs. She hadn't matched her old salary just yet, but combined with what Max brought in, they were doing fine. Having the baby would be an adjustment, but the plan was to try to fit working from home around the baby's schedule, and Nancy had volunteered to babysit when she had client meetings, as long as they were in the afternoons, after she'd finished her shifts as a dinner lady at Weirbridge High School.

Tress was about to sketch out some new design ideas for Mrs Galbraith of Cloverleaf Cottage's bay window, when another yawn made something in her side twinge. She gave it a rub and was rewarded with a swift kick in the abdomen from the baby. Mrs Galbraith's bay window could wait. Clearly, her little guy was demanding a quick rest before starting the day.

Over on the kitchen table, Tress's phone beeped to signal that the battery was just about done, so she retrieved it and plugged it into the charger on her desk, then gently, she lowered herself down on to the cream linen sofa (£50 second-hand, and £50 for the fabric she'd used to recover it herself) and closed her eyes...

She wasn't sure whether it was the sharp pain or the ringing of the landline that woke her, as, in her sleepy fog, both things seemed to happen at exactly the same time.

Tress let out an involuntary yelp, as she rolled her body up into a seated position, just in time for her waters to break. Oh Jesus, no. Not yet. It wasn't time. She still had three weeks. Too early. Too early. TOO FRICKING EARLY. Her heart was racing, fear shutting her reactions down, forcing her limbs to freeze, her mind to blank out. This couldn't be happening. Not now. She needed help.

'Max!' The shout had crossed her lips before she remembered. Max wasn't here. He was on his way to London. And why was that damn phone still ringing?

Deep breath. Deep breath. Calm the panic. Breathe. Make your lungs work. In. Out. It would be ok. That would be Max, calling her before he got on the flight, and she could tell him to come back, that the baby was on the way. Okay, she could do this. There was no choice.

Using every bit of strength her arms possessed, she pushed herself up and off the sofa, but she'd only made it a couple of steps when the phone stopped ringing and the answering machine clicked into action.

'Hello, this is Agnes Wellington from Stonybridge Place. Nancy Jenkins gave me your number because I'm looking to re-do my living room and get a wee bit of glitz in there. If you could call me back on this number, that would be lovely. It's...'

Tress didn't listen to the rest, as, at that exact moment, a surge of anxiety almost took the legs from under her. She gripped the edge of the desk, as her gaze went to the clock on the wall above it: 9.50 a.m. Oh, thank God. Max's flight wasn't until 10.40, so he would still be at the airport.

She picked up her mobile phone and... Damn, the screen was completely blank. She traced her way to the end of the cable and saw that it had fallen out of the USB socket on the wall. Modern fricking technology was not her friend.

She grabbed the landline and... Crap, what was his number? It was saved on her mobile, but the company he worked for had changed their phone supplier the month before and she didn't have the new number memorised yet.

With trembling hands, she scrambled for the piece of paper she'd written it on, just as another sharp pain made her gasp. Oh bugger. This wasn't good. Gritting her teeth, she tried to breathe through the pain, but decided that whoever said that helped hadn't had a bowling ball wedged between their internal organs at the time.

As soon as the worst of it passed, she grasped for her notepad and somehow managed to punch the numbers on the front page into the landline phone.

'Hi,' he answered immediately, before it had even rung at her end.

'Max, it's me! I think the baby is coming—'

Her husband's voice cut her off. 'This is Max Walker of Bralatech. I'm sorry I can't answer your call, but please leave a message and I'll get right back to you.'

Nooooooo!

Desperately fighting to quell the panic rising in her throat, Tress was about to repeat her urgent update when the front doorbell rang. That might be him. Maybe he'd forgotten something. Or had a sixth sense and turned back. She hung up the phone, just as something thudded onto the floor of the hall. Mail. It was the postman.

Easing herself back down onto the sofa, Tress groaned, fighting back tears as she tried to steady her breathing.

This. Could. Not. Be. Happening. Where was Max? Why wasn't he answering his phone? How could she reach him? She needed him here now. Because she was pretty sure that today was the day she was going to deliver their child.

2

NOAH

No amount of coffee was going to make Noah Clark feel better this morning, but he was going to give it a try anyway. He put his mug onto the chrome shelf of the coffee maker, put in an espresso pod and pressed start, then gritted his teeth as the crunching noise of the machine made his eyeballs rattle.

He was in no state to be awake at 8 a.m. and many factors had contributed to this, kicking off with a week of night shifts on the paediatric ward at Glasgow Central Hospital, followed by too many beers after his first day off yesterday. That might have been bearable if he hadn't fallen asleep on the sofa after a huge argument with Anya last night. He only had himself to blame for that. He'd got his hopes up. Thought that he could get to the bottom of what was going on with his wife. Fix the distance that had come between them. Given that he'd spent the night contorting his six foot two inch frame onto the two-seater sofa in the TV area of the kitchen, it clearly hadn't worked.

He dropped his head on to the cool marble of their kitchen island, then jerked it back up as her towering heels click-clicked into the kitchen, the noise of the stilettos hitting the granite floor tiles like bullets being sprayed from an assault rifle. Or perhaps that was just how it sounded in his head.

It took a moment to identify the other noise that came with it, but when he lifted his eyes and squinted in her direction, he saw that it was the wheels of her white Samsonite cabin case. Her matching tote bag was propped on top, her handbag was draped over the handle and her laptop case was now on the floor beside it. Of course. She was going away today for... for... Nope, nothing was coming. Some work trip. He was pretty sure it was on the calendar, so therefore he was 100 per cent sure he wasn't going to ask her about it because it would just open up the 'you don't pay any attention to my career' argument they had on a fairly regular cycle these days.

It was almost as frequent as their depressingly familiar debate about starting a family. That one seemed to be cropping up way too often too, and last night descended into another variation of, 'This is my time and I'm not going to give up my life to stay home and get piles, miserable and covered in pureed carrots for the next two years.'

Yep, that old chestnut had reared its head yet again. Noah had no idea how it had even started. Not that it mattered. It seemed like these days they could turn a 'good morning', into an apocalyptic battle to the death. Thus, he opened with a conciliatory, gentle, 'Hey.'

'Hi,' she answered, in a tone that was as clipped as the sound her heels were making.

'Look, can we talk? I'm sorry about last night.'

He genuinely was. It had all started off so well. He'd cooked dinner for their wedding anniversary, he had the candles lit, John Legend playing in the background, all the things she loved. He'd made his speciality: an amazing fish stew that his Ghanaian grandmother had taught him and Anya adored. He'd timed it for eight o'clock, figuring she'd definitely be home by then. Their anniversary was on the calendar too – their eleventh year of marriage, making it almost fifteen years since they'd met on her first day at Glasgow University. Noah had been in his second year of medicine, and Max was at the same stage of his finance degree, when the new business student had wandered into the freshers' event with undisguised curiosity on her perfect face. Back then, she'd had cornrows down to her waist, and the wide-eyed interest of someone who still couldn't quite believe she was there.

Max Walker, his best mate since they were kids, had spotted her first and nudged Noah in the ribs. 'I think I just fell in love,' Max had whistled, shaking off his Jaeger bomb hangover as she approached their table. They were both on the basketball squad and had got saddled with a two-hour slot on the recruitment desk for the sports teams.

'Yeah, for the tenth time this morning,' Noah had replied, smirking as he pushed Max behind him and gave the new girl his best smile. She was stunning. Almost six feet tall. The easy movement of an athlete. Brush-long lashes framing brown eyes that he could stare at for at least the next hour or so.

Naturally, Max had turned on the charm and went straight to Olympic qualifying-level flirtation. That had always been the order of things. Max was first in there with everything, jumping before he could think anything through. He was always the one to ask a new girl out, the one who signed them up for skydiving, the one who arranged the impromptu party, and the first Noah knew of it was when twenty people and a boom box arrived at the door of their shared flat.

This time, however, Anya wasn't buying what he was selling, despite the good looks and the buckets of charm. Instead, she'd given Noah a side-eye of curiosity. 'So what about you, then?' she'd asked him, and there was a hint of teasing there. 'Do you think I should sign up to devote my entire life to sport?' Her sexy American accent had sealed the deal for him. He found out later that she had an American dad and a Scottish mum. They'd met when her dad had come to Scotland to work on a joint project with the RAF at their Leuchars base, near St Andrews. They'd fallen in love, married, stayed in Scotland while her dad remained posted there and then returned to the USA when Anya was three, coming back and forward a couple of times a year to visit her mum's family in Fife. Her parents were still in America, but Anya had wanted to return to her mother's roots when it was time to choose her university. Noah knew right then that he would be eternally grateful for that decision.

He would never normally flirt with someone he'd just met, and definitely not someone that Max was clearly attracted to, but this woman was irresistible. 'Absolutely not,' Noah had replied, as Max had stared at him, open-mouthed. 'I think you should leave at least one night a week to go out with me.'

Max had thrown his hands up. 'That was the worst line I've ever heard. Don't fall for it,' he'd warned her, 'or you'll need to listen to his crap chat. The last woman he went out with died of boredom. Seriously. It was tragic. They've written medical papers about it.'

'Welllll…' Anya had dragged the word out, leaving the two of them hanging. 'I've a pretty high pain threshold, so maybe I'll take my chances.'

Invoking the two weeks he'd stuck out a drama class, Max literally fell off his chair, faking a faint, while Noah had jumped up and punched the air, making Anya laugh.

'Are you two always like this?'

Noah couldn't wipe the grin off his face. 'Nope. Most of the time, I ditch him for a better offer. Fancy a drink at the bar?'

They'd bailed on Max and by the end of the afternoon Noah

had asked Anya if he could kiss her. She didn't say no. So that's how it had happened. Noah. Anya. Together ever since. Despite the theatrics, Max had been genuinely happy for them and for every one of the next fifteen years, Noah had been grateful she'd chosen him that morning.

Last night, he had been playing that first day back in his mind when the clock had hit 8 p.m. By eight thirty, he was trying to salvage a fish stew. By nine, he'd opened a beer and binned the stew, realising that Anya probably wouldn't come rushing home for their anniversary dinner anytime soon. He'd thought about calling Max up to see if he was at the gym, and then joining him for their regular daily session, but, for once, he had zero motivation. He'd even considered heading over to eat cake and watch endless home décor shows with Tress, but he didn't want his angst and disappointment to burst her pregnancy bubble of joy. Instead, he'd revisited his old medical-student diet by throwing a pizza in the oven and flicked through the channels on the TV, settling for an old war movie. Anything to make his life seem less shit by comparison.

When Anya had come in at 10 p.m., he'd barely been able to look at her.

She'd frozen in the doorway, taking in the scene in front of her. The deserted romantic table. The used pots and plates by the sink. The blown-out candles.

'Noah, I'm sorry, you should have said…'

'I didn't think I needed to. Happy Anniversary,' he'd retorted, hating himself for the brittleness in his voice. This wasn't him. He didn't do petty shit. Max had been telling him his whole life that he was too laid-back for his own good. Well, not tonight.

Anya was still on the defence. 'I had to work late. We've got a big pitch coming up next week and I'm going to be at the conference tomorrow so…'

He'd stopped listening, her rising agitation telling him that she was departing the apology train and going straight on the defensive express.

'Do you still want this, Anya?'

She'd leant down and taken off her black patent heels, one by one, losing at least four inches in height. The tight skirt of her suit restricted her steps as she'd walked to the table and poured what was left of the red wine into the glass next to it. She'd definitely upped her wardrobe game since she'd gone to work at Bralatech as head of sales and marketing. Max had tipped her off that the vacancy was coming up, and she'd approached the directors and nailed it down before it was even advertised.

He could see she was stalling, so the four beers he'd already consumed took over and prodded her on.

'Do you still want us – marriage, children, life, growing old together?'

'Of course I do,' she'd answered wearily, barely meeting his gaze as she perched on the arm of the sofa. 'Look, it's just that this job means something to me. I'm good at it, Noah. I love it. And, right now, it takes everything I've got.'

'And our family?'

He knew he sounded so petulant, but this was two years of waiting for her to come back to him, of putting their lives on hold for a job that claimed all of her time.

'Noah, I can't do this right now. I'm too tired. Yes, I want to be married. No, I'm still not ready for kids.'

'What if I am? We said we'd start trying last year and you've been stalling ever since. If you still want it, I'll wait, but I'm just not sure that it's what you want any more, now or ever.'

How many times in the last year had they had this discussion? And she always said the same thing: 'Yes, I still want to build a family with you. No, not yet, but soon.' Every day at work, he was surrounded by kids, by families, and every day he knew that it was something he wanted. They'd always said they'd start a family in their early thirties. They were thirty-five now and he was past ready. Apparently, Anya still wasn't.

'Then maybe we need to talk about whether or not we have a future,' she'd blurted.

Woah. The shock had made his head snap up.

'What?'

'I don't know if I want kids any more. I just don't know if I see that for me. And if it's a deal-breaker for you then...'

She'd trailed off, leaving the implication there loud and clear. He'd bitten his tongue, even in the red-wine haze, determined not to react with words he'd regret. In a way, at least she was being honest. That was a relief... until she'd started to backtrack.

'I'm sorry, I didn't mean that. Look, I can't talk about this now. I'm tired.'

She'd got up from the couch, her long, athletic body moving with such grace his heart hurt to watch. God, he loved her.

'Don't walk away, Anya. Stay. Talk to me.'

She had kept on going, until he'd heard her feet pad up the stairs, to their bedroom. He didn't follow. Instead, he'd got the first of several more cans of beer from the fridge, and stared at the TV while he drank them, blinded to what was on the screen, just needing some kind of noise, a distraction to stop himself crumbling into a confused, emotional heap.

The TV was still on eight hours later, when he'd woken with a groan, after a night on the couch. He'd run through the conversation, forwards, backwards, rethinking it, desperate to talk about it, but her appearance with her suitcase made it clear that discussion wasn't going to happen any time soon.

Now, despite the aching head and the groaning bones, he had to try.

As she picked her car keys up from the kitchen island, he tried to go for some crumb of resolution.

'Anya, wait... I'm sorry. Can we talk? Five minutes...'

'No. I've got a flight to catch and I'm not going to miss it. I'm taking my car and I'll park it at the airport. We can talk when I get back.'

That was it. With another spray of bullet heels across the tiled floor, she was away. Gone.

Shit.

Noah poured another coffee and took it outside, the February morning chill soothingly cool on his aching head. It was only when he went back inside for yet another refill that he spotted the laptop case, still lying on the floor. Anya must have missed it when she'd grabbed her other bags and shot out the door. He immediately called her to let her know, but it went straight to voicemail.

He didn't leave a message. If she was pissed off with him, there was every chance that she wouldn't bother listening to it.

He tried a different tactic. Anya never went on any flight without speaking to her assistant, Cara, immediately before and after. She was way too work-obsessed to potentially miss a message from a client.

Noah flicked through his contacts for Cara's number, then dialled.

'Hello, you've reached Bralatech Sales Department, this is Cara, Anya Clark's assistant, speaking, how can I help you?'

Damn, that was a mouthful to get out every single time that poor woman answered the phone.

'Hey, Cara, it's Noah.' He'd met his wife's right-hand woman a few times over the years at staff parties, and he spoke to her regularly, usually when she called to let him know that Anya was going to be late home or miss something they had planned because she was held up at work. Anya clearly found it easier to get someone else to do her dirty work. Cara knew it. He knew it. On the bright side, it meant that they'd struck up a bit of a conspiratorial alliance.

'Hey, Noah, how are you doing?'

He was desperate to say he was hungover, pissed off and fairly sure his life was imploding, but instead he went with, 'Great, yeah. How are you?'

'Ah, you know. Overworked and underpaid, but don't tell your wife I said that.'

Despite the thudding head, that made the corners of his mouth turn up. 'Preaching to the choir. Listen, can you give Anya a message for me?'

There was a pause and he realised Cara was probably wondering why he didn't just call his wife himself.

'It's just that… eh… her phone is going straight to voicemail and I'm about to go out for a run, so I thought you might speak to her before I reach her.'

He was lying through his teeth, but he just hoped Cara didn't have some kind of telepathic superpowers.

'Erm, yes, but… the thing is, I won't be able to pass on the message until she's back in work on Monday.' The reluctance and hesitation in her voice was unmistakable. It was the sound of someone who was telling him something that was going to cause a problem, but there was no way out of it.

'Yeah, I know she's not in today.'

'Oh, thank goodness,' she blurted, clearly relieved that she hadn't spoken out of turn. 'I'm sorry. I thought we were having one of those movie moments there, where I tell you your wife isn't where you think she is, and it causes a whole big drama. I was seeing unemployment in my near future.'

Noah forced himself to laugh. 'Nope, you're safe. I knew she wasn't in the office today, but I just figured she'd call you.' This was becoming a lot more complicated than he thought it would be and he wasn't entirely sure that he understood why.

'I don't think so. She said that the spa they're going to doesn't have any signal, so she wouldn't be calling in. I'm so glad she's getting this time to relax with her sister. Feels like she never leaves this place, so I'm sure she'll enjoy the break. Anyway, what was the message?'

Silence. For a full five seconds. Then a panicked, 'It was...' He froze. More silence. His brain wasn't computing, and he was trying desperately to make sense of this. Cara was super-efficient and she didn't get things mixed up. That meant she was providing him with accurate information. But there was a problem. His wife had told him she was going to London for a work conference.

His wife hated spas.

His wife didn't have a sister.

Therefore, if she wasn't at a conference, or somewhere she hated, with a fictional family member, then where was she?

'You're right! I'd completely forgotten about that. No worries, but if she does call in, ask her to give me a ring.'

Noah put the phone down and lowered his head until it once again made contact with the surface of the kitchen island.

So it was going to be today. Today was the day that he was going to find out what was really going on with his wife.

3

NANCY

'She's such a nice lass, that Tress. I've known Max Walker since he was a boy and he was out in that back garden climbing those trees,' Nancy said, nodding out the kitchen window to the branches of the oaks that had grown over her fence. 'I'm so glad he married someone lovely. Urgh, the fumes in here would knock you out.'

The smell of ammonia in her kitchen was enough to alert the dogs on the bomb squad, so Nancy gave a quick blast of Glade coconut air freshener to balance it out. It was her favourite. Always reminded her of the holidays she'd had with her Peter to the Costa Del Bloody Expensive back in the eighties. They'd slap on the coconut tanning oil and fry for four hours, before nudging each other to turn over like spit roast chickens. Then they'd come home and they'd feel like the sexiest things out until the peeling started and they were back in woolly jumpers, smelling of aloe vera and putting a tenner a week away for the next holiday. Those were good times. They just didn't know that, years later, they'd pay an unimaginable price for all those weeks in the sun. Skin cancer. It had taken Peter from her before he'd even had a chance to retire and visit all the other places they'd been planning to go to.

'Ouch! Jesus, Val, you pinged that perming rod like it was yer knicker elastic,' Nancy yelled, making her pal cackle with laughter.

'Oh, doll, if ma knicker elastic was going to ping, trust me, it would echo right down the hall,' Val said, shaking her generous curves as she pulled the clear plastic head cover over Nancy's head. 'Right, that's you. Thirty minutes at gas mark 5 and yer going to come out looking like this.' Val held up the box, which had a beautiful woman of about thirty on the front, her luscious red curly locks framing her exquisite face, all high cheekbones and lips like booster cushions.

Nancy stood up and made for the kettle. 'Aye, only if you attach a bulldog clip to the back of my head at the same time, because I haven't seen my cheekbones since the eighties.'

'It can be arranged,' Angie offered. 'I'm also thinking of offering home liposuction with ma Hoover. There's mugs out there that will fall for anything.'

Chuckling, Nancy flicked on the kettle and reached up to the cupboard above it for the biscuit tin. It wasn't even ten o'clock, but she'd been up since five, so, in her world, it was almost lunchtime. She took the lid off the tin and put it in the middle of the table, then got three mugs and lined them up next to the kettle. Tea for her and Val, but Angie brought her own stuff, some green herbal potion that was meant to help with her flushes. Nancy figured it was all nonsense, but if drinking a concoction that smelled of spinach made Angie feel better, then she was all for it. A glance at her friend located the source of the draught that was chilling the room. That woman and her flushes were a danger to society.

'Angie, I love you, pet, but if you don't close that window, I won't make it tonight because I'll be in Glasgow Central with hypothermia. Then you'll have that on yer conscience. You'll lie awake, thinking "Nancy Jenkins lost her last chance for a bit of romance, because I was flapping my arms out her window first thing in the morning."'

Angie reluctantly closed the white wooden sash window and reached for her hand fans. 'It could be worse. My sister, Joanie, said her vagina was on fire for months. Don't know how I'd get that up to yer kitchen window to cool it down.'

Val shook her head and deadpanned, 'Not without pulling a muscle.'

Nancy added a grave, 'Or traumatising the postman.'

That set the three of them off again.

As soon as Nancy had made their drinks, all three took their seats at the table. The butterflies in Nancy's stomach, however, weren't so keen to take a break. What in the world was she thinking, going to this shindig tonight? The fiftieth anniversary school reunion of Weirbridge High School. Back then, most of them had left after fourth year, when they were sixteen, so this was the class of 1973. She may as well go dressed in a sandwich board that said, 'Lord on a bike, I'm ancient' on the front and 'Pure saddo trying to recapture her youth' on the back. She was a sixty-six-year-old woman, widowed four years now, and if she went through with this, then she'd be meeting many people she hadn't seen since dinosaurs roamed the earth. Including Eddie Tyrannosaurus Mackie. Her first love. Last seen at the Weirbridge High School end-of-year dance in June 1973. But the less said about that night, the better.

'You sure you won't change your mind about coming tonight, ma love?' Nancy asked Val for the hundredth time.

And for the hundredth time, Val shook her head. 'Doll, I'm excited for you, you know that. And I'm thrilled there's a wee flirtation going on there for you. But I'd rather poke my eyes out with a stick and that's the end of it.'

Nancy knew better than to press, but she hadn't given up yet. She figured that if she roped Val into as much of the preparation today as possible, eventually she'd break down her pal's stubborn streak and Val would come along for curiosity's sake, if nothing else.

Unaware that Nancy still had a plan to recruit her as a wing-woman, Val reached over to the biscuit barrel in the centre of the table, took out a caramel wafer, unwrapped it and changed the subject. 'You know, a hairdresser appointment might have been a better idea this week, lovely. I haven't given anyone a home perm since all of our pals wanted to look like Olivia Newton John singing, You're The One That I Want.'

'I know, but it was a panic decision in ASDA at six o'clock this morning. I couldn't sleep, so I decided to pop out for a loaf. Came back with a perm kit, make-up I don't know how to use and a pack of three pairs of knickers that turned out to be those thong things. They're going back. I'd do myself an injury. Oh, and I forgot the bread,' Nancy admitted. 'Thanks for stepping in, though, you two. There's not many people I can call at seven in the morning in a fluster. It's just that... well, last time Eddie saw me, I had long curls that made me look like a windswept surf chick. Now I just look like I've been standing for a week and a half in a monsoon. You saved the day, girls.'

Val waited until she'd swallowed a large bite of her biscuit before answering. 'No worries. Our Mark is over spending the day with his dad, so you got me at a good time. To be honest, it was lovely to get out of the house for a wee while.'

'How's Don doing, Val?' Angie asked.

Nancy was a regular visitor to Val's house, about ten minutes down the road, so she already knew the answer to that. They'd been at school together and had been friends ever since, but they had never lived in each other's pockets. Over the years, they'd had countless nights out, the four of them – Val and her husband, Don, and Nancy and Peter – and they always had a smashing time. With her and Peter not having children, they tended to go somewhere sunny on special occasions like Christmas, New Year and birthdays, but if they weren't abroad, then they loved to meet up with Val and Don, and their kids too.

Nancy had been there for Val when her daughter, Dee, had been killed by a drugged-up driver a few years back and Val had been the first person to knock the door after Peter's diagnosis. And when Val's best pal, Josie, had passed away – och, she was irreplaceable that one – Nancy had stepped in to be there for her too. They'd hoped that was the end of the heartache, but then Don, Val's strapping big, lovely man, had developed dementia and, mother of God, that was a brutal thing. It was shocking how just a couple of years with that disease could change a man from a healthy, active, fun-loving riot to a poor, confused soul. Hard for Val too. Not that she'd wavered for a single second. Nancy had watched in awe as she just took the whole situation by the scruff of the neck and dealt with it. The two women had become rocks for each other over the last year or two, and now they saw each other most days.

Nancy listened into the conversation as Val answered Angie's question. 'You know it's a bugger of a thing, Angie,' Val said with a sigh. 'Some days, he doesn't know my name and other days he's my old Don, and we can laugh like we used to. Those days are getting less now, but they keep me going. That and our Mark. He's been a gem, he really has. He pops in every other day and spends one of his days off with his dad every week. I don't know what I'd do without him.' Val got wistful for a moment, then, true to form, immediately snapped out of it. 'Anyway, I've got a couple of hours to myself and I'm not for dwelling on the sad stuff, so give us the latest then, Nancy. What's Romeo been saying now? Are his loins still lusting for you?'

'Not with his arthritis,' Nancy shot back, before realising she couldn't make her cheeks stop grinning. Who'd have thought it, at her age? When Peter had passed away, she'd never dreamed she would ever feel a spark of attraction or excitement ever again. And then Eddie Mackie had got in touch.

There had been a Facebook page for the reunion tonight. At first, Nancy had ignored it, consumed with sadness that Peter wouldn't be here to share it with her, but then the message had dropped into her inbox just over a month ago.

Nancy, it's been a long time. That doesn't mean I've not thought of you often, so it was great to see your name in this group. I live in Canada now, been here almost fifty years. I'm long divorced, but I've got three sons that don't half make me proud. Didn't think I'd make it back for the reunion, but as luck would have it, I'm over in the UK that week for my granddaughter's wedding in London. I've changed my flight, so I'll fly up to Glasgow on the day of the party, then on back to Canada the next morning. I don't have to tell you that it would be great to see you.
Hope you're well.
Eddie.

Her heart had just about stopped. Eddie Mackie. And he'd thought about her over the years, just as she'd thought about him – although she'd never admit that out loud for a second.

Every single day, from the age of 14 to 16, if anyone had asked her, she'd have said she was going to spend the rest of her life with Eddie. But, in the end, fate had other plans and they included Peter. They'd had a happy life together, but it wasn't without its sadness and heartache and occasionally Nancy wondered if it would have been different if she'd spent it with Eddie. She'd never know. There was no going back, and even if she could, she wouldn't change her time with Peter for anything. He'd been her whole world and she was grateful for it. That said, she couldn't deny that she was curious to know Eddie again. Purely as friends, of course. At least, that's what she'd thought when she began typing out a reply to the message. Her two index fingers battered out the letters and she wished, not for the first time, that she'd done what her mother had wanted and taken a typing course at the local college when she'd left school.

Eddie, what a lovely surprise. It's been such a long time. And lovely to hear you have grandchildren. What a blessing that must be. Sadly, Peter and I never did have children, but we had a wonderful life together. He passed away four years ago now. I'm sorry if that's a shock. I'm not sure how far news from Weirbridge travels these days.

She'd paused and gone to make a cup of tea after writing that much, stomach in knots and not sure what else to say before she pressed 'send'. That's if she was even going to reply. She still hadn't decided and part of her brain had been screaming at her to just ignore the message, ignore the reunion, and ignore the bloody nerves that were making her stomach swirl. In the name of all that was holy, she was too bloody old for this nonsense.

She'd brought her mug of tea back to the computer in the spare room and sat back down, rereading what she'd written a dozen times. *Press delete.* This was a waste of time. The man lived in Canada. What was the point of even considering starting up any kind of contact with someone on the other side of the world. She was sixty-six. A bit too long in the dentures for a pen pal. *Go on, Nancy, press delete and be done with this*, her brain screamed.

But her fingers, the traitorous digits that they were, had a different idea. They kept typing...

I'm hoping to make it to the reunion, so it will be nice to see you there if your plans don't change. What a blast it'll be to get the whole gang back together...

She'd paused, realising that sounded beyond naff. She'd picked up the phone to call Val for help, then realised it was midnight and changed her mind. Instead, she deleted the last line and went for something that didn't make her toes curl.

I'm hoping to make it to the reunion, so it will be nice to see you there if your plans don't change. Take care and safe travels, Nancy. Xx

Nope, no xx. Delete, delete.

Take care and safe travels, Nancy.

She'd thought that would be it. End of conversation, and then small talk over some sausage rolls at the reunion tonight, but no. His next message to her had pinged back almost immediately and it had been the start of a conversation that had stirred up the kind of feelings she thought she'd left behind on the day she'd last said goodbye to him.

She'd chosen Peter. She'd never believe that was a mistake, but could she and Eddie have had something more than a teenage romance? In a few hours, she was going to find out.

Today was the day that she was going to see the first love of her life again after almost fifty years. And there was a piece of her heart that had begun to think it might not be too late for them to give each other another chance.

4

MAX

As soon as Max jumped into the taxi, he turned around to wave at Tress, and kept that going until they turned out of the end of the street.

'Motorway is busy, mate, so it's going to take us a good half-hour to get to the airport,' the driver informed him, making no effort to hide the half-eaten roll packed with a thick Lorne sausage, onion and tomato sauce that was sitting on the passenger seat next to him.

The sight of it made Max glad he'd sat in the back. He was a low-carb, healthy-eating, one-cheat-day-a-week kind of guy. He had no idea how anyone could put that stuff in their bodies every day.

'Listen, there's been a change of plan, pal. Can you drop me at the hotel down at Erskine Bridge? Car park there will do fine.'

In the rear-view mirror, he saw the driver look back at him with a raised eyebrow, but he didn't respond. It was none of his business, and Max didn't need to justify himself to anyone. Although, swapping the airport for a hotel car park a few miles away from it did give off dodgy vibes. The driver probably thought he was a drug dealer, keeping his movements fluid to escape the cops.

The truth wasn't much better.

He hated lying to Tress. She didn't deserve it and especially now, with the baby on the way. He just reminded himself that what he was about to do today was for Tress and for his boy. For their family.

Just thinking about his son released a gush of pure joy that made Max's shoulders relax. He was going to be a dad. An actual father. And he wasn't going to be the kind of disinterested, half-hearted, distracted dad that he'd grown up with. Nope, no way. Max's priority was going to be the son who would be here in a few weeks' time. It wasn't even a question, because he'd been on the other side of that situation and he never wanted his boy to feel the same way as he'd felt for so much of his childhood.

To the outside world, Max had had the best life ever as a kid. Two fairly comfortably off parents who had spoiled him with every material thing he could want. He'd been the first of his pals to get a BMX bike. The first to have a disco in the garden for his birthday. The first to visit Disneyland and the first to get a tenner-a-week pocket money.

He was the luckiest kid in the village and he didn't keep quiet about it, so most people had no idea that the material stuff was just compensation for two parents who didn't give much of a toss about anyone but themselves.

His chiselled jaw clenched as one of many memories from the locked box of his childhood found a way to escape and bubble to the surface.

It was Christmas Eve, sometime in the mid-nineties. He was seven or eight and he could barely sleep, too excited about what was coming the next day. He knew his friend, Noah, would still be up because his family celebrated on Christmas Eve too and Max had begged his mum to do the same. For once, she hadn't given in to him and Max didn't understand it. When he lay in bed, staring at the ceiling, and heard the sound of all his parents' friends arriving, he realised why. They were having a party without him. His mum had always loved him the most, and now she didn't.

There were voices he recognised. There was Nancy next door and her husband, Peter. He was a cool guy. He'd fixed the chain on Max's bike for him when it came off the week before and he'd given him 50p for sweets.

Max wasn't sure what time it was when he heard voices outside in the garden. A man, whispering, and he knew straight away who it was. The only person who'd be outside in the cold was Santa, but he wasn't going to be able to leave any presents because there were so many people in his house. He tiptoed over to the window and peeked out the side of the net curtain to see…

It wasn't Santa. It was a man he didn't recognise. And his mum. And they must be really cold because they were hugging.

Max ducked back down under the window in case they spotted him, and he only popped his head back up again when he heard Nancy from next door outside and she didn't seem happy.

'You never bloody change, Georgina, do you? Not even now that you've got a boy in there that needs a decent mother,' Nancy hissed, just loud enough for him to hear.

His mum didn't like that. She spoke in her angry voice, the one she used if he got out of bed during the night. 'Don't you dare speak to me like that, you—'

'You what? Georgina, you don't have a single thing you can say to me, so take that boney backside of yours and shoogle it right back into the kitchen before your husband comes and punches that one's lights out.'

Max really, really, really hoped that wasn't Santa after all, and next morning, he was sure it hadn't been, because he woke up to a whole room full of presents and everything was great again.

Years later, he'd realised exactly what had been going on and discovered that his dad wouldn't have punched anyone's lights out, because he'd probably been too busy inside hitting on someone else. He knew it. They knew it. Hell, the whole village had known it.

Max had been in his teens when he'd found out that his parents had an unspoken agreement that they could find pleasure wherever they wanted, just as long as the other one didn't have to see it or hear about it. His dad had broken that little nugget of parental knowledge to him when he'd turned eighteen and he'd taken him out for an official pint for the first time. Turned out he was having a fling with the barmaid at the Weirbridge Arms.

Sometimes Max wondered if that was why they'd buggered off to Cyprus as soon as they'd retired, but, more likely, they'd just run out of opportunities for extracurricular activities and had gone in search of fresh exploits.

The taxi pulled onto the M8 and immediately got stuck in the gridlocked lanes, the irritation shaking off the melancholy of Max's step back in time. Ach, it was all bollocks. He wasn't down with the theory that you could blame your adult mistakes on your childhood. Nope, too convenient. It would be so easy to claim that his upbringing had left him with a skewed view of fidelity that shaped his views on monogamy as an adult, but that would be a lie and he knew it. If anything, it should have made him more determined to choose a different path.

He'd been a bit late getting to that junction, but he'd finally arrived. He was going to be better. He just had to tie up a few loose ends first.

He took his phone out and fired off a text to the person he was about to meet, deciding not to call in case it was a bad time. That done, he pulled out his laptop, fired it up and answered his emails. Anything to keep his mind busy and off the fact that he'd just left his pregnant wife and lied about where he was going. He'd make this up to her. He definitely would. And then he'd never do this again. This was it. It was all fun and games when the stakes were lower, when they were all just messing around and making the most of life, but it was different now. He was going to be a dad. He had his son to think about.

Max felt the tempo of the car change and glanced out of the window, to see that they were coming around the slip road off the motorway. After a couple of hundred metres, they took a sharp right into the car park of the hotel. Over in the right-hand corner, he spotted her.

'Just over there by the Range Rover, pal,' he told the driver, whose gaze had already been captured by the gorgeous woman climbing out of the car.

The driver swerved across, coming to a halt a few feet away from where she was standing, leaning against the car. It could have been a scene from a Range Rover ad.

'On account?' the driver asked him, making an understand-able assumption that someone in a suit, with the whole briefcase thing going on, would probably have a corporate account with his firm.

'No, cash is good,' Max replied, pulling forty quid from his wallet, hoping a £10 tip was enough to ensure that that the driver wouldn't be pissed off and moan to anyone that would listen about the bloke who booked a taxi to the airport, waved goodbye to his wife, then changed the destination and had a dodgy drop-off with a cracker of a woman in an out-of-the-way hotel.

'Cheers, bud,' the driver chirped, tucking the cash into a wallet that he then stashed in the glove compartment.

Max grabbed his stuff, climbed out, then waited until the cab drove off before turning to the woman waiting for him, arms folded, hint of a smile on her face.

A switch inside him flipped on. For the first decade or so that they'd known each other, he could honestly say there was no sexual attraction. Now there was way too much and it had changed him into a man that he no longer wanted to be. He didn't want to be the scumbag who was cheating on his pregnant wife with someone from work. He didn't want to be the scumbag who was cheating on his wife with an old friend from uni. He didn't want to be the scumbag who was cheating on Tress with his best friend's wife.

Max stepped forward, saw Anya's eyes flaring as they met his, dancing with the danger that, somewhere along the line, they'd both become addicted to. There had been guilt too, but they'd both managed to lock that away in another of those mental boxes, telling themselves that no one would ever know, that no one would get hurt, that they both knew exactly what this was. A moment in time. One that was ticking to an end.

'You ready for this?' he asked her, hating himself for wanting her so much that he'd gladly check into this hotel right here and now and they'd be naked before the taxi driver was halfway back to Weirbridge. But no, they'd both decided that what they'd had together deserved a better ending than that. That's why they'd planned this trip to their favourite place, to be together one last time, to say goodbye properly to this secret part of their lives.

They both accepted that this was the right decision. Anya would move on with her life with Noah, and Max would relish every second of the fatherhood that was ahead of him. This 'Max and Anya' thing would always just be a game they'd played for a while, one that ended in a draw and then was archived, never to be replayed.

'One last dance?' she asked, her pillow-perfect lips forming a teasing smile.

'One last dance,' he told her, taking her hand, all thoughts of real life – of Tress, the baby, Noah – blocked out by the here and now.

Reality had been put on pause, but only for a short while.

Because today was the day that his affair with his best mate's wife was going to end, and tomorrow he was going to start being the husband, father and friend that the people he loved deserved.

10 A.M.–12 NOON

5

TRESS

Tress took a calming breath and tried to focus and squash the panic. She could do this. This happened to other women all over the world, and they managed fine. It just hadn't happened to her yet.

Getting pregnant had been the biggest surprise and thrill. At forty-one, she'd been pretty sure that ship had sailed, so when the blue line had appeared on the white stick, she'd been over the moon. They both had. Max had always insisted that having kids wasn't top of his priority list, and that he didn't mind at all if they didn't have them, but she wasn't convinced he meant it. His reaction to the news had confirmed her suspicions that he'd been playing down his desire for a family. He'd been so thrilled, and ever since then, he'd been even more attentive than usual. This was the most wonderful time of her life, and she had no idea what she'd done to get this lucky. Although, granted, her timing didn't feel too lucky right now. Why couldn't this have happened before Max left this morning?

Okay, stay calm, Tress. Take another breath. This is going to be fine. You've got this.

The mobile phone on the charger next to her finally sprang into life. 10.10 a.m. Okay. Calm. There hadn't been another contraction since the first one twenty minutes ago, so she had a little bit of faith she wasn't about to give birth on the floor. At least, not in the next five minutes.

Her first call was to the hospital. Max had put the phone number of the maternity ward at Glasgow Central into her phone on their first visit there.

For a horrible long thirty seconds or so, she thought he'd entered the wrong number because it just rang and rang. She was just about to give up when it clicked.

'Hello, Maternity, how can I help you?'

'Hi, this is Tress Walker. I'm under the care of Dr Greyson. I'm not due for another three weeks, but my waters have broken, and I think I had a contraction.'

'Okay, how long ago was that?'

The voice on the other end of the phone was calm and pragmatic and that helped. See, women did this every day. No need to panic. No. Need. To. Panic.

Tress gave all the details, being reassured at every stage that she was doing fine. It was the last question that just about caused her to unravel.

'And are you on your own at the moment or is someone with you?'

Tress felt her bottom lip start to tremble. 'I'm on my own. My husband left for a business trip this morning...' She stopped herself, fearing she would either cry or spill out her life story. 'But I can call my neighbour.' She realised how pathetic that sounded and wished she'd said 'friend'. Which was true, too. What with the renovations and starting up her own business, she hadn't had a chance to meet many people since she'd moved here, but she hoped that joining mother and baby groups would help that. In the meantime, she had Nancy, who was definitely so much more than just her neighbour.

'Great. Well, normally I'd say to wait and see when the next contraction comes, and when they're half an hour apart, make your way in. But, for once, we have a couple of spare beds on the ward, so since your waters have broken and you're on your own, just make your way here this morning and we'll get you admitted.'

'Thank you. Thank you so much. I'll do that.' The kindness in the nurse's voice almost turned her to mush, but again Tress held firm. No rush. She had a plan. Now she just needed a husband.

Another call to Max's phone had the same result as before. Straight to voicemail. He must be at the boarding gate by now and maybe they didn't have signal there. Or perhaps he'd already boarded and was waiting on the runway. She did a quick calculation in her head. Even if he took the flight to London, and got there on time, as long as she caught him before he left Heathrow airport, and there was a return flight he could jump on (a lot of 'maybes' but she was naturally optimistic), then he could be back here by around two or three o'clock. By then she'd have been in labour for just over four hours, which was nothing for a first baby. She'd read all the info. First babies usually had longer labours and she hadn't even had a second contraction yet, so maybe this was all going to work out. She'd rest. Take it easy. Wait a little while longer before heading into the hospital and hope she got hold of him before she went and that he'd be back here before the little one was even close to making an appearance.

She called him again, this time listening to his voice on his recorded message, then adding her own.

'Hey, honey, so it looks like our little guy didn't want to wait around after all. My waters broke and the hospital has said that I should make my way in, so I'm going to get organised and do that.

I'll have my mobile with me, so please give me a call back and let me know when you can get here. Thanks, baby. Love you. And your boy is gonna love you too.'

Gingerly, taking it easy, Tress went through to their bedroom, showered in the ensuite and then dressed in fresh clothes. Feeling better, she picked up the baby bag that lay, half-packed on the cream ottoman at the end of the bed, trying desperately to remember what was still to go in there. Everything for the baby was packed already, as were her pyjamas, change of clothes, maternity bra and most of the other things she'd found on the lists that she'd copied from the mum and baby websites that she'd been scouring for the last month or so. That meant she just needed to throw in the things she had still been using on a daily basis: toiletries, phone charger, her Kindle – not that she antici-pated having any time to read. She collected it all, threw it in and then tentatively picked up the bag.

On the way back through to the kitchen, she paused at the room next to theirs. The nursery was decorated in shades of grey, white and pale blue and looked exactly like the one she'd envi-sioned in her mind for years on the outside chance that she should ever, in the future, have a child. She'd drawn it up as soon as they'd found out they were having a boy at their eighteen-week scan and then set about turning her imagination into reality.

Max and Noah had spent a whole Saturday last month building the cot. There had been swearing. Shouting. Exclama-tions of frustration. A finance director and a doctor, yet they couldn't work a fancy screwdriver. And then a victory lap when those two blokes, with not a single construction gene between them, had finally managed to build something that didn't look like it would collapse in a stiff breeze. It had taken a six-pack of beer and two hours of the second *Top Gun* movie on Netflix to restore their emotional equilibrium.

If she'd had to pick the perfect mate for Max, it would have been Noah. She could see why they'd been friends since they were children. They were one of those duos that perfectly balanced each other out. Max was spontaneous, unpredictable, an adrenaline junkie, whereas Noah was the guy who thought things through and had a plan. Max was raucous and an extrovert, while Noah was smart and hilarious, but he was definitely more reserved. Max was the ideas guy, Noah was the planner. Later that night, as she'd lain in bed, she'd heard them discussing Max's impending fatherhood.

'You know, I'd have wagered good money that I'd have been the first to do the kids' thing,' Noah had mused, making Tress wonder if his wife, Anya, had decided to wait and focus on her career. Tress had never asked her. Anya was lovely, but she'd always sensed a distance between them that she put down to Anya, Noah and Max having been friends for ever and Tress being relatively new to their lives.

'I just got lucky, I guess,' Max had replied, and Tress had drifted off to sleep with a smile on her face.

Standing in the nursery doorway now, that memory was eviscerated from her mind by the sudden pain of the next contraction. No slow build-up. No gradual tightening. Just wham – pain so severe that she dropped the bag and buckled over. *Breathe. Breathe. Damnit.* The soft inhalations and exhalations that had seemed so easy in her childbirth class were now taking every muscle in her body to master. Oh crap. Oh crap. It wasn't just the physical pain – she was blindsided by a visceral, searing need for her mum.

Squeezing her eyes shut tight, Tress tried to pant through the pain, sending a prayer to wherever in the universe her mum now rested. 'Mum, I don't know if I can do this. I think I need some help here. Look out for me today, look out for my boy, and please, please help us through this.'

Panting, panting, inhaling, exhaling, breathe, breathe... And just when she thought it was never going to stop, that she'd left it too late, that she was going to give birth to her baby on the floor alone, the pain subsided, retreated from her front, round to her back and then disappeared, leaving her forehead damp and her nerves tighter than the skin on her pregnant belly.

Tress checked her watch. It had been an hour since the last pain, but this one was sharper, so much more severe. Something inside her instinctively told her that taking it easy was no longer an option. It was time to get to the hospital and make sure that she was safe, that her baby was safe.

She dialled the number again.

'Max, change of plan. I'm going to head to the hospital now. Just get there as soon as you can.'

She flicked up her favourites list to make the next call, then paused, not sure whether to make it. Nancy had her big date tonight and she was so looking forward to it. She'd been talking about it for weeks, fretting over whether she was going to go. They both knew she would. Tress was pretty sure Nancy had never backed away from anything in her life. Now Tress was going to wreck her plans.

Or maybe not. She could just call a taxi and go on her own. Yes, that's what she would do. But... what if something happened on the way? What if there was a problem and she had to give birth alone? That thought terrified her.

Okay, what about Noah? She could call him, but he was probably at work, and he had packed clinics every morning. She couldn't stand the thought that she'd drag him away from kids or families who needed to see him.

And besides, Nancy would be furious if she wasn't at least given the first option to be there. She'd been so invested in this pregnancy, stopping in every day for a cup of tea and an update and supporting Tress every step of the way. She'd even come to two scans because Max was working in London and couldn't be with her. 'To be honest, love, you're doing me a favour,' Nancy had assured her, when they'd gone for a cup of tea and a scone after her last trip to the hospital. 'I've never had this experience, and with me and my Peter never having kids...' Tress hadn't missed the fleeting sadness on Nancy's face when she'd said that. 'Well, I'd always thought this – the being involved in this whole blooming miracle – wouldn't be a part of my life, so I'm grateful. It's fair been a tonic for me over these last few months. A real treat.' Tress had felt every word of that, because until just a few months before, she'd thought it would never be part of her life either. Did she really want to take that away from Nancy now?

Damn, what should she do? *Think, Tress. Think it through.*

A solution started to form. Maybe if Nancy could just come with her now, then as soon as Max arrived back this afternoon, he could take over, and Nancy would be away in plenty of time to get to her party and rediscover the long-lost love of her life. So win-win. Tress would have her friend with her, and Nancy would get to share the experience, but she'd be tagged out by Max in time for her school reunion tonight. Yep, that was a plan.

She gave her stomach a rub, trying to somehow calm the child inside it.

'Hey, little guy, don't you worry about a thing, okay? I've got you. It's just me and you, but we're going to be fine. I promise.'

Time to get going. This baby was on his way. Tress just hoped for all their sakes that his father was too.

6

NOAH

This was ridiculous. A misunderstanding. It had to be. Maybe Cara had opened the wrong month on Anya's calendar or there was a software glitch that had merged Anya's schedule with one of her colleagues – one that actually had a sister and who would perhaps join her sibling at a spa. But...

'*She said that the spa they're going to doesn't have any signal.*'

There had been a conversation about it, not just some random assumption based on entries on an online diary.

Thoughts ricocheted around Noah's head, desperate to settle on a logical explanation, something that would allow all this to make sense.

He replayed a dozen conversations in his head in the space of seconds. Last night. She talked about her trip. About taking the car to the airport. About parking it there and flying to London. A conference. Preparing for a big pitch.

No, he hadn't got this wrong, so where was the disconnect? Why wasn't his wife right now sitting on a plane on the way to Heathrow?

He had the first obvious thought: Max would know. They

worked for the same company, so, of course, he would have the correct information.

He picked up the phone and dialled his mate's number. Straight to the 'leave a message' bit. Shit.

'Hey, mate, it's me. Give me a call back when you get a minute. Cheers.' Keeping his voice steady had taken effort, but Noah didn't want to look like an over-emotional, overreactive tit when it turned out that there was a simple explanation for all this.

He thought about calling Tress, but it was still early and the last thing he wanted to do was wake up a pregnant woman, or lay his troubles on her shoulders. No. Not an option.

His mind buzzed back to Anya. Did she just want time away, some space to think, to make some life decisions without the craziness of work or Noah's hopes getting in the way? But why the secrecy? That wasn't Anya's style. If she was feeling pressure or needed a break, she'd have said and she'd know that he'd understand and be fine with it. They'd been together almost fifteen years, through years of medical school, long days on the wards as a junior doctor, exhaustion, lack of time together, followed by an almost incomprehensibly challenging couple of years for everyone who worked for the NHS and the soul-crushing pressure that came with it. Many of his colleagues and friends had gone to work in the private sector, but Noah loved his job too much to change a thing, no matter how tough it got. He'd stuck in there and Anya had stuck by him. They'd survived it all, and they hadn't managed that without cutting each other some slack and working through their problems.

He picked his coffee back up and didn't even realise that it was cold as he took a slug, every brain cell too focused on replaying the conversation with Cara.

It was the 'sister' element of the story that bothered him most. Why would Anya say that? One possibility rose from the swirling cauldron of confusion. Her girlfriend, Mischa. The two of them had been close since high school and had a bond that was as tight as any siblings. Could Anya have been referring to her? It was strange that she wouldn't have mentioned that she was meeting up with her, and even stranger that she'd spin a story about work to cover her tracks, but, again, maybe they were plotting something totally innocent, perhaps for his birthday or something, and there would be an explanation for this that they'd all laugh about later. Maybe on his birthday. Five months from now. Yeah, even he could see that was either meticulous forward planning or a real stretch.

Back on his phone, he dialled Mischa's number, praying that he was right and there would be no answer because Mischa was in the same telecommunications void as his wife.

'Noah! How are you doing, you big sexy thing? How's my favourite doctor? You know I still can't get through an episode of *Casualty* without thinking about you.' Mischa's voice belted down the line. Shit. She was there. And in the background, he could hear the riotous sounds of two of her children – the under five year olds - running as wild as ever. Despite the stress of the circumstances, he couldn't help but smile. Mischa came from a loud, exuberant Jamaican family, the kind of clan that made everyone welcome and – as three holidays to the island had proven – liked to love, laugh and party until everything hurt. Mischa was carrying on all those traditions with her own brood of four and counting.

'Yeah, I'm good. Great. Better for hearing you and sorry about the *Casualty* thing,' he blustered, trying to sound as upbeat and normal as possible. Crap, he hadn't thought this through. He played for time, realisation dawning. If Mischa was with her kids, then she wasn't off on some bloody spa weekend with his wife.

He fought to keep his voice warm and casual. 'It sounds like chaos there.'

'It's always bloody chaos here. I'm making a cake with the young ones for Ray Junior's tenth birthday tomorrow. He's demanding that his party start today and last for three days. It's ridiculous, but I kinda like his style.'

'Me too.' Thinking on his feet, Noah came up with the first thing that came into his mind. 'Listen, I won't keep you then. I was just calling to talk about Anya's birthday. Got a bit of a notion to take her away somewhere and I was thinking you and Ray might want to join us. Have a think about it and let me know.'

'I don't need to think about it, I'm there. An escape from this crazy house and spend a solid weekend where I don't stand on Lego and no one throws up on me.'

'I can't promise that,' Noah joked, trying to make his conversation sound as normal as possible. 'Glad you're up for it. I'll keep you posted. And I was going to make this a surprise, so please don't say anything to her. I've still got a few weeks to get it organised.'

'Don't worry, lips are sealed. I'm so sleep-deprived, I'll have forgotten about it by next weekend anyway. We were planning to do a long FaceTime with wine next Sunday night because it's been ages since we caught up. Be a bloody miracle if I can stay awake long enough to get to the bottom of the glass, but I'll give it my best.'

Despite the kind of rising anxiety that made the nerves under his skin prickle, Noah managed to keep the normality going until he'd wished Ray Junior a happy birthday, then they said their goodbyes. He ended the call and threw the phone on the sofa. Fuck. Fuck. Fuck. Dead end. And in the process of getting nowhere, he'd lumbered himself with planning a surprise weekend away for Anya. He'd worry about that later. Right now, his worry beads had other issues to keep them busy.

He paced over to the kitchen, poured a large glass of water from the tap and popped two paracetamol. He needed a clear head, one that didn't contain a brass band, so that he could think.

Who else could he call? What would make sense? His gaze fell on the obvious answer, right where he'd left it, on the breakfast bar in front of him. Anya's laptop.

No. He couldn't. That was crossing a line. Invading her privacy. Bordering on stalking. But even as those thoughts were going through his head, he was opening the white leather laptop case, his gift to her when she landed the job at Bralatech, and pulling out her MacBook.

He opened the lid and stared at the screen as it came to life. This was it. The moment he started the ball rolling on a path that he couldn't backtrack on. He'd never been the kind of husband to check on his wife. Was this really who he'd become?

As he typed in the first attempt at the password, he knew the answer to that question.

ANYA0908

The month and year that they'd met. It was the password that she used for most things, or at least she had, until the head of cybersecurity at the firm had given her a lecture about online safety.

Incorrect.

Shit.

He thought for a second, then typed again. It was a long shot, but...

NOAH0908

Incorrect.

Damn.

One more try, then he'd be locked out.

He stared at the screen, the wallpaper image so familiar to him. Her favourite picture. Kobe Bryant. He'd always loved that Anya was as into sport as he was. They'd never been the couple that chose separate rooms when he wanted to watch a game, because his wife wasn't interested. They'd both been on the basketball teams all through uni and it was her passion. Her father had played throughout his career in the US Air Force, and her mum had been a track star at university in St Andrews. That combination of DNA had given Anya an athletic superiority that she still had to this day. She ran most mornings, played for a local team when she had a chance, and she still could out-shoot any player on the court. Including him. That's why that man right in front of him, Kobe Bryant, had been her hero. On their honeymoon, they'd gone to LA to watch him play for the Lakers and she still teased Noah that it was more thrilling than their wedding night. She'd been devastated when Kobe had been killed in a helicopter crash with his daughter, Gianna, and their friends back in 2020.

He typed his final attempt.

KOBE2408

It was a gamble –24 and 8, the two numbers forever associated with Kobe, his jersey numbers when he played for the LA team.

Enter.

The screen opened to her home page. He was in and that made him hate himself just a little bit more. Not that there was any turning back now.

He started with her emails, scrolling down over the last

month to see if anything stood out. Nothing. That was strange in itself. No mention of this weekend. No agenda for a conference. No flight details for the journey.

Cara hadn't made a mistake. Noah had no idea where his wife was, but she definitely wasn't on a company trip to the capital.

He wasn't sure where to look next. He scanned her home screen and found her collection of shortcuts to travel apps. He opened Booking.com and checked for reservations. None pending. Hotels.com was next. Nothing. The third option was Expedia and when he opened her future bookings link, his heart thudded. One reservation. Two people. To... Paris.

He scanned the page and finally managed to breathe again when he saw that it was for 23 October. His birthday weekend. And it was to their favourite hotel on the Left Bank, one they'd visited many times over the years. This was a birthday trip for him, and that thought made him feel like crap. Here he was, spectacularly invading her privacy, and she was planning a romantic escape to Paris for his birthday. Who was in the wrong here?

Enough. Whatever was going on today, he had to trust that Anya had her reasons and he'd find out what those were when she got back. In all their years together, she'd never given him a single reason to doubt her, to be suspicious or to question her integrity, and he had no right to start now. He had faith in his wife. She was the best person he knew, and she would never do anything shady. It just wasn't in her heart.

Sighing, he reached over to close the lid on the laptop, when another idea cut right through his attempt to assure himself that nothing was happening here. Her history. There might be a clue there. If she had plans for this weekend, she might have checked them in the last couple of days.

The internal tussle started. No, he had to stick with the voice of reason from a few moments ago and trust his wife. That sentiment was fighting against the other voice that said, fuck it, you've gone this far, you're as well investigating some more.

That voice won.

He clicked on the history tab and watched as the drop-down box revealed the last few websites she'd visited. Facebook. Twitter. Instagram. The Financial Times. Forbes. Sky News. The LA Times. ESPN. Harpers Bazaar.

All her usual choices. Nothing surprising in there. Until he got to the final link on the list.

The Cairn Luss Lodge.

Noah knew exactly where that was. He and Anya had spent a weekend there years ago with Max and Tress, not long after their wedding. It had been glorious. They'd had an uncharacteristically three sunny, warm days in a row and had taken advantage of it with picnics on the edge of the loch, hikes up a nearby mountain called The Cobbler, long walks in the early evening, morning runs as dew burned off the heather, and jet skis on the water in the afternoons. They'd talked about going back for years but somehow never got there.

Maybe Anya was putting that right.

He clicked on the link and it took him to the hotel home page. Dread and anxiety started to rise again, but he settled them with reassurance. She was organising another trip for them. Maybe for her birthday. Perhaps their anniversary. It was the kind of thing his wife liked to do; to surprise the people she loved with trips that created memories they'd always have.

On the page, he clicked on the log-in and used the same password he'd used earlier. Right first time. Another couple of clicks and he was staring at the My Bookings section.

February 9 2023. One king suite. One night.

And no matter how many times he read that, it didn't change.

February 9 2023. One king suite. One night.

So she was in a hotel only an hour and a half away and she'd lied to his face about where she was going? Why not just tell him that she needed space, time on her own?

The next piece of information on the booking gave him the answer.

Number of occupants: 2.

What. The. Fuck.

Over the last few hours, weeks and months, he'd wondered many times what was going on with his wife. Flipping back through his memories, he tried now to put a more specific time frame on it. Probably six months or so. That's when he'd first noticed a detachment developing between them. She'd sometimes be snappy. Distant. He'd occasionally catch her staring into space, or he'd notice a frown between her eyes when she didn't realise he could see her. He'd gone through a million reasons. Pressure at work. Uncertainty over whether to start a family. Maybe she'd changed her mind. And the truth was, if she had actually voiced that to him, he'd known it wouldn't break them. He'd always truly believed that they could get through anything. Or maybe not...

The one thing that he'd never thought for a second was that she could be with another guy, but the information in front of him suggested that was what was going on here. Anya. Someone else. Staying in a hotel less than two hours away tonight. King-size bed.

Noah got up, picked up his car keys and headed for the door.

If his wife was being unfaithful, he wanted to look her in the eye, he wanted to know the truth, and he wanted to see the man that was taking his place.

7

NANCY

Nancy held up the perm box, so that it was just inches from the frizz on her head and pointed to it. 'If I ever meet this woman on this box, I'm having a serious word with her about false advertising.'

Val and Angie were struggling to keep straight faces, because she wasn't wrong.

'I mean, seriously,' Nancy stormed on. 'She's all bouncy curls and I look like I've been blasted by a fire extinguisher.'

That broke the dam of Val and Angie's restraint.

'Oh, love,' Val howled, 'give me a hairdryer and I'll make you look gorgeous, I promise.'

Nancy wasn't convinced. Val had unapologetically worn her platinum-blonde hair in the same over-sprayed bob style since the seventies, although it seemed to get wider with every passing year. If they were ever in a hostage situation, Val had volunteered to be used as a battering ram to open steel doors.

'I would so love to stay for this, but I need to get to work. The buses of Weirbridge wont drive themselves. At least, not until they replace us with robots who won't moan the face off everyone about the roadworks on the High Street,' Angie announced, climbing off the kitchen chair with a wince. Her menopause was also serving up joint pain and mild irritation. 'Ladies, yer fab. Have a great day. Val, give Don a squeeze from me. And, for what it's worth, I agree with Nancy that you should go tonight too. It'll do you good to let your hair down and have a bit of a dance to some Abba tunes. Nancy, I'll be in tomorrow morning before my shift to get the gossip on your big date tonight. Just don't be doing anything too bendy or energetic. At your age, you've got to think about osteoporosis.'

Cackling, Nancy threw the perm box at Angie's back as she giggled her way out of the door. 'Aye, you might be younger, but get a bit of "Hi Ho Silver Lining" on and I could still run rings around you on a dance floor.'

With a last chuckle from the hall, the front door banged behind her pal, leaving Nancy amused as she took a seat at the kitchen table. To her side, Val unplugged the toaster and plugged the hairdryer in instead and then pulled a can of mousse from her bag. Although, 'bag' was probably a conservative term. Her leather tote could easily accommodate the entire contents of the Superdrug hair care section.

Nancy's jaw dropped. 'Do you just randomly carry mousse with you every day?'

Val shrugged, like this was completely normal. 'Never know when you might need it.'

'I feel the same about my microwave and my kettle, but I don't take them out with me,' Nancy countered, before shaking her new curls back. 'Right, doll, do yer worst.'

Val got to work with the mousse, some spray and a round brush (all of which materialised from the bag), singing Patsy Cline's 'Crazy' over the sound of the hairdryer.

The effect was so weirdly relaxing that Nancy had almost nodded off by the time she was done.

Val stood back to admire her work. 'Yer not Kate Moss, but yer pretty close.'

Nancy harrumphed and crossed to the wall mirror at the back door and almost gasped when she saw the reflection staring back at her. 'Val, I don't know how you did it, but it's fab. Thank you, love. I mean, it's huge and I'll need to keep a safe distance so I don't take someone's eye out, but it looks smashing.'

Her voice cracked on the last word and she felt a strange sensation that she eventually recognised as the urge to have a good cry. It wasn't Nancy's way. Or Val's. They weren't criers. They came from the 'pull yourself up and get on with it' breed of women. Val always said it was something to do with having mothers that lived through the war years and never let them forget it.

Nancy retreated to her seat as two fat tears rolled down her cheeks.

Val looked horrified. 'What is it? Aw, Nancy, I was joking about Kate Moss. You're her double.'

'Ah, shut up, you daft thing.' Nancy couldn't help but laugh through the tears.

Val grabbed a roll of paper towels from the holder on the worktop and joined her at the table. 'Tell me, love.'

Nancy took a moment to compose herself. 'Am I being an old fool, Val? I mean, look at me. I'm sixty-six years old and I'm acting like a teenager, all bloody butterflies and excitement. And how would my Peter feel about this if he could see me? I mean, we didn't have a bad marriage. He was a good man and we loved each other. I keep thinking he'll be spinning in his grave if he could see me...'

'Stop that right now, Nancy Jenkins,' Val warned her with

such ferocity the pink baubles dangling from her ears vibrated. 'If Peter could see you now, all he'd care about is that you were happy. Since the day he died, there's been a cloud of sadness above you and all this had lifted it for a wee while. Hopefully forever. We're not done, Nance. We've got a good twenty years in front of us if we're lucky, so what are we supposed to do with that? Just give up? Sit at home and wait to die. No thanks, love. We deal with the hard stuff that's in front of us, but we need to make the best of it. And if that means doing something wild and sheer bloody crazy sometimes, then good for us.'

The speech had obviously taken something out of Val, as she was now unwrapping a second therapeutic caramel wafer. They went through so many of them they should undoubtedly be awarded brand ambassador status and given a free lifetime supply.

Nancy pulled off another two sheets of kitchen roll and blew her nose.

'I'm not so sure about that, Val. I know Peter would have wanted me to be happy, but with Eddie? You know how he felt about him. About what happened back then.'

Val sighed. 'I know. And I don't disagree. But that was nearly fifty years ago. I think Peter might give Eddie the benefit of the doubt. We all need to do that. People change, sometimes for the better.'

Nancy thought about that for a moment, then sniffed loudly and pulled back her shoulders. 'I suppose I'd be daft to back out now. I mean, this hairdo deserves an outing.'

Val took a sip of her tea, then nodded. 'Oh, it definitely does. It would be a criminal waste to keep it hidden.'

The tension that had worked its way through Nancy's body eased, her confidence bolstered by the encouragement from her pal. Val wasn't one to mince her words and if she thought this wasn't right, or that Nancy was making a show of herself, she'd be the first one to say it. And that worked both ways. Maybe it was time to gently deliver a home truth in the other direction.

'Thanks, Val. I don't know what I'd do without you,' she said, leaning over and putting her hand over her friend's, ignoring the inner self that had spotted the state of her hands and was now screaming something about dipping them in a vat of Nivea for the rest of the day. God, this whole aging process was a bastard, it really was. All those types that preached self-acceptance and self-love had never woken up with two hands that looked like they had just crawled out of a sandstorm. She filed that trifling issue away for later. Right now, she had a bigger one to deal with. 'But while we're on the subject of dealing with the hard stuff and making the most of it, you know what I'm going to say again. Same as Angie. I still think you should change your mind and come with us tonight.'

Now it was Val's turn to blink back the tears. 'Dear Lord, what was in that perm lotion?' she wailed, pulling a paper towel off the roll for herself. 'Look at the state of us.'

Nancy didn't say anything, just waited for Val to gather her thoughts. After a few sniffs, she was ready.

'I can't, Nancy. I just can't. It would break my heart. I couldn't go without Don and then have to answer questions about why he wasn't there, or take the awkward glances of people who know he's ill and don't know what to say. And I just wouldn't enjoy it without him. I'd spend the whole night reminding myself that he should be there too.'

'Then bring him with you,' Nancy suggested, watching as a single tear rolled down Val's cheek and splodged on to the table.

'I would love to, but it's not that easy...' Her gaze drifted off and Nancy wanted to weep for her friend.

'Look, Val, many of our gang from back then didn't make it

this far. Don's health is heart-breaking, but he's still here and he's still got you loving him and taking care of him. That's something to be celebrated, no?'

Val was pensive. 'I know you're right, but… I don't know if my sore heart could take the hurt, Nancy, and that's the truth. Every day I look at him and think I'd give anything to have my old Don back. Anything at all. He's been beside me for fifty years and I've loved him every minute of that. Now, every day it's like a bit of him disappears and inside, hidden right in my gut, where nobody knows except me, that kills me. I feel terrible saying that, love, because I know your Peter isn't here with us…'

'But the Don you married isn't here any longer either,' Nancy said sadly, feeling every sting of her pal's pain. 'And I get that. But I just don't want you to stop living either. When was the last time you went out, Val?'

'I'm here!'

'Don't be smart. You know what I mean. You're exhausted, Val. You've been looking after him day and night and you need a wee break, to be around people and have some good chat. When was the last time you had a night off? Had a bit of fun. Let yer hair down, like Angie said. Not that that hair of yours has budged since about 1982, right enough.'

That earned Nancy a playful raised eyebrow of scorn, before Val shrugged. 'I don't know. Probably year before last when Mark stayed with Don for a few days, and I went over to the States with our Carly.' Val's niece, Carly, had married an actor and spent half the year in Los Angeles. Val had gone to visit her, and Nancy had made several requests for Val to bring her back a gift-wrapped George Clooney, but she was still waiting for him to turn up at the door. Val did come back with a life-size cardboard cut-out of Al Pacino, but she'd kept him to herself. He stood in her little summer house in the garden, so she could see him from the kitchen window.

'Exactly. Nearly two years ago. Come on, love, that's not good for you. Look, think about it. And if you decide you can face it, I'll ditch Eddie and be yer partner. Just watch yer hands if we're slow-dancing.' Humour had got these two through so many things in life, and it wasn't failing them now.

'I'll try, but you're hard to resist,' Val quipped, grinning. 'Anyway, enough of this. Let me see the outfit you're wearing tonight. Did it arrive from the catalogue?'

Nancy stood up, and Val must have caught the expression on her face, because she flicked straight to inquisition.

'What is it? Is it terrible? Oh bugger. What are you going to do? It's too late to find something else. You'll just have to wear that thing you wore to Betty from the Baking Club's funeral.'

'You realise you just had a whole conversation with yourself there? I actually think the dress is lovely. A bit... erm... unusual, right enough. Hang on, I'll show you...'

She disappeared into her bedroom, and a few minutes later, came out singing 'Big Spender' and strutting across the lino like it was a catwalk.

Val's hand flew to her mouth to cover the jaw-dropping shock that was all over her face.

Nancy did a pirouette, to ensure that her pal got full view of every aspect of her frock. It was pale yellow, off the shoulder and trimmed with a generous amount of huge feathers along the neckline, the cuffs and the hemline.

'Oh, pet,' Val whimpered.

Nancy braced herself for the brutal truth. Not that she'd let anyone put her off. This dress wouldn't be for everyone, but she adored it and that was all she cared about. Her Peter used to tell her he loved the fact that she liked a show-stopping frock and this was definitely that.

'Go on then. Let me have it,' Nancy demanded, amused. 'That's what pals are for. Just as long as you don't mind me ignoring your opinion.'

'It's lovely…'

'But?'

The dam opened and a whole river of Val's hilarity gushed right through as she added, 'Someone might want to put a call out to see if anyone has murdered a field of ostriches, because you appear to be wearing their feathers. Nancy, that's a lot of wildlife there.'

'Apparently, feathers are in,' Nancy aped the line she'd heard from the fashion expert on *Lorraine* a few months ago.

'Aye, *feathers*, Nancy. Not the whole bloody bird.'

That set them both off again, heaving with laughter until there were tears in their eyes and Nancy was having to hold on to the back of a chair and bend over not to pull something in her sides. A feather, probably.

When she eventually regained the power of speech, she had to splutter out her words of defiance. 'I care not a jot. I love it.'

'And that's all that matters, ma darlin',' Val agreed. 'I just hope Eddie doesn't have an allergy to chicken.'

Irrepressible shrieks overtook them yet again and only stopped when the sound of the ringing phone forced them to get hold of themselves. Nancy picked it up, cleared her throat, forced out a greeting.

'Hello?'

'Nancy, it's me. Tress. Listen, I'm really sorry and I hate to do this, but my waters broke and I can't get in touch with Max. Is there any chance you'd come to the hospital with me? I know you've got your night out tonight, and I'm so sorry to do this, but I'm sure Max will get there soon and then he can take over and—'

'Tress!' she cut off the needless apology. 'I'm on my way. Have you called a taxi yet?'

'No, I—'

'Well, no need. Val is here with her car, and it's one of those Jeep things, so we'll get you into that and we'll have you at the hospital in no time.' Nancy looked at Val, hoping she was saying the right thing, and, of course, Val nodded back. Her boxy Jeep thing was far more practical and she didn't fancy Tress's chances of folding herself into Nancy's Smart car.

'We're on our way, love. Be there in two minutes.'

They were out of the house and racing along the road when Nancy realised she was still wearing her feather dress and her slippers. No time to do anything about that now.

At Tress's house, Nancy ran to her friend, who was bent double, holding on to the front door frame for support, jaw clenched, trying to pant through gritted teeth.

'I can't move, Nancy. I just can't move. I think this baby is about to make an appearance.'

8

MAX

Max kept his head down as he jumped into the passenger seat of the car and then waited for Anya to climb back into the driver's seat. No public displays of affection in car parks. It was a small world and who knew who could be watching.

'You okay?' she asked, eyeing him quizzically.

'Yeah, I'm just tired. Not been getting much sleep.' He didn't say why. The truth was that Tress had been restless during the night and her tossing and turning had kept him awake. Not that he minded. He was aware that she was the one doing all the work in this situation. The thought pre-empted a tiny spike of guilt, but he didn't vocalise it. Hadn't he and Anya agreed at the start of this that guilt was a waste of time?

Anya didn't respond, just pulled out of the car park and hit the familiar road towards Loch Lomond, to the hotel that had become one of their regular spots.

For a moment, Max felt a strong compulsion to just call this weekend off and go back home. Why did they need this proper goodbye anyway? It wasn't like they weren't going to see each other any more. The four of them – him and Tress, Noah and

Anya – had already arranged to have dinner down at the local Indian restaurant next Friday. The truth was, he'd suggested this weekend as one last bit of fun before going their separate ways, because he knew that after the baby was born, that's where all his time and focus would be.

Until now, he'd been too selfish to end his affair with Anya because he loved the time he spent with her and had convinced himself that they weren't doing any harm. Not really. Anya wasn't going to leave Noah, he would never leave Tress, and neither Noah or Tress would ever find out, so they were all good.

It was the blue line on the pregnancy test that had changed everything. When he'd first met Tress, she was thirty-eight and they'd been pragmatic about not being parents because they both knew it might not be a reality. Now that it was, the imminent arrival of his son had focused his mind on what really mattered. His parents had moved abroad, and he didn't have any siblings, so Tress and his son were all he really had. Instead of running around hotels and having wild nights of passion, he wanted to spend every spare moment with his wife and his boy.

Now was the right time to let go of the relationship with Anya, and she felt the same way.

'You sure you're okay?' Anya asked again, snapping him back to the present.

Bizarrely, given their history, he knew this whole affair wasn't Anya's style. They'd talked loads of times about how she'd never have been unfaithful to Noah if it hadn't been with Max, and he believed her. And, yes, when she said that, it made him feel even more shit. There was no getting away from the fact that he'd betrayed his wife, his best friend and corrupted the only other person in the world that he genuinely loved. His kid deserved so much more than this and it wasn't too late to give him the dad he should have. Screwing around when you had kids was his parents' deal, not his. The difference with his folks was that they were both into it, whereas he knew Tress would be horrified and it would be a deal-breaker for her.

'Yeah, I'm just thinking about my mum and dad,' he replied, half-truthfully. They had one rule in their relationship, an agreement that never wavered – they were not allowed to talk about Noah or Tress. They'd decided that right at the start, aware that discussing their partners just made the betrayal real, rubber-stamped the fact that they shouldn't be doing this. It was so much easier to just block out all the negativity and betrayal and just take each minute, hour, and day they were together as an escape from reality. One that came with no responsibilities or regret. And every time, when they said goodbye, they just locked what they had in another one of those mental boxes until the next time.

Only, now there wouldn't be a next time and he was fine with that. He really was.

Anya didn't take her eyes off the road as she reached over and turned on the heating. 'How are they doing?'

'Oh, you know... probably shagging their way across Cyprus.'

It wasn't the first time he'd said that, but it still made her gorgeous face melt into a rueful smile.

'I always thought open marriages were just something that they made up in movies until I met your parents.'

'Yep, they're peaches,' he shot back, used to handling the situation with glib irreverence.

Was there any difference between him and them? Not really. Except perhaps that he really hadn't mean it to happen. Not the first time.

He leaned his head back and closed his eyes, letting the memory flood his mind, hoping that somewhere in there was a shred of defence, but knowing that there was none.

He'd been in London for a meeting with the directors of the company and Anya had flown down for an interview. He'd recommended her for the job, told her exactly how to pitch for it, so it wasn't a surprise when they'd offered it to her at the end of her final presentation in front of the panel. Damn, she'd been brilliant. And sexy as hell. She'd worn a cream trouser suit, her long ebony hair now cut in a short, pixie style that framed those incredible cheekbones. All through her presentation, he hadn't been able to take his eyes off her lips. He'd caught himself several times throughout the day, thinking about her in a way that had never happened before. For ten years, since they'd all met in uni, they'd been mates, like family: Noah, Anya, Max and whatever girl he was seeing. When they were younger, she used to joke that his bedroom had a revolving door, but he was in his early twenties, living his best life, enjoying himself – wasn't that what you were supposed to do?

Back then, he'd thought that, if anything, it was Noah's life that was messed up. Sure, he had that whole medical-degree, planning-to-be-a-doctor thing going on, but he never once used it to impress women and play the field. What young guy wants to settle down with the girl he met when he was twenty? But there had been no telling Noah and Anya. Even when Max and Noah had moved out of the twin-bed room they shared on campus, to a two-bedroom flat in Glasgow's Merchant City, giving them the freedom to run riot and do whatever they pleased, Noah only had eyes for Anya.

Not that Max minded. She was great company, and she was fiery, always quick to tell him when he was messing up, but sisterly enough to love him anyway. They were a trio and it worked brilliantly. He was the best man at their wedding. He slept on their sofa after countless nights out. He even lived with them whenever he was between houses.

Not once had he ever tried anything on with her, because he knew that she'd reject him, just like she'd done on the day they met. And sure, it had stung, that she'd chosen Noah over him, but he was over it by his second drink that night at the Student Union. Never, in all the time they'd hung out as three best mates, had he had the feelings he was having that day in London, as he watched her slay the company directors with her knowledge, her quick wit and her market expertise. She was a natural. But, of course, it went against the grain of their relationship for him to say that out loud.

In the hotel bar later that night, he'd raised his glass of Jack Daniel's and Coke to meet her gin and tonic. 'Congratulations. Although, you only got the job because I recommended you, you know that, don't you?' The ribbing was a core fundamental of their relationship.

As always, she was ready for him. 'Ah, you poor deluded soul. They said the reality was that I ticked every box except the one that judged the company I keep. "Could do better", apparently,' she'd teased.

Their banter had been interrupted by a FaceTime call from Noah, congratulating his wife on her new job. Max had envied their closeness, their easy conversations and their absolute devotion to each other. He'd never had that. But then, he'd never given anyone the chance to get that close.

She had turned the phone to face Max for a second, so that Noah could speak to him directly. Max could see he was at work, white coat and stethoscope slung over his neck as he delivered a warning. 'You're asking for trouble now, mate – you'll have my wife on your case if you slip up at work and she's pretty fierce.'

Anya had turned the phone back and giggled into the camera. 'Only with you, bae, only with you.'

'I think I'll cope,' Max had quipped, leaning in so that he was on camera again. 'She won't want to get on the wrong side of her husband's best mate. Noah, we all know if you had to choose between me and Anya, I'd win.' That made her shriek with laughter, especially because they all knew it wasn't true. Much as Noah was his non-genetic brother, Max knew he'd choose his wife over him in a heartbeat.

Noah had confirmed that without the slightest hesitation. 'Not a chance, pal. Not even close.' Someone in the background had interrupted him with a 'Dr Clark?' and Noah had wrapped up the call. 'I need to go. I'll let you guys get back to the celebrations. Wish I was with you. Have a drink for me.'

'We will,' Anya had promised, blowing kisses into the phone.

The massive love and affection between them gave Max another twinge of something... Yeah, definitely envy. And it wasn't an emotion that sat well with him.

For the next four hours, they had knocked back drinks, forgetting their dinner reservation as the alcohol flowed. It was the first time Max could remember having a one-to-one conversation with her, a real connection, the kind where your eyes lock and you're captivated by every word that is being said.

He had no idea what time it was when the bartender told them they were closing for the night, but he knew that they'd both drank way too much, and he knew that he didn't want the night to end.

They'd fallen out of the lift on their floor, both creasing with hilarity as they staggered along the corridor. Of course, their rooms were close to each other.

Anya had stopped at her door first. 'Goodnight...'

'Or...' he'd countered.

Even in their drunk, celebratory state, he'd registered her flinch of surprise.

'We could raid the mini-bar and clock up all the booze, the nuts and the Toblerone to expenses.'

'I don't think the finance director would go with that. I've heard he's a bit of an arse,' she'd teased.

'You're right, he is. But I'll persuade him.'

Laughing again, she'd opened her hotel-room door and they'd staggered inside. He'd made straight for the bar, while she plonked down on the crisp white duvet of the king-size bed and took her shoes off one by one, tossing them to the side.

If there was a moment when one of them made the first move, he couldn't remember it. He'd handed her a drink, they'd both ended up lying on the bed, sharing an extortionately overpriced jar of pecans, and at some point, they'd melded into one, when they'd both leaned together and kissed. Neither of them had instigated it. It had just happened. After that, all restraint was gone. It was a frantic rush of discarded clothes, of grabs of passion, locked lips, of hands touching places they'd never been before and, damn she was spectacular. It was the most thrilling, the most horny, the most un-fucking-believable night of his life.

The next morning, the guilt had come thundering down at the same time as the hangovers.

He'd woken a split second before Anya, and when she'd rolled towards him and opened her eyes, there had been a visible moment of confusion before, 'Oh fuck. Oh fuck no. Fuck. Fuck.' She'd grabbed at the sheet, pulling it up to cover her naked body. Horse bolted. Stable door shut. 'What did we do?' she'd gasped. 'No, don't answer that. Oh Fuck. We did. How could we? Noah...'

The final word had trailed off, as the realisation sank in for both of them. Her husband. His best friend. And yet...

'I'm so sorry this happened,' Max had said softly. 'But, at the same time, I'm not.'

Her brown eyes had fixed on his and he could see it there too. She felt the same.

Anya had sighed, closed her eyes. 'I'm never leaving Noah.'

'I would never ask you to. This, whatever this is, can never be a thing in the real world, but Anya, last night was incredible. I felt things that I've never felt before. We both know that what you've got for Noah is for life…' He'd paused there, his brain trying to catch up with what his mouth was saying. 'But maybe we could have something too. Something that was just for us.'

Part of him had expected her to slap him, to yell, to tell him where he could shove his proposition, but she didn't. Instead, she'd stayed silent, as he reached over, lifted her chin, kissed her. Then another kiss. Then her hand was in his hair and her leg was wrapped around his and they were back to the night before, to the most explosive, carnal, incredible sex of their lives.

Their understanding was clear. In the real world, nothing changed. She was married to Noah. Max was their closest friend. But when they were on work trips, it was something else, they were two people that milked every bit of pleasure from each other.

Meeting Tress hadn't changed that. He'd bumped into her about a year after, and it had been the start of the biggest love of his life. But the biggest lie of his life had never ended. He and Anya had just carried on as normal. Conferences in London. Sales trips to Europe. And the occasional overnight like this one, where they were just using work as an excuse to escape and have a couple of days to themselves, to talk, to stroll, and to stay in bed all day making love and eating room service.

In the five years they'd been occasional sex-buddies, they'd never discussed calling it off. Not even when he met Tress. Or when she first got pregnant. He'd thought about it, but then, the month after he'd found out about the baby, the company had sent them to a week-long research conference in San Francisco. He was never going to resist Anya when they were in a five-star hotel, with an unlimited expense account and way too much free time on their hands. He justified it to himself by thinking, why shouldn't they make the most of it? What harm were they doing? It wasn't like they could put the genie back in the bottle. They'd been unfaithful, so what did it matter if they carried it on for a little while longer? They were just two consenting, attractive, fun-loving adults making the most of their days. And nights. He'd held on to that perspective until a few weeks ago, when they'd been lying in bed in the London hotel they always stayed at when they were down at head office. Anya had opened her eyes and caught him staring at her.

'What? Is something wrong?'

There had been a flinch of panic, so he'd immediately replied with, 'No, nothing. Everything is fine.'

Max could have left it there, but the thought on his mind wasn't budging. He hated confrontation. Or bad news. Denial and fun had got him through his whole life, but something inside him was in charge. 'Anya, I...'

His words had drifted off when she reached out and hushed him with her finger. 'You don't have to say it. I know. This has to end. For me too.'

That had shocked him. She'd never so much as hinted at calling it a day before.

The sheet pulled around her, as she sat upright and rested her chin on her knees. 'Time to go back to the real world. Do all that adult bollocks.'

He couldn't have put it better himself. 'It is. Are you okay with that?'

She'd nodded slowly. 'You know, I've been using this as a distraction from facing some big decisions.'

'Starting a family?' he'd asked.

Of course, Noah had discussed her reluctance with him a few times.

'Thing is, I'm really not sure that's what I want any more. I want to spend my life with Noah, but maybe this is all I can give him.'

'You know he'd take that. If you just told him.' It had felt weird, talking about the others, breaking their rule.

'I know, but what if that's a mistake? What if I regret that later? I just... I'm panicking on the inside. I've never in my life been unsure of myself, but now I am. I don't know what to do.'

They'd talked about it a little more, and it hadn't felt right to just call it quits when she was in turmoil, so that's when they'd planned this weekend. Just the two of them. And, for once, they were going to talk about everything. Say goodbye, and then say hello to the next chapters of their lives.

They made small talk as the car swerved and bumped on the deserted country road. The hotel they were heading for was near Loch Lomond, but it wasn't one of the grand, picturesque ones on the water. Those were too popular, too busy, which made them too risky that they'd bump into someone who knew one or both of them. No, their destination was the Cairn Luss Lodge, a small twenty-bedroom lodge in the hills between Loch Lomond and Loch Goil. It was remote. Isolated. And completely hopeless for a phone signal within a ten-mile radius. Not that it mattered. They'd both switched their phones off when they were meant to be on their flights. This wasn't their first infidelity rodeo.

It was almost noon when they pulled up the gravel drive to the reception area and stretched their aching muscles after the car journey.

Anya opened the boot and took out her trolley case, her tote, her handbag, her...

'Shit, I forgot my laptop. I must have left it in the kitchen. Damnit. How the hell did I not notice?'

They both knew the answer. She got highly strung and nervous right before they met up, every time without fail, and he had no doubt that it would have been even worse today. He knew it was why she'd stayed late in the office last night and why she'd probably left even earlier than necessary this morning. She'd struggled to deal with the guilt. Just not enough to stop her doing this.

'Will it be a problem? Is there anything on it?'

She understood exactly what he was saying and shook her head. 'No, of course not. I wipe all the emails that could be an issue, and besides, it's password-protected. It'll be fine.'

A distinct chill ran through his veins. 'Are you sure?'

'Positive. I promise. I changed the password months ago, not that Noah would ever dream of going through my laptop anyway. You know him. That's not in his nature.'

She wasn't wrong. Noah was the most laid-back, chilled guy and he'd never, for a second, suspect that Anya would do this. And it didn't escape Max's irony gene that if Noah did suspect anything was amiss with his wife, the first person he'd turn to was him, his best friend.

They checked in at reception, paid cash for the room, and handed over the company credit card as a guarantee for incidentals, knowing that they'd pay cash for those too, so no charges would register on the account. When she handed it back, the receptionist gave them a beaming smile. 'Welcome back to The Cairn Luss Lodge. We have the room you reserved online. The Wi-Fi code is on the back of the room key. If you need anything at all, please don't hesitate to call down. Would you like me to make a dinner reservation?'

Max thought about it. Maybe 8 p.m. That would give them

time to talk, to have closure, then spend tomorrow saying goodbye and enjoying their last hours together.

'That would be great – 8 p.m.?' he suggested, and Anya didn't disagree.

Details settled, they took the familiar route up to their favourite room. As soon as they closed the door behind them, Anya dropped her bags, turned and wound her hands around his neck. He felt himself immediately stiffen and he reached for her, pushing his hands up under the jacket of her suit, peeling it off, then feeling for her skin under her white silk bouse. God, she drove him crazy.

His lips went to her neck, to her shoulder, and were working their way to her collarbone when…

All hell broke loose.

Their phones obviously still had the Wi-Fi codes in their memories after the last visit, and both of their handsets started ringing, beeping and vibrating at the same time.

'Leave it,' Anya panted, as her hands went into his hair, and he was going to, almost did, but then a little voice in his conscience told him to stop being a dick and check his phone, so he pulled himself away.

'Two seconds, just in case it's…' He didn't want to say the word, once again abiding by the general rule that they never discussed their partners. He'd pulled the phone from his jacket pocket and he was staring at the screen now and… 'Fuck.' Six missed calls from Tress and one from Noah. What the hell?

'Oh shit. Noah has called me twice,' she said, brow creased with worry, before she shook it off. 'It's fine. He'll just be trying to tell me I've left my laptop. Or maybe he's been called in on his day off. Yeah, that's what it'll be.'

Max was barely listening. His trembling thumb pressed the touchscreen, taking him to his voicemail to play back his messages. The first one was just a click, indicating that Tress had hung up before saying anything, but it was the second one that turned the chill in his veins to pure icy panic.

'Hey, honey, so it looks like our little guy didn't want to wait around after all. My waters broke and the hospital has said that I should make my way in, so I'm going to get organised and do that. I'll have my mobile with me, so please give me a call back and let me know when you can get here. Thanks, baby. Love you. And your boy is gonna love you too.'

Oh no. No. No. No. Fuck.

He'd been holding the phone up between them, and as Anya heard Tress's words, her eyes widened. She and Tress had never been best buddies, but they were friends, part of their foursome, and despite the current situation Max knew Anya cared about her too.

'Oh God. What are we going to do? Max?'

He couldn't speak. His voice box was paralysed, his feet rooted to the spot. What was he going to do? What was he going to do? There was only one thing he could do.

'I need to go back. Fuck, I can't believe we did this. How fucking stupid!'

A flash of hurt crossed her face, but she didn't disagree.

'What will we say though?' She checked the time on her phone screen. 'We're supposed to be in London right now. How are you going to explain that you got back so quickly?'

He was pacing now, backwards, forwards, backwards, forwards, one hand on his hip, the other running his fingers through his hair in a subconscious stress reaction. 'I don't know. I'll say...' He tried to think. 'I'll say that the flight was delayed. Or that we missed it. Fuck knows, but I'll make up something. We can just both stick to the same story. It's not like anyone will check.'

That seemed to satisfy her. 'Okay, let's go.'

Max grabbed her jacket from the floor, where he'd tossed it a lifetime ago, gathered the rest of his things and they both fled at speed back down to reception.

Max dropped the key on the mahogany reception desk. 'Sorry, but we've just had news of a family issue and we won't be staying after all.'

Before the receptionist could even respond, they were out of the door and throwing their stuff in the back of the car.

'I'll drive,' he insisted.

'No way, you're too stressed.'

'Anya, my son is about to be born and I'm not fucking there. I'll drive,' he repeated forcefully, jumping into the driver's seat. It was a keyless ignition, so when Anya got in the passenger seat with the key, he pressed the ignition button and it sprang into life.

Okay, this could work. It could be fine, he told himself as he threw the car into reverse and screeched in a semicircle so that he was pointing in the right direction. 'Damn, I should have called Tress and let her know I'm coming.'

As he reached for the phone, he spoke under his breath, as if saying the words would get some kind of cosmic message to his boy.

'I'm on my way, son. Just hang on.'

NOON – 2 P.M.

9

TRESS

'Overtake him in the penis extension, Val,' Nancy ordered, pointing at the Porsche in the outside lane. 'OVERTAKE HIM!'

Val shushed her. 'Jesus wept, Nancy, you just about took out my eardrum there. I've got this, don't worry. How you doing back there, Tress? Not long now. The bloke in the sat nav thingy says fifteen minutes.'

'I'm fine, honestly. I'm starting to feel like a bit of a fraud. I really thought I was in trouble with that last contraction back at the house, but that's nearly twenty minutes now and there hasn't been another one.'

'That can happen, love. When I was having my Mark, the contractions stopped and started all day, and then all of a sudden, they came thick and fast and then he shot out like a can of Coke from a vending machine.'

The mental image made Tress laugh, and then wince, as there was a tiny spasm in her side. If she had to predict all the ways that she thought she might build up to the birth of her child, careering along a Glasgow motorway, in a Jeep Renegade with two sexagenarian women, one of them literally spitting feathers, wasn't one of them. But, weirdly, she was glad of it. The two of them were keeping her entertained as well as reassured that, no matter what, they were going to take care of her. Somewhere up there, she knew her mother was looking down and feeling grateful to them for taking care of her family.

Her family. It still felt weird to think of them that way. All her life, it had been just Tress and her mum, and then for that awful year, just Tress. When she'd met Max, it was as if her mum had sent him. The perfect guy. Within a week, she had known that she wanted to be with him, within a month they were engaged, and six months later they got married on a beach in Bali, just the two of them. Since they'd got together, she'd only been spending weekends in Scotland, so they'd gone back to Newcastle after the wedding, had a party there to celebrate with her friends and say goodbye to her workmates, and then she'd travelled north for the final time and made Weirbridge her permanent home.

It was perfect. Her. Max. And now the baby. Their own little trio. It was all she needed. In a weird way, the fact that she and Max were both only children, both alone, had made them some kind of kindred spirits. Even if, right now, he was missing in bloody action.

'Nancy, I don't want to be rude, but do you normally wear that kind of outfit around the house in the morning? Because, if so, I really need to upgrade my loungewear action.'

'Sure do, pet. Yellow on a Thursday, same outfit in different colours every other day of the week.'

Val ran right along with it. 'It helps her with the housework. If she walks within two feet of her blinds, they get a good clean with those feathers.'

Tress instinctively put her hands around the bottom of her belly as she laughed, fearing that it would set off another contraction. This was helping her to stay calm. In fact, strangely, she felt totally at ease, completely sure that this was going to work out. Besides, her son didn't need a stressed-out mum adding anxiety to the list of things that were floating about in there. He needed her to be relaxed, to be strong, and to get to the hospital before he decided to enter the world.

'I can't thank you ladies enough for doing this for me. I really can't.'

'Are you kidding? This is the most excitement we've had since Nancy got one of those gadgets that opens tins from the catalogue.'

'Remember that?' Nancy chuckled. 'We were eating crushed pineapple for a week, just so we could use it. Okay, love, we're getting closer. Any word from Max?'

Tress checked her phone again. Nothing. But that was to be expected because he'd only just have landed in London and he probably didn't have a signal yet. Or maybe he was trying to organise a flight back and was waiting to call her when he knew for sure what time he'd be arriving. She had another thought.

'I'm going to try Noah,' she informed the others. 'If he's at work, he should be out of clinic by now and he'll want to know too. And he might have some other way to track Max down. I think Anya is probably at this conference too.'

'Och, she's lovely, that lass,' Nancy said, approvingly. 'She's a good match for Noah. That boy has been a wee gem since the day he was born. And him and Max – it was a blue moon if you ever saw one of them without the other. I was their dinner lady all through primary school and I don't think they ever missed a lunch together.'

'They're still the same,' Tress chirped. 'I just hope this wee one finds a pal like that too. If nothing else, I know Noah won't mind coming over after he's finished his shift. Or if he's off today, maybe he would just come now. He's been my go-to medical person for every ache and pain since I got pregnant. And that would let you away to finish getting ready for the big date night. That dress is too good to waste.'

'Sweetheart, all that matters is taking care of you, so don't you worry about a thing. If I don't make it tonight, you'll be doing me a favour. Last time I went dancing, I tore a ligament.'

'Thanks, Nancy. I love you both and can't thank you enough, but I'll try to rally the troops just in case.' Feeling teary-eyed with gratitude, Tress dialled Noah's number from her favourites list. Straight to voicemail. 'Does no one answer their phone any more?' she wondered aloud, as she listened to Noah's recorded greeting.

'Hey, Noah, it's Tress. No panic, but I just want to let you know that's me on the way to hospital because I think the next basketball champion of the world is about to make an appearance.'

Noah had already said he was going to train the little one to be an NBA star. Tress had a vision of lots of broken kitchen windows.

'But I can't get a hold of Max, so can you see if you can track him down for me, please? I'll keep trying too, but I'm not sure if I'll be able to use my phone in hospital. I'll be at Glasgow Central Maternity, but tell Max not to worry because Nancy and Val are with me and we're doing great. Talk to you soon. Oh, and your nephew can't wait to meet you.' She was unashamedly going to do that thing where their close friends became his uncles and aunts even though they weren't related by blood. They didn't have a large biological family, but they wanted to have as many people to love their boy as possible, so they were just going to pick a family for themselves.

Aunty Nancy and Aunty Val had already secured themselves invitations to his birthday parties until the end of time for their emergency services work today. They careered into the hospital grounds and screeched to a halt in front of the doors of the maternity wing, like something out of a *Fast and Furious* movie.

Nancy was out of the car and round opening Tress's door like a flash. 'Just put your arms around my shoulder, pet, and I'll support you. Don't let the feathers fool you – I'm stronger than I look. My Peter used to say I could toss cabers.'

'You'll get a job on the dodgy channels with a talent like that,' Val said, deadpan, coming round the other side of the vehicle.

Tress put her hand out and clutched the door as she slid out. 'I'm okay, honestly. I can walk fine. It's only bad when... when... Oh God.' Even though she'd experienced the pain a few times already, it still took her by surprise. She was on her feet, but bent forward at the waist, one hand holding Nancy's, the other still gripping the door. Val was off and running through the sliding doors into the hospital building.

Nancy assumed coaching duties. 'Just breathe, pet. That's it. Keep breathing. You're doing great. Oh Tress, you're a natural. That's it. Just keep breathing. Val is away to get help. We'll get you in there and organised in no time. And no pressure, love, but try not to let this pregnancy escalate in the next thirty seconds because I've never done this before and I'm not sure I'll be quick enough to catch him.'

'It's okay. It's okay. It's okay,' Tress panted, as the pain began to ease again, coming down from somewhere near 'removal of internal organs' to 'still excruciating'.

Just at that, Val came thundering back out of the doors pushing a wheelchair and accompanied by a bloke in scrubs. 'Okay, ma love, sit yourself down here. I know this nice man looks about twenty-one, but he assures me he's a real doctor and that he's done this before.'

Tress felt sorry for the poor guy being under the scrutiny of Nancy and Val, but, to his credit, he took charge of the situation and whisked them inside. He pushed her straight up to the admitting ward, where a nurse was the epitome of calm at the reception desk.

'Thanks, Declan, I'll take this,' she offered.

Tress glanced around her. There were rooms on both sides of the corridor, with its pale green walls and forest murals painted along one side. She could hear a baby crying in one of the rooms, immediately followed by a woman's voice gently shushing it. Despite the havoc of their entrance, there was an atmosphere of calm competence. This was where her son was going to be born.

The nurse, a soft-spoken redhead in her twenties, lifted a clipboard and was obviously preparing to take her details.

Nancy got in first, and began shooting out information like she was an intern on *Grey's Anatomy*. 'This is Tress Walker. She's forty-two years old. Eight and a half months pregnant. First child, which, let's face it, is bloody marvellous. She's been having contractions since... what time, Tress?'

'About ten o'clock. They're only every forty minutes or so, actually maybe thirty minutes for that last one, but I called and they said I should come in.'

'Ah yes, I think it was me you spoke to. Okay, let's get you to a bed, and I'll call Dr Greyson. She's on duty today, so she shouldn't be long. She can give you a check-over and see how things are coming along. Ladies, you're very welcome to stay with Mrs Walker...'

'Call me Tress,' she interjected with a smile.

'Tress,' the nurse repeated. 'But I need to ask you to have a seat in the corridor here until I get her settled.'

To her credit, Tress mused, she didn't even bat an eyelid at Nancy's frock. They must see all sorts in here. For what Tress thought was maybe the first time in their lives, the two older women quietly did as they were requested.

The nurse introduced herself as Marie as she pulled the curtains around the bed. It was a ward of four beds, but the one across from Tress was empty and the other two had curtains around them, so she wasn't sure who else was here.

While she changed into one of the pyjama sets she'd brought in her bag, Marie continued to ask questions and jot the answers down on the form. She checked Tress's pulse and blood pressure, then held her arm out to support Tress while she climbed onto the bed. Tress pulled her handbag onto the bed, so that her phone would be handy.

This was it. It was really happening. But where was Max? Where was he?

'That's you all sorted,' Marie chirped. 'I'll just go check on Dr Greyson, and I'll say to your friends to come in now. I'll be back in two minutes to hook you up to the monitors.'

Tress thanked her, then tried Max's phone again. Still not going through. Buggering damn it. Where the hell was he? She felt the first twinges of anger and she immediately chided herself. This wasn't his fault. He would be here if he could. And when she finally got hold of him, he'd do everything short of hiring a private jet to get back. Actually, she wouldn't put the private jet past him. It was the kind of spontaneous, over-the-top gesture that would be totally in character for her husband. His wild side was just one of the reasons she loved him. She'd woken up on their first anniversary to find out that he was whisking them away, first-class, for dinner and an overnight stay at the Plaza Hotel in Paris, and she'd been blown away that this man could be so loving and romantic. As the call went to voicemail yet again, that thought calmed her right back down again.

'Darling, it's me. I'm at the hospital now and all checked in, so just come straight here. I'm not sure how long it will be. I've had a few contractions now, but they're not very close together. Nancy and Val are with me, though, so I'm not alone. Could be ages yet, so don't panic, but just get to me when you can. I love you.'

She slipped her phone back into her bag. She had no idea how he was going to do it, but she had never felt surer that, no matter what it took, Max would find a way to get to her.

'He's coming, little one,' she whispered. 'Just hang on in there a little longer.'

10

NOAH

The clock on the dashboard told Noah it was just after noon when he jumped into his car. Going from memory, he was pretty sure it would take about an hour and a bit to get there. Maybe less, if he ignored the speed limit, but the last thing he needed was to get pulled over by the police today.

'Where are you travelling to, sir?'

'Well, the thing is, I'm pretty sure my wife's shacked up with another bloke in a remote hotel near Loch Lomond, so I'm just going to go check that situation out.'

He plugged his phone into the car's audio system, punched in the destination, and tried to regulate his breathing as he made several turns to get out of Weirbridge and onto the route to the motorway. He automatically turned his head left as he passed the end of Max's street and saw Tress's car in the driveway. No sign of Max's Mercedes – the flashiest company car he'd ever seen, and way more impressive than Noah's trusty ten-year-old Volvo. Not that he cared about that kind of crap. He wasn't spending his hard-earned NHS salary on a £60K car. The third-hand Volvo would do him just fine.

He glanced over again just to make sure Max wasn't there. Nope, definitely no car. Although, he often put it in the garage, so that didn't mean anything. For a split second, he thought about stopping to check, but decided against it. He could really do with speaking to his mate right now, but he didn't want to disturb Tress. She was due soon, and the last thing she needed was Noah's dramas on her doorstep.

Besides, he didn't want to put any negative speculation about Anya out there in the universe, because he still couldn't believe that she would do anything to hurt him. It just wasn't her. This was much more like the kind of shit Max used to pull before he married Tress. He'd been the biggest player in the West of Scotland back then. Anything for a good time. But from the day he'd met Tress, he'd been a one-woman man. He'd settled down and was finally acting like the decent guy Noah had known he really was all along.

He pulled onto the access road to the motorway, and the traffic ground to a halt. Roadworks. Shit. Why today? Drumming his fingers on the wheel for the next ten minutes just made his anxiety levels rise further, so he pressed shuffle on his playlist and let the car fill with music. Okay, deep breath. There was going to be a simple explanation. It was going to be fine. Optimism was the way to go here. He forced himself to go with faith and positivity, until the song changed from Snow Patrol's 'Run' to Diana Ross's 'Ain't No Mountain High Enough'. That was one of Anya's contributions to his music catalogue and immediately sparked a different set of emotions and a barrage of memories.

Twelve years ago. They'd moved from the halls of residence to a two-bedroom flat in the Merchant City area of Glasgow. He and Anya had one bedroom and Max had the other, although his mate was dating a wannabe model with a shared flat in Park Circus, so he was staying there most of the time. Noah had been pretty sure it wouldn't last. It never did with Max. Clichéd as it was with him, it was all about the chase. As soon as he got what he wanted, he was bored and on to the next thing. Noah loved him like a brother, but he wasn't blind to the fact Max had been spoiled his whole life, by parents who were rich in cash, but not so much in affection. Noah's mum and dad had been the opposite. His dad, Leo, worked for the council, and his mum, Gilda, was a legal secretary, but to them, Noah, his brother and his three sisters were everything.

Argh, why wasn't this traffic moving? Hang on, green light at the roadworks. He was moving again. On to the motorway and heading west.

Where had his mind been going? Yep, Anya. 'Ain't No Mountain High Enough'. Their flat in the Merchant City. It was a Saturday night and they'd been out for dinner. They didn't have much money, but there was a little Italian place down at the Trongate that did a Saturday night special of two pizzas and a bottle of cheap plonk for £20. They'd come back from there, happy, a little tipsy, and definitely drunk on lust for some Saturday night passion. They'd fallen in the door and the first thing Anya had done, as always, was to press play on the CD player. Diana Ross. 'Ain't No Mountain High Enough'. She'd pushed him down on the sofa and then begun to dance, singing at the top of her voice as she performed an impromptu strip tease. Man, she was glorious. Spectacular. Only when she was naked did she come to him, easing herself down on his lap, kissing him, pulling his T-shirt over his head, their breathing frantic, desperate, rushed and...

'Aw, for fuck's sake, you two. I'll never be able to sit on that couch again.' Max, at the door, howling with laughter, his girlfriend behind him, eyes wide with surprise. 'We thought we'd come hang out with you tonight. So. Up to anything?'

Anya had her back to him, so she wasn't totally exposed and

that's probably why she could see the funny side of it. 'Shut your eyes right now, or I'll remove them while you're sleeping, Max Walker.'

He'd done as he was ordered, and she'd used the moment to pull her clothes back on, then flip around and sit on the couch next to Noah. When she was sorted, she acted as if nothing had happened.

'Max. Molly. Nice to see you. We were just about to watch *Mission Impossible* if you fancy joining us.'

That was one of a hundred unforgettable moments they'd all had when they'd lived together back then. Anya was always a class act. Funny. Smart. Decent. Just a really good human being. Someone who loved him fiercely, every bit as much as he loved her. When had that changed? When had they let this distance creep up between them? Stopped being on the same page?

If he really thought about it, it was when she'd joined Bralatech. Up until then, she'd had a pretty demanding job but still prioritised their relationship and their time, still shared his family dreams and his dedication to making their lives together amazing.

After joining Bralatech, that had changed. Just a little at first. Longer hours. More travel. Personal time spent at the laptop doing work stuff. Noah understood it completely. Was proud of her, even. She was a thirty-four year-old woman out there killing it in the corporate world, making changes, breaking glass ceilings, claiming her rightful place. But then, if he was honest with himself, he had started to resent the changes a little. She'd become so wrapped up in what she was doing, that he'd started to push back, to ask for their time together. He just wanted his wife. The one who hung out with him, the one who wanted to make love, the one who shared her life with him. He knew this was a stressful time for her, and he didn't need to come first, but he did need to matter.

Over the last six months or so, it had got even worse. It was as if nothing he said or did was right. As if she was just irritated with him on a permanent basis. And no matter how many times he asked, she would never tell him why.

Was that what had pushed her further away? Was this his fault? Or... The reason for this drive nudged into his mind with another possibility. Was it because she'd met someone else?

His heart rate started to speed up as he veered off the motorway slip road, down to a roundabout and then took the B road that ended at the Cairn Luss Lodge, about ten miles further along. There had been about thirty songs since Diana Ross, but he couldn't remember any of them, or a single thing he'd passed on the road, too wrapped up in his thoughts and memories to register what was going on outside his head.

The road was a single-track lane, with passing places every hundred metres or so. As he drove along, forced to keep his speed frustratingly slow because of the blind corners at every turn, he had the sudden realisation that he hadn't thought any of this through. What exactly was he going to do when he got there? Stalk the corridors of the hotel shouting for his wife? And if she was there and – it was excruciating to even form the thought – was... with... someone... else... what was he going to do? Was he ready to face that possibility? Could he handle being confronted with something that could destroy their marriage, their future, their lives? The answer was no. Definitely not. But he couldn't face not knowing either. He couldn't turn round and just go back to his life, always wondering what this was about, always suspicious, always terrified that he'd lost her. He had to know.

Not a single car came his way, but still the going was slow until, a few miles along the road, he heard a siren behind him and checked his rear-view mirror. An ambulance. Without thinking, he pulled into the next layby and let it pass, part of him wondering why it was out in such a remote spot, the other part of him thankful that he could tuck in behind it and get along this road quicker. It was the first stroke of luck he'd had all day, but he squashed that thought because it came with the reality that it was at someone else's misfortune. Hopefully, there was nothing serious happening to the person who was waiting for it.

Foot back on the accelerator, he drove another couple of miles, the ambulance slowing down frequently to go round blind corners. This bloody road was a minefield. Why would she choose this place instead of one of the far easier, larger, more luxurious hotels that were right off the motorway and down on the edge of the loch?

Thankfully, Noah was paying attention when the ambulance started to brake. This wasn't good. Either some clown was forcing the ambulance to pull in and let it past, or the injured person was out here, still a couple of miles from the nearest civilisation. He moved the steering wheel slightly, drawing his car out a few inches to the right and saw the answer. Up ahead, a police car, a police officer on the road, signalling to the ambulance to stop.

Noah had no choice but to do the same.

He jumped out as soon as he'd come to a halt and ran forward, catching up with the paramedics – one male and one female – who'd just climbed out of the ambulance and raced to the cop.

He held up his medical ID card. 'I'm a doctor. Glasgow Central. Can I help?'

Now that he was out of the car, he could see a van in the passing point ahead of him. Slumped on the ground next to it, a man Noah presumed was the van driver, maybe in his sixties, his face ashen white, a woman in cycling gear crouched down, holding his hand as he just kept repeating the same words.

'It wasn't my fault. Too fast. He was going too fast. It wasn't my fault. Too fast. He was going too fast.' The panic and confusion were in every word, and Noah could see he was in shock.

'We could do with your help,' the cop shot back, before addressing the paramedics. 'The van there,' the cop was saying to them, gesturing his head to where the man was propped against it, 'stopped to let a couple of cyclists past. One of them is over there,' he said, this time motioning to the woman Noah had already spotted. 'The other one drove on to the hotel to call us.'

Noah's brain was already in work mode, weighing up the scene, computing the possibilities, searching out answers. Had the van driver had a heart attack? Was that the issue here? But who was going to fast? What wasn't his fault? Something wasn't making sense.

'The van driver needs attention, but I think it's more shock than injury,' the cop was saying, spraying the facts out at speed, 'but the bigger issue is over there. He pointed to a wooded area that ran along the side of the road, and stretched back as far as the eye could see. 'There's a car in there. Came up behind the van. Didn't see it. Going too fast. Swerved. Went off the road. My partner is over there with it now. Two casualties. Pretty bad.'

'Got you,' one of the paramedics replied, and then took off, ploughing through the wood, Noah racing beside him, while his partner ran to the van driver to check him out.

Now that it had been pointed out, he could see it. About thirty metres to the side of him, a vehicle on its roof, tyres in the air. He could also see the trail through the bushes, coming from the other direction, where the car had come off the road and skidded through the shrubbery. Then he spotted the broken branches on the huge oak next to it. It must have hit the tree, flipped, and... oh shit, this wasn't good.

More details came into focus as he ran towards the wheels, feet slipping on the wet foliage. It was white. Run. A Range Rover. Run. An Evoque, just like Anya's car. Run. The driver's door and window were the only ones he could see. Run. Damn. A person there. Run. A guy. Eyes closed. Not moving. Run.

Stop.

The guy. Eyes closed. Not moving.

It was Max.

Noah dived forward to look further, a sickening twist in his guts, a prayer going out of his mind and into the universe.

Please don't let Anya be there too.

11

NANCY

'How is he doing?' Nancy asked Val, when her pal rejoined her at the chairs in the corridor, just along from where Tress was getting settled in. Val had nipped out of the ward to make a quick phone call home to check on Don.

'Mark says he's fine. They've had a walk around the park and they're just about to have a bit of lunch. Mark had set the TV planner to record the footie last night, so they're going to watch that this afternoon. I've told him where I am and what's going on here, and he says not to worry about rushing back because he can stay as long as I need him to. Tara and a couple of her girlfriends are taking all their kids to the cinema tonight, so he was at a loose end and thinking of staying over anyway.'

Val's son, Mark, was a lovely boy who'd married a lass from Australia and had two children, Claudie and Lochlin, who were about six and four. Val adored them all and she'd been thrilled when they'd moved back from Sydney to Scotland a couple of months ago. Mark had told Val he wanted the kids to know their roots, but they all knew that the big-hearted lad had really come back so he and Tara could support his mum and dad. He was a credit to Val, that boy, he really was.

Nancy couldn't miss the sadness in Val's voice, even though, as always, she'd tried to cover it up with her trademark cheeriness. 'You know, you don't have to put a face on with me, pal,' Nancy told her gently, nudging Val's shoulder with hers.

Beside her, Val sighed. 'I know that. And thank you. But it's like I was saying this morning, it doesn't feel right to moan about life with my Don, when you don't have Peter any more, because if I was given the choice between losing him altogether, and keeping him with me, even the way he is now, then that's what I'd choose every time.'

'I wouldn't blame you if you sometimes thought otherwise, Val. It's not an easy life you've got there.'

Val gave her a sad smile. 'I suppose. But you know something, Nancy, no matter how bad the day is, I know that at night, when he's asleep, I can lie beside him, and then, just for those hours, he's my Don again. I can feel him breathe and I can pretend that everything is fine. Sometimes I tell myself stories, you know? When I'm lying there, I close my eyes and imagine that we've been out that night, that we've had dinner somewhere lovely, with a whole gang of pals, and then we've all come back to our house for nightcaps and got the music on, a bit of Tom Jones and Elvis. And I picture Don, like a thousand nights gone by, belting his heart out and swivelling his hips, like he did that time he slipped a disc at your birthday barbeque and I had to take him to hospital. He'd had a few shandies, so he was still singing "Delilah" in A&E.'

Nancy's grin was wide as she nodded. 'Aye, that was a great night. Although, someone stole my garden gnomes and I've never seen them since. I think it was...'

'Josie,' they both said at the same time, laughing.

Josie had been Val's best friend for years and Nancy didn't even try to take her place. Josie was one of a kind. A free spirit, a force of nature, a fiercely loyal shining light with the gob of a sailor and a soul that absolutely refused to buckle under anything life threw at her. Val had told Nancy many times how, even on the night she'd died, Josie had been at a wedding, dancing and singing and drinking until dawn. Nancy knew that Val missed her every day of her life. She could see it now, as Val spoke.

'Yep, she had a pathological hatred of garden gnomes. Said they were just an advert for blokes sitting about doing nothing.'

That set off another gale of amusement, before Val switched back to what she'd been saying about Don, moving seamlessly between sadness and laughter, the same as they'd always done, the way that got them through every trouble and struggle in life.

'Anyway, those nights, those hours, when I can tell myself that everything is fine, they make every heartache and worry disappear, because I fall asleep with my arms around him and he's my Don again. I don't need to think any other way until I wake up and remember. If that's all I get now, then I'll take it, Nancy, because it's better than not having him here at all.'

'I hear you, love, and I don't think for a second that I'd choose any differently. Sometimes I think it was a mercy that my Peter was taken so quickly, other times I'd give anything to have spotted the cancer earlier, maybe given him more time. Not that he wanted all those treatments, as you know.'

He'd been a stubborn one, Peter. That's why it had taken him so long to even go to the doctor to get the mole on his scalp looked at. He'd always had a fierce head of hair, but in his early fifties it had finally begun to thin. Of course, he didn't go with all that baseball cap nonsense that the young ones wore these days, so they'd carried on as usual, with their two holidays a year in the blistering sun. Then there were all those days on the golf course, walking for miles on a sunny day, and endless hours in the garden too, out there with his top off at the slightest hint of sunshine. Tango Man, his work colleagues called him, because he made it his life mission to have a permanent tan. It was Nancy who'd first noticed that the mole on his scalp had grown. She'd been using clippers to shave the back of his neck the day before they flew to Tenerife for a fortnight. 'Jesus, Peter, that thing on your head is the size of a raisin now.'

He'd nodded, almost causing a near-death incident with the clippers. 'Aye, I noticed that. Age, darling. That's all it is. There's things growing where they shouldn't be and there's other bits falling off. There'll be no two bits of us hanging the right way soon.' His arms had slid around her waist and given her a squeeze. All those years and he still loved a cuddle at every opportunity.

She'd finally persuaded him to have it checked when they got back from holiday and the results had been swift and devastating. Skin cancer. Malignant melanoma. It had already spread to his lymph nodes and ravaged his body. Turned out he'd been hiding the fact that he had been feeling awful for a long time. Until it was too late. By the time he had it investigated, it was terminal, they'd said. He'd refused all chemo options, determined to enjoy what time he had left. And they did. Two more holidays and countless days of golf, until he was gone, barely six months after diagnosis. Just like that.

Many times in their marriage Nancy had wondered if Peter was the right choice back when it came down to deciding who she would spend her life with, but they'd had more ups than downs and there wasn't a day since then that Nancy hadn't missed him. That thought sat with her for a moment.

'You know, I think this is a sign from the heavens,' she said with a sigh.

Val raised an eyebrow. 'That you shouldn't spend yer day impersonating an ostrich?'

'I swear to God, Val Murray, don't make me talk about the time you turned up at Hogmanay in that floaty dress that went transparent under the fairy lights. You'd get put on a register for that these days – you flashed the whole village.'

Val nodded, nonplussed. 'Aye but I got a dozen invitations to parties the following New Year, so it wasn't all bad. Anyway, what's the sign from the heavens then?'

Nancy idly brushed her feathers with her fingers. 'Well, I've waited fifty years to meet Eddie Mackie again and I admit that occasionally I've wondered what my life would have been like with him. And I suppose, silly old fool that I am, maybe I thought I could have the best of both worlds. A great life with Peter and then time with Eddie. Maybe a second romance. Another chance to see if we'd been right for each other after all.'

'But?' Val prompted.

'But I'm sitting in a hospital, in a frock that I'll be paying off to my catalogue for the next six months, because the heavens have called on me for the first time ever to take care of someone who's about to have the biggest moment of her life. Me! Who has never even had kids and wouldn't know one end of a breast pump from the other.'

'That could make your eyes water,' Val quipped.

Nancy ignored her and carried on, 'And all this happened on the one day – THE ONE DAY – that the only love of my life, other than my Peter, is going to be in the same country. If that isn't a sign from the gods that I should swerve the whole reunion idea, then I don't know what is.'

'You could be right,' Val agreed solemnly. 'Either that or Peter is up there bribing the gods with what's left of his pension to sabotage your plans. If this doesn't work, I'd look out for banana skins and meteor strikes in your street.'

They were still laughing when the nurse they'd seen earlier came out of the side room. 'Ladies, you can both go on in now. Dr Greyson is on the way, and she'll be here shortly, so I'll have to ask you to nip out again while Mrs Walker is being examined, but you're welcome to keep her company until then.'

Nancy and Val both jumped up, Nancy as quick as her skin-tight frock of feathers would allow. As soon as they got on the ward, they saw that Tress was hooked up to a couple of monitors.

'I had another contraction there, so the nurse did all my vitals and then hooked me up to check the baby's heart rate. She said that everything looks okay. The doctor is going to examine me, and they'll decide then whether to move me to the labour suite. It depends how dilated I am.'

Nancy and Val both slid into the plastic chairs at the side of Tress's bed. 'Any word from Max yet?'

Tress shook her head and Nancy could see that the poor lass was apprehensive.

'Then don't you worry, pet, we've got you. Me and Val can stay here as long as you need us.'

'But your party…'

'Max will be here by then, surely. And even if he isn't, I'm having second thoughts about that anyway.' She'd just got the word out when there was the beep of an incoming text on a mobile phone. Val and Tress both grabbed their phones and checked their screens.

'Max?' Nancy asked Tress, but she didn't even need to wait for an answer, because the poor thing's face fell, and she turned the blank screen for Nancy to see. 'Nope, not Max. It wasn't my phone.'

Nancy went for the next logical option. 'Was it Mark, Val? Is everything okay?'

Val was still fidgeting with her phone and Nancy got that. They were both convinced that being of a certain age gave them an affliction that caused severe delays at every stage of mobile phone use. Wrong password. Face ID not working. Thumbprint buggered. And then when they did get in, they had to suss out if they'd just received a Facebook message, a snapchat, a Whats-App, a text, or an alert from an energy company to say their next electricity bill was going to require them to remortgage the house. After Val had worked her way through all of those options, she shook her head. 'Nope, wasn't me either.'

'Och, bugger...' Nancy mumbled, pulling her bag onto her lap and having a rummage, before finally liberating her phone. She hadn't even thought to check because she didn't expect anyone to be looking for her. Unless it was Angie and she needed new batteries for her hand fans.

Thumbprint? Not working. Two attempts to enter the password? Finally in. Text? Nope. WhatsApp? Nope. Facebook message? Yup, there it was.

'Right, girls, hold on to your knickers.' She cleared her throat and started reading.

'New message from Eddie Mackie.

Nancy, I couldn't sleep last night for thinking about seeing you again tonight. We've got so many years to make up for. Counting the hours. Love, Eddie.'

The other two didn't say a word, just eyed her expectantly, waiting for her reaction. Ten minutes ago, she'd decided she wasn't going, and she stood by that decision. She wasn't the kind of woman to be swayed by mushy words and romantic fairy tales. No. It didn't matter. She was too old and too long in the tooth to go chasing after fantasies.

Wasn't she?

Oh, bugger it.

'Tress, love,' she blurted, 'I just need a word with the wee one.' She leaned forward so that she was speaking to Tress's bump. 'Son, I know you're probably comfy in there floating about without a care in the world, but if I could ask a wee favour. Could you hurry up and get ready to slide down that chute the second yer daddy gets here, because Aunty Nancy has a party to go to.'

12

MAX

The pain.

Max didn't understand.

The pain was everywhere. He tried to breathe, but that hurt more.

Why couldn't he see?

Why was his body not working?

He couldn't make sense of it.

Why wasn't he driving? He'd been in the car, he was rushing to Tress. Tress. The baby. He had to get to the hospital for the baby. A memory. He'd been leaving the hotel. He'd dropped the phone. Picked it up.

Driving.

Out of the entrance to the lodge, along the dirt track road. Speeding. Had to get to the hospital. Eyes to the phone, tried to call, wouldn't go through.

His son was coming.

Tried to call again. Still no success. Had to get back into a signal area.

Anya was screaming at him to slow down, but he wasn't

listening to her. She wanted to wait. To talk. To plan out what they were going to say, but he didn't have time.

Driving. Racing.

Every time he went around a corner, she was yelling at him to slow down, but he knew this road. He'd been here many times and he'd see if someone was coming. Even on the blind corners, he'd hear them. One corner. Two corners. Slowing down a little on the bend but not too much because he didn't want to lose time.

Another corner.

He went round it. See. No problem.

Wait.

A flash of something. A van. It was stopped right there in front of him.

Fuck.

He swerved to avoid it, but he was too late. Going too fast.

The car clipped the back of the van. A bang. Then they were in the air and they were flying. Spinning. Once. Twice. Three times. Another bang. They hit something. A tree. They dropped. Hit the ground. Metal crunching. Rolled again. Glass smashing. Stopped. But...

Dark. It all went dark.

His eyes tried to open again.

The pain. So much pain.

Upside down. Why? What had happened? And Anya. Was she okay? Was she next to him? Where was she? Fuck. Was she there? Hurt? Safe? Going for help?

It hurt to move, but he tried to turn his neck. More pain.

Had to see. Forced himself. Had to see... Oh God. Anya. Her face. Blood. Her eyes closed. Hanging. Like him. Inside the car. Seat belts on. Upside down. Oh God, Anya. Anya.

The smell. Petrol. It was all round him. Burning. Rubber. Metallic. Blood.

Make this make sense.

Where was he? He had to get to the hospital. Had to move.

A dream. Was this a dream? Was he asleep? Was his wife in hospital? Was there a baby?

Yes, a dream. It was all a dream.

Dark. It all went dark again.

Awake. The smell. Worse now. Petrol. Blood. The noise.

Someone was banging on the window. His eyes. Blurred. He couldn't see properly. A woman's voice. Shouting. Trying to open the doors. Wouldn't work. Trying to smash the window. Couldn't do it. Going for help, she was screaming. Going for help.

Tried to move. His arms wouldn't work. He couldn't see why. Eyes. Sore. Blurred.

Make this make sense, he begged again. Make this make sense.

The pain. Everywhere. His head exploding. His back on fire. His legs throbbing.

Darkness.

His eyes flew open. Light again. A new noise. A man's voice. Yellow. Maybe a jacket.

'Hello!' he was shouting. 'Hello! Can you hear me? We're going to get you out of there. Can you hear me? Can you move?'

Only my eyes. And when they move, I see Anya.

So much blood. So much.

Cold. So cold.

The man. He was pulling trees away. Branches coming off the windows. Then a hand. At Anya's side. Coming through the smashed glass. Pressing buttons on the door. Nothing working. Doors still locked.

Voices outside. Male. Female. People shouting. We need to get them out of there. The petrol is leaking. Risk. Explosion. Can't wait for the cutters. Need to move now. Get me tools. Running. Shouting. Okay, here. Use this.

The voice. He knew the voice. Noah. His mate was here. Thank God. Noah was here. Everything would be okay now.

But Anya. Shit. Noah would see Anya. She shouldn't be here. He shouldn't be here. Fuck.

Blackness.

Awake.

Anger. Frustration. Why couldn't he speak? Why couldn't he shout? Help. Get me out of here.

A dream. Had to be a dream.

No. A car. Upside down. He'd been going too fast. Driving. Bang. Confused. Had those thoughts before.

Don't think back. Think now.

Noah was here. Everything was going to be okay. He was going to get him home. To Tress. To their baby.

'Anya!' Noah was screaming. 'Anya, speak to me!'

More movement. More talking.

'Anya, we're going to get you out of there. Hang on, babe. I've got you. I've got you.' Noah was shouting now. Orders. More voices. Smashing glass. Then he was reaching into the car. A click. Anya's seat belt. A sudden movement. A drop. Noah caught her. He had her. Touching her face. 'I've got you, babe. I've got you.'

She was moving away. Out of the window. The ground was rocking. The car moving.

Stopped again.

Someone coming towards him. In the car. Through the window.

'Max, can you hear me?' Noah again.

Beside him now. Touching his neck. Pulling up his eyelids. A light. Shining.

Touching him again. His head. His neck. His shoulders.

'We need to get him out right now.' Noah shouts.

Another voice. A man. Can't make out what he's saying.

Noah again. 'We haven't got that long. We need to get him out now. Get the backboard ready.'

Movement. Next to him.

'Max, I'm going to move you. Try to stay with me. Can you hear me? I'm going to take your seat belt off and then I'm going to hold you and pull you out.'

Okay, Noah. The words in his head. Couldn't say them. Getting out, though. Noah was going to get him out. A jolt. Pain. Chest.

Try to speak. Can't. Want to smile. Want to say thank you. Help me. Please. Get me to Tress. To my baby.

'Okay, Max, we've got you.'

Lying down. On a board. Lifted up. People shouting. Running.

'Get him in the ambulance. She's already in there.'

'Stay with us, Max. Stay with us.' Noah again. 'We're going to get you to the...'

A bang. So loud. And a smell. Fire. Petrol. Heat.

Shouting. Fuck. Swearing. Rushing. Moving faster now.

Another noise. Sliding. Doors slamming. Moving again. Inside a car. No, a van. An ambulance. The sirens. They were going with him.

All the time, Noah's voice. Talking to someone. A woman. Conversations.

Something about oxygen. Keep it going.

Someone touching him again. 'Max, can you hear me?'

I can hear you, Noah. Just can't speak. Can't tell you. Thank you. Thank you for coming for me.

And Anya. Thank you for coming for us both.

Us both.

I'm sorry. I'm so sorry, Noah. Please don't hate me. I didn't mean to...

Pain. Chest.

But it was okay.

Noah was here.

He would fix everything.

He was already helping.

The pain. Going away. Cold. So cold. No more pain. All gone.

All gone.

Everything black.

2 P.M. – 4 P.M.

13

TRESS

Dr Greyson had that calm way about her, the reassuring manner of someone who had helped a thousand mothers and birthed a thousand babies, with one hand tied behind her back, before lunchtime. She came into the ward with another woman, whom she introduced as Sally, the midwife who'd be looking after Tress today.

'Love that dress,' Sally said to Nancy with a smile and Tress liked her even more. That wasn't a frock for the faint-hearted.

'Just some casual daywear I threw on,' Nancy replied, with pitch-perfect nonchalance.

'These are my friends, Nancy and Val,' Tress explained, pushing herself up in the bed, trying not to think about the fact that she'd be flashing her vagina to strangers any second now. 'My husband is away on a business trip today – bad timing – and we're having trouble getting a hold of him.'

Dr Greyson was the epitome of calm. 'Don't you worry. Let's take a look and see how you're doing then, shall we?'

Val and Nancy were already on their feet and heading out of the curtained area.

'We'll be right outside, lovely,' Nancy told her. 'In fact, we'll just nip down to the café and we'll bring you back some coffee and lunch. You must be starving.'

Tress felt another overwhelming wave of gratitude. If it wasn't for these two women, she'd be doing this completely alone.

Dr Greyson picked up her chart, read over it and then gently gave Tress instructions so that she could examine her.

Tress stared at the ceiling the whole time, trying to disassociate from what was happening. It was okay. It was all going to be okay. How many times had she told herself that today?

The truth was that on the inside, she was starting to panic. Where was Max? Why hadn't he called back? He must have landed. Must be in London by now, so why wouldn't he have returned her call? The obvious suggestions flicked through her mind. He'd lost his phone. It wasn't working. The flight had been hijacked. Okay, that one was probably a long shot, but it was getting to the stage where some kind of natural disaster or cataclysmic event was going to be the only justifiable reason that he hadn't fricking answered her texts.

Or maybe... maybe he just wasn't ready to face fatherhood.

She felt a rise of heat soar up her neck at the very thought of that. There it was. It was out. The thing she'd been blocking for months, her worries, her doubts, her fear that he wasn't ready to put someone else before himself.

She adored her husband, but she wasn't blind to his faults. He could be selfish. Self-centred. What if he'd left her? What if he'd just done a runner and she was going to have to do this all alone, bring up this child by herself? Just like her mum had done?

Tress had never known her dad, didn't even know his name. A holiday romance, her mum had always told her. Julie had gone to Corfu, her first holiday with her girlfriends when she was eighteen years old, and come back with a sun tan and a baby on the way. Every time Tress watched *Long Lost Family*, she wondered if she should try to track down the man who shared her DNA, but the truth was she didn't want to know. There wasn't a thing she'd change about her childhood or her life now, so adding a stranger into it just because he shared her genetics held no appeal. Besides, it was such a romantic tale that she was always worried she'd find out it wasn't true and her dad was actually a one-night stand after a boozy night out in The Bigg Market. Didn't matter. Her mum had made sure Tress always felt enough love for two parents. Why wasn't she here? Why couldn't she have hung on for just a while longer, to see her married, to meet her grandchild?

'Are you okay, Tress?' Dr Greyson had stepped back from her nethers and was now looking at her with tender concern.

Tress wiped away the silent tears with the palm of her hand. 'Yes, I'm just... sorry. A bit overwhelmed.'

'That's to be expected,' she said sympathetically, then transitioned effortlessly back into business mode. 'Right, well, you're only a couple of centimetres dilated, so I'm going to keep you here for now. Everything looks perfectly straightforward, though, so nothing to worry about. I have a couple of deliveries down in the labour suites, so Sally will take over your care and she'll keep me posted. Try to rest. To eat. Keep your energy for later.'

Tress had a feeling that was something she said every day.

'Do you want the curtain left closed or open?' Sally asked her, and Tress warmed even more to the soothing kindness in her manner.

'Closed, please.'

'No problem. I'll check back in on you every half-hour or so, but your buzzer is there if you need me.'

Tress lay her head back on the pillow and closed her eyes, suddenly exhausted, but absolutely sure that sleep wasn't an option.

'Are you decent? Don't want to come in there if I'm going to see bits of you that you don't usually show your neighbours.' Nancy's voice.

'Definitely decent. Just an emotional wreck and prone to teary outbursts,' Tress replied.

'That's just a day ending in a Y for me,' Val quipped back, as she came through the curtains first, clutching a cup holder with three beverages on it. She turned back to Nancy, who was coming in behind her, balancing a tower of paper bags topped with three bananas and a plastic box of grapes, face like thunder. 'And you straighten yer face, Nancy Jenkins. It was an easy mistake to make.'

'What was?' Tress asked, pushing herself up to a sitting position and pulling the wheely table towards her so that it was over the bed in front of her.

Nancy wasn't forthcoming, so Val filled in the blanks. 'Bloke down in the canteen took one look at those feathers and her slippers and asked her if she was one of the entertainers. Apparently they put on a show over at the day room in the children's ward once a month. They thought she was Big Bird.' Val let that sit for a moment, as Tress tried to contain her laughter, before going on, 'Easy mistake to make. Anyway, here's your coffee. Decaf. And water.' She pulled out a bottle from the depths of her handbag and put it on the table. 'Chicken or ham? Miss Stroppy Knickers over there is offering a choice of both.'

'Chicken please.'

Nancy shuffled over, throwing daggers at her pal. 'Val Murray, your Don deserves a medal for putting up with you all those years. I'd have put gaffer tape on that gob by now. Here you go, lovely.' She plonked the fruit and one of the paper bags down on the table next to the drinks, then opened another bag to reveal a

Jenga-sized supply of Kit Kats. 'Have you had another contraction yet, pet?' she checked.

Tress picked up the sandwich, her hunger genes suddenly activated by the food in front of her. 'No, nothing. Doctor says that can happen sometimes, but they've checked everything and it all looks fine.'

Val reached over and squeezed her hand. 'You're doing great, Tress, you really are. You're strong, and you're brave and there's nothing you can't handle because you're a warrior.'

Tress saw that Nancy had frozen, ham sandwich halfway to her mouth and was surveying Val with clear surprise, until she couldn't keep her thoughts in any longer and exploded in a gale of laughter.

'What was that? Sweet Jesus, Val, you sounded like a Hallmark card there.'

Val raised her eyebrow and drew herself up as if she was going to slay her critic, then dissolved into cackles. 'Was it too much? I read it on a card down in the gift shop while you were in the loo, and I thought I'd use it. They're always saying on *Loose Women* that we should lift each other up, so I thought I'd give it a try. That kind of lingo is all the rage now, Nancy. Positive reinforcement, it's called. Our Tara is always going on about it. It's all about self-care and affirmations, these days. You need to get with the times.'

Nancy's shoulders were trembling with amusement. 'You do that then, doll – but if you're going to try to lift me up, I'd prefer a couple of vodka and lemonades and a night at the bingo.'

'Noted,' Val grinned. 'Anyway, Tress, heard from the bold Max yet? I don't want to overreact, but if we don't track him down soon, I'm thinking Interpol or a national TV campaign.'

'Nothing. To be honest, I'm starting to get worried. It just doesn't make sense. Even without the baby, he'd normally have called and checked in on me by now.'

Nancy put her ham sandwich down. 'Right, let's really think about this and see if we can get to the bottom of it... Supposing his phone was lost. How else could you contact him?'

'I don't know. I think he was going straight to the conference, but I've no idea where that was being held. To be honest, I'm not even sure what hotel he's staying at.' Just saying that out loud, Tress could hear how crazy it sounded, but she'd just always called him on his mobile when he was away. It had never crossed her mind to reach him any other way. 'I mean, I know the one he usually stays at...'

Val sprang to attention and – after the standard umpteen clicks and a swear word – managed to get her phone open and held it up ready to go. 'Right, what's it called?'

'The Hilton in Kensington,' Tress answered confidently, feeling better that at least they were doing something that might help.

Val began tapping something on the screen with her pearly pink painted thumbs.

Nancy sighed. 'This baby will be born before you finish typing that.'

Val ignored her, concentrating furiously before giving a triumphant smile. 'Got it.' She pressed the screen again and the phone burst into life with a loud ringtone. 'Bugger!' Val hissed, frantically pressing the side of the handset until the volume decreased, just as the call was answered.

Tress watched as Val got her phone voice on.

'Hello, yes, I wonder if you can help me. I'm trying to track down one of your guests. Mr Max Walker. He's staying there tonight, and his wife has just gone into labour, so it's crucial that we speak to him as soon as possible.'

Nancy leaned closer to Tress. 'She can't buy a pint of milk without telling the folk behind the counter her life story.'

Tress watched, hope rising, then... Val's face changed.

'Are you sure? And definitely not checking in later?'

Another pause.

'Okay, thank you.' Click. 'He's not there. And they have no reservation in that name for tonight.'

'He must be staying somewhere else,' Tress mused.

'What about calling his office and asking?' Val suggested.

Tress jumped on that one. 'Yes!' Damn. She should probably have done that before now, but it hadn't crossed her mind. Not once, in all the years they'd been together, had she had a need to call his office. 'It's Bralatech. In the city centre. Argyll Street.'

Val was off and typing again. 'Got it.' Dial. 'Yes, I wonder if you can help me. I'm trying to track down Max Walker. I need to speak to him urgently.'

Val held the phone in the space between them so they could hear.

'I'm sorry, but Mr Walker isn't in the office today. Can I take a message?'

'Yes, I realise he's not in the office, but it's crucial I speak to him.'

'I'm sorry, as I said, he's not here today. If you'd like to leave your number, I'll have him call you back.'

'And *as I said*, it is urgent,' Val was going full-scale Princess Anne, posh voice and full of authority. 'Can you contact him now and ask him to call me straight away please?'

'No. As I said...' That was the third time that phrase had been thrown into the conversation and the person on the other line was speaking slowly and with attitude now, clearly not getting the urgency of the situation, 'he is not available today. I can have him call you back on Monday.'

Val rolled her eyes and Tress could see she was getting impatient, her voice becoming more insistent with every word. 'Look, dear, I don't think you understand. I'm his mother...'

Nancy spat her tea across the table.

'And I'm actually with his very pregnant wife, who is about to have their child, so, again, please contact him immediately and have him call his wife.'

That seemed to have the desired effect as they got a curt, 'Hold on, please.'

After what seemed like an age, the woman came back on the line, more hesitant and unsure this time.

'I'm sorry, but Mr Walker isn't answering his mobile at the moment.'

Tress thought Val's head was going to explode, but she managed to keep her cool.

'Yes, we've tried that already. That's why we're calling you. We need you to call wherever he is in London and interrupt his conference and tell him to get back here pronto. This. Is. An. Emergency.'

Another pause.

Tress could feel her anxiety rising. What was wrong with this woman on the other end of the phone? Why wasn't she all over this and trying to help? Max would be furious when she told him about this.

'Mrs Walker...' Tress was confused for a second, then she remembered that Val had claimed to be Max's mother. 'I really do understand that, but... but... I think there must be crossed wires somewhere. Mr Walker isn't at a conference today. And I'm not sure if he's in London, but if he is, he's not on company business. Mr Walker is off today.'

Tress felt every muscle in her body deflate as Val clarified, 'Off?'

'Yes. He took a personal day. So, I'm sorry, I really do have no way of contacting him.'

Val disconnected the call and the three of them stared at each other in stunned silence.

Tress felt a wave of nausea erupting inside her body, fighting its way to the top until she couldn't contain it. Thankfully, Val saw it coming and grabbed a cardboard toilet pan from the unit beside her bed. Tress heaved until there was nothing else to bring up.

'I don't understand. None of this makes sense,' she said, voice hoarse from vomiting.

'There will be an explanation, love,' Val was saying, as she rubbed her back, but Tress caught the look of worry, or maybe suspicion, that passed between the two women.

'Has... has he left me?' she whispered.

Neither of them jumped to answer. Instead, Nancy got up from her chair.

'Of course not. I've just had a thought. Noah Clark works in this hospital, doesn't he? Paediatrics?'

Tress nodded. 'Yes, but I don't know if he's working today. I couldn't reach him either.'

'Well, I'm going to go and find out. Because those two boys have always been thick as thieves and if anyone will know where Max is, it's Noah.'

14

_____

NOAH

The ambulance must have hit a pothole, because there was a sudden bang and a swerve and Noah was thrown from one side of the vehicle to the other. Only quick reflexes saved him from slamming against the compartments on the side wall.

Recovering his balance, he dropped back to a crouch position between the two stretchers. Anya on one side of him. Max on the other. His brain wasn't even capable of trying to process this situation and was just batting away the questions that sneaked through his focus on what was actually happening in front of him. Anya and Max were together? Swipe away. Why were they in a hotel? Swipe away. Why had Anya lied to him? Swipe away. Was there something going on between them? Swipe away. Were they having an affair? Swipe away. Had his wife and the man who had been like a brother to him all their lives betrayed him? Head explodes.

He couldn't deal with any of that right now, because at this moment, things were not good, and every single synapse and cell of his brain had to be focused on the people in front of him. Not his wife. Not his friend. His patients. Because if he connected the bloody face of the woman on the stretcher with the wife that he adored, then he'd fall apart.

It had been the toughest thing he'd ever done to keep it together at the scene, but the urgency and years of professional training blocked everything else out and he'd started to shout out information to the paramedic and the police officer he was working with.

The car had come to rest upside down, pressed up against a tree on one side and thick foliage on the other. As soon as he'd reached it, the fumes had told him that the petrol tank had burst, and the engine was still running, still firing, smoke everywhere. Added to that, both of them had been suspended upside down, which could have fatal consequences, depending on their injuries.

'Male. Thirty-five. Driver. Female Thirty-four. Passenger. Both unconscious,' he'd rattled out as he'd dived to the ground, trying desperately to see how they could get them out of there.

The paramedic who was with him had the obvious questions, raised by the fact that Noah had barked out their ages. 'Wait, you know them?'

Noah had still been lying on the ground, trying to prise open a door, or work out a way to get in through the crushed windscreen. 'She's my wife, I was on my way to get her.' Right then, right there, he couldn't even remember why. All that mattered was in front of him. Ten minutes ago, an hour ago, this morning, last night... none of that existed any more.

He had soon sussed out that there was no way to right the car, no way to open the doors, no easy way to get to them and get them out. In any other situation, it would have been preferrable to wait for the fire service to cut them out, but there was no time.

Option one: follow best protocol for potential back and neck injuries by cutting the passengers out and removing them to a stretcher in a controlled manner. Potential issues: car could explode at any minute, and position of victims could be fatal for certain categories of internal bleeding.

Option two: get neck braces on and get them out of vehicle as quickly but as safely as possible, mindful that the movements could exacerbate back or neck injuries while, quite honestly, knowing that the slightest jolt could have catastrophic consequences.

They'd gone for option two. No contest.

Max's side of the car was in thick foliage that was going to take more than the tools they had available to get through, so they'd worked out that the quickest way in would be through Anya's side. The front windscreen was already smashed, but the car was tilted forward so there was no way he could go in that way. Between the police officers and the paramedics, they'd managed to use crowbars and cutters to clear enough of the tree branches away to smash the side window. That had given him enough leverage to reach in and put a brace around Anya's neck, undo her seat belt, then pull her out.

The paramedics had immediately taken over, getting her onto a stretcher and clearing the scene.

'Are you sure you want to go back in there?' one of the cops had shouted. 'I don't know how long you're going to have.'

Noah hadn't even got the reply out when the officer had shouted, 'Fuck!' and sprang into action. Noah had followed his movements and saw the problem. A flame. Over at the back wheel. The officer had already unpinned his fire extinguisher and started blasting.

'Doc, I think you need to leave him. Wait till the fire service get here,' he'd shouted over the noise.

Noah knew there wasn't a choice.

He threw himself back into the vehicle through the same side window, fixed Max's neck brace, then released his seat belt, supporting his weight and turning him as he pulled him out. One of the paramedics was already racing back to him with a second stretcher. They had managed to get Max on it and start moving. Seconds later, they'd just made it back to the road when the back end of the car exploded, sending them all diving for cover.

'There's another team on the way for him,' the female paramedic had shouted to the police, gesturing to the driver of the van, who was still in shock but coherent on the other side of the road.

Noah had leaned into his car, grabbed his phone, then shouted to her over the noise and the chaos, 'My keys are in still in my car. Do whatever you need to do with it.' He didn't care. All he cared about right now was in this ambulance.

Doors had slammed, the engine had started and they were away, lights flashing, sirens blaring, slowing only once to pass the fire engine and second ambulance that had pulled into a layby to let them past.

That had been about an hour ago, maybe more, maybe less. Noah had lost track of time, knowing only that the drive had been smooth for a while now so they were on the motorway. He no longer even registered the noise of the sirens or the speed that they were travelling at, too busy counting the seconds until they reached their destination. A couple of times, he felt the inner panic rising, the questions resurfacing, the chilling fear that this was going to be a life-altering situation for them all, but every time he felt his emotions surface, he squashed them right back down again. Later. No time for feelings or doubts right now. All that mattered were the patients.

The paramedic riding with him was monitoring Max, while Noah tended to Anya. From what he could see, her injuries were extensive. She was still unconscious, and they hadn't been able to bring her round despite their best efforts. Her blood pressure was way too high but consistent with this level of injury, and she was tachycardic, with a pulse of over 150. It had been over ten years since he'd done a rotation in A&E, so he was out of date and out of practice on emergency treatment. He had let the paramedic do her work and she was an absolute personification of calm but urgent efficiency. Right now, he'd classify both Max and Anya as critical.

Noah pushed Anya's hair back from her face. She had severe cuts to her cheek, her lips and her forehead, probably from broken glass. Just by looking at her, he could see that her nose was broken and at least one of her wrists had obvious fractures, so he'd strapped her arm to her chest in a splint. On the surface, none of those things should have rendered her unconscious, so it was the bloody mass on the top of her scalp that was worrying him the most. They'd stopped the bleeding, but she'd clearly sustained a massive head trauma and if he were to make a clinical judgement, he'd say there were major internal injuries in her abdominal area too. Her blouse was torn and their examination showed widespread bruising already forming on her stomach and side. He couldn't even hold her free hand, in case it aggravated any potential fractures there, so, without thinking, he settled for the lightest touch on the side of her hip, just hoping that, somewhere in there, she knew he was with her, and that his touch gave her strength or comfort or just the basic human need for reassurance.

Max's injuries were more difficult to assess. He'd been unconscious since Noah had got to the car, apart from a few seconds when he'd mumbled incoherent words. There was definitely a significant head injury, indicated by a massive swelling to his temple, just into his hairline. That was the only visible damage, which made Noah even more concerned. Until they got him into a scanner, they wouldn't know what they were dealing with.

The paramedic beside him had stopped working on Max now and radioed forward to her colleague. 'What's our ETA, Bob? Goes without saying, mate, but we're on a time crunch back here.'

'Five minutes, Jodie. Road is clear. A&E standing by and ready.'

The ambulance swayed to the left, so Noah knew they were coming off the slip road and would be travelling a couple of hundred metres along a city-centre road to the entrance to Glasgow Central A&E. Every day he drove the same route to his work, and not once had he ever imagined this scene, that he'd be racing here in an ambulance with his wife and best friend, both badly injured, both unconscious.

'Noah?'

It was the faintest whisper, the smallest movement of her lips, so barely discernible that at first, he'd thought he'd imagined it, that, like a mirage in the desert, he'd manifested it through sheer desperation.

'Noah?' A second time. Definitely not imagined.

'I'm here. I can't hold your hand because you're hurt, my darling, but I'm here and I'm taking care of you. Don't worry, I've got you. I've got you.'

Another tiny movement and words that were almost like the softest of breaths. 'I'm... sorry.'

That almost broke him. He'd been holding it together the whole way, but now he could feel his throat being strangled by pain, his eyes furiously blinking back the pools of water that were forming there.

'It's okay, baby. It's okay. We're going to fix this. We're going to—'

The furious beeping of the monitor to his right shut down his words, swiftly followed by the murmured 'Shit!' from Jodie, who almost knocked him out of the way as she spun around and grabbed an oxygen bag from somewhere behind him.

'We're just pulling up, so I've got her airway, you do compressions, let's get her inside before we shock her,' she ordered, and Noah snapped right back into doctor mode.

He somehow managed to keep his balance as he stood over his wife, two hands on her chest, trying desperately to push her life back into her body, one press on her chest at a time. One. Two. Three. Four. Five. He didn't even register the ambulance stopping, or the doors opening, or the swarm of people who had jumped in and who were now helping to get Anya out of the vehicle. They were pushing, pulling, while Noah was still pressing. One. Two. Three. Four. Five.

Doors banging open. Lights blinding. Into a cubicle.

'You take over compressions. You on defib. I need...' Another doctor, a woman, he didn't even register who it was, was calmly issuing orders to a team of people who snapped to work, doing the jobs they were trained to do. 'Noah, step back, we've got this,' the doctor's voice was saying now.

Someone who knew him then. He'd worked his whole career in this hospital so that wouldn't be unusual.

'Noah!' The voice was insistent this time and it registered. Dr Cheska Ayton. They'd come through the ranks together and been friends since medical school.

Noah felt hands taking his away from Anya and he fell back, hit a wall, slumped down and then he heard it – the solitary sound, the constant note that was coming from the monitor in the corner.

She was gone.

Noah wasn't a religious man, but all he could do was pray that they would get his wife back.

15

NANCY

Nancy shuffled into the lift, pressed the button to go down to the ground floor, then alighted to a busy lobby area. The maternity wing was just off to the right-hand side of the main Glasgow Central building and was the nearest hospital to the village of Weirbridge for expectant mums. Nancy had been here many times in her life, but always as a visitor, never the mum.

That thought would always make her sad. Not that she felt a woman needed children to have a lifetime of happiness. Hell, no. Her pal, Angie, and her cousin, Dora, had both decided that they didn't want kids and Nancy absolutely respected that choice. Envied it, even. It just hadn't been Nancy's.

For the first couple of years that she'd been married to Peter, they hadn't given it a second thought. They'd gone to Majorca on their honeymoon, the first foreign holiday for both of them, and oh, it had given them a taste for it. They'd drunk sangria, and danced until dawn, and then slept on the beach all day to recover. Fourteen days of that and they'd both gone home thinking they'd had the best two weeks ever, and vowing that they were going to save like demons and repeat the experience as often as possible.

Back then, she'd got a job in the council office's canteen, and all the other lassies the same age that worked there were of the same mindset. No responsibilities, just work hard all week, then use their wages to shop, or to buy new clothes, or maybe to go to a concert. She'd seen David Bowie and Blondie at the Glasgow Apollo theatre in 1978 and both times she'd sung so loud, she'd lost her voice for a week.

But gigs and nights out weren't the only priority for her and Peter. There were no credit cards or any of that nonsense back then, so they'd put money by every week into a tea caddy in the kitchen cupboard to save for the next trip. She'd eat egg and spam for months if it meant she could have an extra week in Palma Nova every year.

It was only when she hit her mid-twenties that she started to think it might be time to start a family. She'd been using one of those new-fangled cap things as contraception, so she'd cut it up into little pieces and put it in the bin – God forbid she'd left it whole, and a fox had got into the black bin bags outside and trailed it through Weirbridge. She'd never have been able to show her face in the village again.

Anyway, when it came time for the summer holidays again, there was still no baby, so off they'd gone. Palma Nova. That winter, still no sign of a pregnancy, so there was a wee week away in December so they'd have lovely tans for Christmas. The following year, still not pregnant. Back off to the beach. It had gone on like that for years, until she'd had enough of people telling her just to be patient. Worries rising, she'd gone to the doctor's, had all the tests, only to be told that she was perfectly fine. Nothing wrong with her tubes at all. They were delighted and relieved, until a couple more years passed and Peter finally gave in to her pleading to get checked. Low sperm count. That was that then.

She'd thought long and hard about adoption, but Peter was so bloody optimistic that even though his swimmer volume was low, he'd have one wee Rambo (as he put it) that would find a way through.

That wee Rambo never made it. And by the time he'd accepted that, they were too old to adopt and they'd ran out of options.

That was life, wasn't it? You didn't always get what you asked for. Nancy had decided she could either be bitter or get on with making the most of things, and when it came down to it, that wasn't really a choice, was it?

Anyway, she'd been an auntie and pal to half the kids in the village when she moved from the council canteen to the school dinner hall and she'd seen thirty years of Weirbridge kids coming through those doors, served up tens of thousands of scoops of mash and made enough gravy to float an oil tanker.

Noah Clark was one of the best of them. She'd had such a soft spot for that kid. It didn't surprise her in the least that the sweet wee thing he'd been back then had grown up to be a doctor. He'd always had that caring side to his nature. He could be a wee rascal, like all of them sometimes, especially when he was with that Max Walker.

He was another lovely boy, but, good Lord, he was wild. Those parents of his gave him everything and let him do as he pleased. Spoiled rotten he was. Nancy always thought it was to make up for the fact that they weren't much as parents. Always out. Always partying. And she knew exactly what was going on in that house next door when other couples started to arrive on a Saturday night. Car keys in the ashtray. The whole village knew it. They'd invited her and Peter over one night, but Nancy had declined and had a lie-down to recover from the suggestion. Bloody cheek. As if Georgina Fancy Pants Walker hadn't done enough damage in Nancy's life already.

Nancy shut that thought down. If she did make it to the school reunion tonight, she wasn't going to go there lugging memories from fifty years ago.

The front doors of the maternity wing slid open as she reached them and she stepped out into the chilly February afternoon. At least it wasn't raining. She could handle the strange looks she was getting for her outfit, but she couldn't handle dragging a dress full of soaking wet feathers around.

Dodging cars, she crossed over the narrow road that separated the main building from the maternity wing, then went past the front doors of A&E and into the main entrance of the building. There, she scanned the huge information board in the foyer.

Paediatrics. Level three.

Past the packed café, she nipped into a lift, where there was already a family of four waiting for the doors to close.

There was a little boy of about five at the front, holding his mum's hand.

'Are you a bird?' he asked, with nonchalant curiosity.

'Sorry,' his horrified mum blurted. 'Aiden, shush.'

'That's a perfectly understandable question,' Nancy reassured the mum with a smile, before turning her attention back to inquisitive Aiden. 'Nope, a superhero. Bird Woman,' she informed him, in her best matter-of-fact tone. 'Only, I've been running about fighting crime all day and my feet are killing me, so that's why I put my slippers on. Nobody ever thinks superheroes get sore feet, but let me tell you, they do.'

He gazed up at her, awestruck. In a mind that accepted Batman, Spiderman and Antman, Bird Woman was perfectly reasonable. 'My dad gets sore feet when he runs a marvelon.'

'Marathon,' his dad corrected him with a grin, obviously enjoying the conversation.

'Yeah, I gave them up,' she whispered to the kid. 'Too easy. Much more fun chasing bad guys with Spiderman and Batman.'

His gasp was louder than the noise of the lift doors opening when they got to their floor. Holding a hands on hips superhero pose, and a chin up expression of power, Nancy waited for them to close again, then went back to her original mission. Tracking down Noah Clark to find out if he knew where the hell Max Walker was hiding.

Sweet Mary and Joseph, she couldn't even imagine how poor Tress was feeling.

The whole confusion with Max's work saying he had a day off? Something was very wrong here. Of course, there was the obvious assumption that he was up to no good and had just been caught out, but Nancy couldn't bring herself to believe that. She ran through the standard list of vices. Gambling? He'd never even joined the street syndicate for the Grand National. Drugs? Surely not. She couldn't imagine Max lying on the floor of a crack den – he'd always been far too concerned about how he looked. That man didn't leave the house without pressing his trousers. Messing around with another woman? Nancy felt a twist of nerves in her stomach. Surely he wasn't a rotten apple that had fallen from the Walkers' swinging tree? Especially with a lovely lass like Tress and, worse, a baby on the way.

If that boy was up to no good, he'd get the toe of Nancy's slipper delivered swiftly to his arse. In fact, even if there was an innocent explanation, he was going to get a piece of her mind when she got a hold of him.

The lift doors opened again and Nancy shuffled out and followed the signs to the children's ward. She knew she was getting near when the walls were decorated with cloud murals on one side and jungle scenes on the other. When two double doors blocked her path, she pressed the intercom on the wall beside them.

She took a note out of Val's book and channelled Princess Anne's voice of authority. 'Hello, my name is Nancy Jenkins and I'm trying to get hold of Dr Noah Clark on a very important matter.'

'Hold on, please.'

Nancy almost punched the air. Yes. That sounded hopeful. Maybe Noah was there. Maybe – and, yes, it was a long shot – but maybe Max was with him, had popped in to see his pal at his work.

A few seconds later, one of the doors buzzed and a very friendly-faced nurse pulled it open. If she had any thoughts or judgements on Nancy's outfit, she chose not to share them, just beamed a lovely wide smile. 'Hi, sorry, it was me who spoke to you on the intercom. I double-checked because I've just come on shift, but Dr Clark is off today, so I'm afraid he's not here.'

Nancy felt her weary, superhero bones sag. 'Are you absolutely sure?'

'Positive. I'm sorry. I checked the rota and then I double-checked with the charge nurse too. Definitely not here.'

'Okay, thank you. Can I just leave a message then please? If he does come in, or if he calls, can you please tell him that Nancy Jenkins would like to speak to him urgently? His friend's wife is over in the maternity wing, and we'd just like Noah to know.'

It wasn't strictly the truth, but, unlike Val, she didn't feel the compulsion to share every detail of every story with every person that she met.

The nurse pulled a phone out of her pocket and punched in some letters, speaking aloud. 'Nancy Jenkins. Friend's wife in maternity. Got it. I'll ask Charge Nurse if I can call him and let him know,' she added conspiratorially.

'You're a gem, pet. Thank you.'

Dejected, Nancy headed back to the lift, racking her brain for some other idea that would help. She couldn't go back to Tress with nothing. She must be worried out of her wits. By the time she reached the ground floor, she still hadn't thought of anything. Nothing else for it. She was just going to have to keep Tress's spirits up, stay with her and keep reassuring her that everything was going to be okay.

Leaving the building she wasn't paying much attention to what was going on around her, until the sirens got so loud she couldn't hear herself think. Bloody hell, what a racket. As always when an ambulance passed her, lights and sirens blasting, she sent up a wee prayer that whoever was inside would be okay.

This time, it looked like she was going to find out. The vehicle swerved right in front of her and then stopped a few metres ahead at a side door to A&E. For the first time, she noticed a whole crowd of medics there waiting for the ambulance, and as soon as it stopped, they all kicked into action. This was like an episode of *Holby City* unfolding right in front of her. She could walk on past, but she was too terrified that she'd get in the way or fall over someone, so she decided to change direction, take the long way around the edge of the car park. She was just about to start walking again, when the full-scale commotion escalated, a whole lot of frenzied activity and orders being barked all over the place as they pulled out...

Nancy froze. It wasn't that there was a stretcher, and she could see that there was a woman on it. It wasn't even that the whole atmosphere and level of activity made it clear that this really was a life-or-death situation. It was the sight of the man who had once been that sweet little boy, Noah Clark, his face a picture of abject devastation, his clothes and hands covered in blood, kneeling on top of the stretcher as it moved, straddling the injured person as he pressed on her chest, giving her CPR. And as the angle changed and they went right past her, she realised who the woman was. Anya.

A sob stuck in Nancy's throat as her hand flew to her mouth. Oh dear God, that poor lassie. Nancy didn't know whether to stay, to move, where to go, but there was no decision to be made right now anyway, because there was still frantic activity in the back of the ambulance. A couple of minutes passed, Nancy still rooted to the spot, scared to move, trying desperately to compute what she'd seen, trying to make sense of it, dread rising with every second that ticked past. Her mind was throwing up thoughts that she didn't want to process. Anya. She worked with Max. Was she going to the airport with him this morning? Had there been an accident? Or... oh God forbid... a plane crash? But Noah had been with her. This didn't add up. What in the hell was going on?

All of a sudden, her thoughts shut down when they pulled a second stretcher out. This time, she was close enough to see exactly who it was straight away.

That was the moment that Nancy knew that for Tress, for Anya, and for those little boys she once knew, Noah and Max, now grown men, life was never going to be the same again.

Before she even considered what she was doing, Nancy was off and running behind Max's stretcher.

16

MAX

Max could hear voices again. Lots of them, all fussing around him. Noises from machines too. He could feel people prodding him, opening his eyes, putting needles into his arms, but all he could do was lie there and take it. It was like walking through a fog, hearing things going on around you, but not being able to see anything, or to shout out, or call for help.

They were saying a load of things. Numbers. Words. He recognised the odd one. Years of sharing a flat with Noah and helping him prep for exams had given him some basic medical knowledge. How many times back then had he laid on the floor while Noah practised on him? He'd had more fake heart attacks than a bad actor on a hospital TV show. A thought. Noah. He'd been with him, but Max couldn't hear him any more.

He just wished he could work out how he got here, but for now all he could do was listen to them work and talk. There was no pain now. He was in a hospital and they were taking care of him. He knew that. So where was Noah? Why wasn't he here now?

Time passed. Max didn't know how long.

'Hey Richard. Cheska. Barry. I brought this guy in. He's my mate. What can you tell me?' Noah. He was back.

'Noah,' the female voice said. 'I'm so sorry. How's your wife?'

'They got her back, stabilised her,' Noah replied. He sounded sad. Dazed, even.

Max tried to think. What was wrong with Anya? Was she hurt? Was she here too? He felt like he should know this. Thoughts kept coming into his head and then leaving again and it was so hard to keep track. One minute there. The next minute gone.

Noah was speaking again. 'There's internal bleeding. Blood in the abdomen. Facial bones broken. Her hand too. She's gone up to X-ray and CT and then they're taking her straight into theatre, so we won't know anything for a few hours. I just feel useless. How is he?'

The woman spoke again. 'Stable. There's significant head trauma, but we can't see the extent of it until we get him upstairs for a CT. Anya took priority, so we're just waiting for her to clear and then we'll take him up. Blood pressure and pulse high. No obvious signs of any body fractures, but we'll need X-ray. Maybe internal bleeding too, but, again, we need to get him upstairs to check. Barry, can you go call and ask if they're ready for him. I don't want to move him until we're good to go. If he's going to destabilise, I'd rather he was in here.'

'Are you sure you're okay, mate?' The guy was talking now. He sounded like someone in charge, so maybe a doctor too.

'Yeah, Richard. Look, thanks for working on Anya and then jumping in here too. I appreciate it.'

'No worries. I'd just come down from ICU to check on something, so it was just right place, right time. Do you know what happened yet?'

'No,' Noah replied. Other people wouldn't hear it, but Max

recognised an edge in his voice. 'They were in the same car. Travelling on a back road. He was driving, Anya was in the passenger seat.'

Max was taking all this in. He was driving?

Thoughts in. Thoughts out again. Still trying to process it.

He was driving with Anya, and he was speeding. A memory flickered like a dandelion spur in the breeze that he just couldn't catch, but he saw it for the briefest moment. He was driving. He was agitated. His phone was on the floor and he was trying to reach it. Got it. He picked it up. He was trying to call. Anya was screaming at him to slow down, but he wasn't listening. Trying to make the call again, but his phone wasn't working. What the fuck was wrong with it? Kept driving. Kept calling.

Another puffball of fluff went by, and he grabbed it. Tress. He was trying to call Tress. To tell her that he was coming to her. Why was he doing that?

Noah was speaking again. 'They came around a corner too fast, swerved to avoid a collision, car took off, flipped, rolled a few times and then landed on its roof in some trees. We were lucky to get them out.'

We. Noah said we. So he must have been with them? No. It was only Anya and him in the car. So how did Noah get there? This didn't make sense. Please let it make sense.

'It blew just as we got them away from the scene.'

'Jesus, Noah, that's a nightmare. What can we do for you? I want to tell you to go home, but I know that you won't, and I get it.' The woman said that.

'I can't leave them, can't go, knowing that Anya is upstairs. I'm going to change into these scrubs, then I'll wait in the on-call room. Can you keep me updated on him?'

The guy answered first. 'Of course. I'll stay with him, then come and find you as soon as we get out of X-ray. Let you know what we're going to do.'

Footsteps coming back into the room. 'They're ready for him upstairs in ten minutes. Said to make our way up now.'

'Okay, Barry, go grab a couple of the team and I want a defib on standby. If we're going to move, I want to be prepared.'

'I'll get out of your way.' That was Noah, but almost immediately there was a new voice.

'Dr Clark?'

A pause, then Noah replied with, 'Yes?' His mate sounded weary. Exhausted. Strained. What had happened? Max couldn't remember. Why was he here? What was wrong with him?

The woman was speaking again. 'I'm sorry to bother you, but there's a lady in reception who asked me to pass on a message. She insists she's a friend of yours and of the patient.'

'What was the message?' He knew that tone. Noah used it when he was confused.

'She said that the patient's wife, Mrs Walker, is in the maternity ward and she's in labour. She said you would want to know.'

'I'll be right there!' Noah blurted. 'Richard, Cheska, I'm sorry. I need to go. Please keep me posted. On both of them.'

Lots of steps. Noah. Running out.

Max was still trying to work out what had happened. Mrs Walker. Wait. Was that Tress? His Tress was in labour? His boy was coming. And he was lying here. He had to get up.

In his head, he screamed, 'Wait for me. Take me with you. Take me to her.'

But nothing came out.

'His pulse is elevating. His blood pressure too.'

The woman again. 'Damnit. What the hell just happened? Get him upstairs now. I need scans and I need them now. If there's bleeding somewhere, we need to get it under control. I'm not telling Noah that this guy didn't make it.'

4 P.M. – 6 P.M.

17

TRESS

The pain in her back was starting to throb and every couple of minutes it would be so sharp it would make her wince. Tress was trying not to think about it. Seconds after Nancy had left, she'd had another contraction and it had been the longest one yet – right up there on the pain scale with the ones she'd had earlier. Val had let Sally know and she'd checked everything out. 'Baby's heart rate is still good, and yours is fine too, but I can see he's getting a wee bit more active. Let's give it another hour or so and we'll have a look and see how you're getting on. I'll buzz the labour ward and let them know we'll probably be heading their way soon.'

'Another one coming?' Val asked, getting up from the chair and moving to her side.

'Not a contraction. Just some pain at the bottom of my spine.'

'Lean forward and I'll rub your back for a bit and see if that helps. I used to love a good back rub. Saying that, my Don always took that as an invitation, so I bought one of those back massagers off the telly instead. Quicker and more hygienic.'

Tress almost choked on her laughter, which caused another

shooting pain and another wince. For the umpteenth time, she wondered what she would have done without these women today. Although, Nancy had been gone for so long, Tress was starting to worry. It had been way over an hour now.

'Do you think Nancy is okay? She's been away for ages.'

Val didn't even pause in her rubbing of the back. 'Och, yes. She'll be down there calling Interpol and setting up that TV appeal. Either that, or she'll have got lost and she's wandering about the corridors like an escapee from *Sesame Street*. How are you bearing up, love?'

Tress shrugged. 'I'm just trying not to think about it. I know if I get stressed, then it's not good for the baby, so I just need to put everything aside for his sake. And I know it sounds fishy that Max isn't in London, but there has to be a good reason for it because Max has never given me a single reason to doubt him. We've been so happy, Val. And he's either with me, or Noah, or at work, so I've never had concerns about where he was spending his time. I trust him. I truly, honestly believe that there's an explanation for all of this. He's going to walk in that door with that grin of his and he's going to be mortified that he worried me, and he'll tell me some wild story about his day and it'll all make perfect sense.' There was a sharp pain in her lip and Tress realised she was biting it. 'Am I being crazy?'

Val shook her head. 'Not at all. I think it's a lovely trait that you always think the best of people. I always say that you should trust someone until they give you a reason not to. And if he's never given you that, then you're right to stick with him. I'd usually make all sorts of comments here about cutting off his bollocks and putting them in a pickle jar if you find out differently, but I realise that's probably not the most sensitive line to take given the circumstances.'

'Val, right now, the relief I'm getting from you rubbing my

back would make me forgive you anything,' she murmured, the aches oozing out of her. But only for a second. The pain came roaring back with a vengeance. 'Oh God...' she hissed through gritted teeth.

'Just squeeze my hand,' Val said urgently. 'Squeeze it tight. I've been taking calcium supplements since the menopause, so the bones can take it. That's it. That's it. You've got this, Tress. Remember what that card said. Total warrior. And I know I'm talking pish, but I'm just trying to get you through this. That's it, love. Breathe. Breathe. Breathe. I punched my Don for saying that every two minutes when I was in labour with my Dee. He had to get his crown replaced.'

Tress felt the sweat prickling in her pores, and the tightness of the skin on her stomach was excruciating, but just when she thought she couldn't endure it for another second, the pain faded and released its grip. The worst thing was, she knew that she was closer to the beginning than the end. She could have hours of this ahead of her. That thought shot tears to her bottom lids, and she blinked them back. She just wanted Max.

'I'm okay, I'm okay,' she reassured Val. 'But please don't stop rubbing.'

'Of course I won't, but I'm expensive. You'll faint when you get my bill.'

'Yeah, well, Max can pay it. In fact, charge him double,' Tress went along with the joke, before a sigh changed her mood. 'I just want him here with me, Val. Not because I need his help, because your rubs are honestly sensational,' she placated her friend, 'but because this should be a special day for us. This should be something we do together, something we share, a memory that we can talk about when we're old and sitting out in the back garden listening to Nancy over the fence signing Dolly Parton songs.'

'I've warned her about that. She sounds like two drunk geese in a fight to the death at a karaoke.'

'Just so you know, I'll never tell her that. You're on your own with that one.'

That made Val laugh, but she still kept rubbing, so Tress went on.

'I've pictured today so many times. You know, I didn't think I was ever going to be here. I was thirty-eight, I had never met anyone…'

'Never?'

'Well, not never. I'd had relationships. A couple of years here, a couple of years there, but no one I could see myself spending my life with. No one I wanted to keep. When I was a kid, my mum was the best mother ever, but, oh my God, she dated some dodgy men, and I knew it was just because she craved the company, was desperate for someone to love, someone to love her. I think that made me see the futility of it. I wanted love but only the right kind, the kind that was worth having and keeping and I'd never felt that until I met Max. He swept me off my feet. I know that's a romantic slushy thing to say, but he really did. And it stayed that way. Every day. Sorry. I don't know what made me feel the need to tell you all that. I'm not usually one for big emotional chats.'

'You chat away, Tress. It's good to say things out loud sometimes. Makes them more real. And I understand every word of what you're saying. We're lucky, you and me. Don't get me wrong, we've had pain. You losing your mum must have been so hard, and when our Dee was killed, I thought I'd never have another minute of my life without the kind of pain that makes you want to die. Even now, sometimes that feeling comes along and it cuts me to the bone. But I've known real love too. My Don has been the only one for me my whole life. Except Tom Jones, but I've never been to Wales, so I wasn't up for relocating.

Thing is, I didn't love Don because we were married. Or because we had a family. Or even because I was scared of being alone or missing the boat. I loved him, and still love him now, because he's my person. And if I lost him tomorrow, I'd be heartbroken, but every day I'd know that I've had that love in my life, and I'd be grateful for it, whether it lasted for a year, or ten, or fifty.'

Tress listened to every word and thought about what Val said. She was right. Her mum had never had that love, and that made Tress's heart ache for her. She'd been chasing it her whole life, and she'd made some terrible decisions in the process, stayed too long with men who didn't deserve her, or gave up too easily on others because she was too scared to give it time. Tress had never realised as a teenager just how much she'd absorbed, but when she got into her twenties, she'd almost subconsciously begun to set boundaries and expectations and if those weren't met, she just simply and happily moved on. When she got to Max, that's when she'd realised it had been worth every moment of the wait.

Val broke her contemplation with a grumble. 'I've just realised I'm beginning to sound like one of those bloody cards again. Must be old age.'

Tress was about to reply when she sensed movement outside her curtain. Max. He'd got here. He'd found her.

Val sensed it too, because she stopped rubbing and both of them were suspended in time until the curtain opened and...

'Nancy!' Val blurted. 'Sweet Jesus, you got our hopes up there. We thought it was... Nancy, are you okay? Oh my, love, you're a terrible colour. Did something happen?'

Now that Val mentioned it, Tress could see she was absolutely right, and a cold shiver made her tremble. Something was wrong. She could feel it.

'No, not at all,' Nancy countered, and Tress thought for a

horrible moment that she could be acting, until she said, 'As a matter of fact, look who I found.'

It was only when she moved to the side that Tress realised who was behind her and squealed, 'Noah! I have never, ever, been so happy to see you.' The tears shot right back up into her eyes again, but this time they were caused by pure joy and relief.

It took a few moments to register that he was wearing scrubs.

'I'm so sorry if we've dragged you away from work. I shouldn't have called you earlier, but I was just panicking a little. Pathetic, really, I'm absolutely fine.'

Before she could say another word, or ask if he knew where Max was, Noah, her gorgeous big pal, came forward and hugged her. She held on to him for dear life and he let her stay there. 'I'm so sorry. So sorry. I didn't know you called. It's been... it's been a crazy day.'

Tress heard a catch in his voice and wondered what this poor man had been through today. Noah was always so chilled and positive, but on a couple of occasions she'd seen a sombre side to him. Max had told her that was how Noah handled those days at work where he lost a kid or had to deliver bad news to a family. The strength it took to do that and to keep going must be incredible. Today must have been one of those sad days. Now that she'd let him go and he'd pulled himself back, she could see it on his face too. She decided it was better not to ask.

'I guess if you've been working, then you've not seen Max then? We've been trying to get him all day, Noah, but he hasn't returned our calls. I'm starting to get worried. He was supposed to be going to London, but when Val called his work, they said he was off today. I don't understand.'

Noah shook his head. 'You know what he's like, Tress. I've put some calls out, so hopefully we'll hear something back soon. There will be some crazy explanation for the whole thing.'

Noah's words reassured her. 'That's exactly what I was just saying to Val. The baby has come so early that there's no way he'd have been expecting this to happen today. I'm not mad at him. Well, maybe a bit. I just want him here.'

Noah sat on the edge of the bed and took her hand. 'Well, I know it's a small consolation, but I thought maybe I could be his stunt double and step in for him for now?'

The cold chill she'd been feeling now turned to something much warmer. 'Thank you. I really appreciate that. I know Max would too.'

Tress thought for a second that he was blinking back tears, but she didn't get a chance to ask, because the curtain opened again and the midwife, Sally, was standing at the foot of her bed.

'Sorry, folks,' she began but then caught sight of the new arrival. 'Dr Clark! Lovely to see you. Business or pleasure?'

'Friend of the family and uncle to this little guy,' Noah replied, and Tress had an inkling that his smile was still forced. He must have had a terrible day, but it was so typical of Noah that he was here and taking care of everyone else.

'Well, you certainly know how to pull strings,' Sally teased Tress. 'Your own personal doc and one of our favourite ones too.'

That didn't surprise Tress one bit.

'But if you'd all like to step outside for a few minutes so I can examine Tress, that would be lovely. Tress, if it's time to get this show moved along to the labour suite, I'm afraid we can only have one person with you in the delivery room.'

Tress glanced up at her three friends and knew the choice was an easy one to make. 'Nancy, you need to go to your night out and meet the first love of your life again. I honestly couldn't have your eternal singledom on my conscience. Val, I love you for being here today and calling me a warrior, but I know you need to get back home to your Don. So, Noah, fancy the gig? Just until Max gets here?'

Tress noticed that Sally just about swooned when Noah answered, 'There's nowhere else I'd rather be, Tress. I'll stay as long as you need me.'

18

NOAH

Noah, Val and Nancy did as Sally asked and stepped out while she checked Tress over. Out in the corridor, Noah watched as Val's head dropped into her hands when he told her about the accident. Nancy had already crumbled into tears and they were streaming down her face.

It took Val a minute to regain her voice. 'Wait, I don't understand. Max and Anya were in a car together? Were they rushing back from the airport? Tress said that's where Max had been headed this morning.'

Noah took that one. He'd already told Nancy everything in the five-minute chat they'd had in the on-call room while he was changing into his scrubs, before they'd both raced here. He couldn't believe this. Not today. This morning, all their lives were perfectly normal, and now two of them hung in the balance and another one was facing one of the most important moments in her life.

Val was part of this too, so he felt he owed her the truth. He'd known her for as long as he could remember, as one of his older sisters had been friends with her daughter, Dee, and he knew she could be trusted.

'No, not the airport. It seems that they were at a hotel in Loch Lomond. One we've all been to before. I think that maybe they got there, and then for some reason – maybe Max got one of the messages Nancy said Tress left for him – they decided to come back. And I think they must have been in a hurry, because Max was driving and the eyewitnesses said he took the corner way too fast. He's driven that road before, so he would have known how dangerous it was.'

'And they were there for work?'

Val was still struggling to process this, and he didn't blame her. He was too. He thought about lying, but he wasn't sure if that would just make everything more complicated. He opted for the truth. There had been enough lies told today already.

'I don't think so, Val.' That was all he said. There was nothing to be gained from speculating, but it was enough for Val to draw her own conclusions.

'Oh, son, I'm so sorry. I don't even know what to say to you except you don't deserve that. Neither you nor that poor lass in there.'

He couldn't argue, but all he could think was that no matter what they'd done, Max and Anya didn't deserve this either. How the fuck had it all come to this? He wanted to scream and rage, to cry and to punch a wall. He wanted to wake Max up and ask him what the fuck he'd been playing at. He wanted to tell Anya that that no matter what, he loved her and he'd still swap places with her if it meant that she'd be okay. He wanted to do all of those things, but right now all that mattered was taking care of Tress and the baby.

Next to him, Nancy cleared her throat and Noah felt for her too. She'd been his dinner lady every day of primary school, his best friend's next-door neighbour, and the safe place that he and Max always knew they could go to as wee boys when they needed a jam sandwich and a juice. 'We didn't know what to do, Val,' she whispered, 'and, lord knows, I'm still conflicted, but we decided not to tell Tress. If you think we've done the wrong thing, you tell us right now.'

Noah watched an expression of pure compassion come over Val's face as she reached over and hugged her friend, then held her close and let her sob into her chest. 'Nancy, I don't know how you acted like nothing was wrong in there, how you kept your composure, but I've never been prouder of you,' she told her, while her gaze went over Nancy's shoulder and met Noah's eyes. 'Son, I'm struggling to process all this right now, and my head is too scrambled to decide what's best, so tell me your reasons so I can understand.'

Noah sighed and slumped against the wall. 'If I put my doctor's hat on, then I don't want to deliver devastating news while Tress is in labour. Medically speaking, there's no definite answer as to what that level of stress would do to her or the baby, but I don't want to take the risk. I'd never forgive myself if it caused complications.'

Val had released Nancy now, and she was nodding as he went on.

'But, even as a friend, I think it's the right thing to do too. Anya is in surgery and will be in there for at least a few more hours. Max is unconscious, but when I left him, he was stable and they were waiting to take him for scans and X-rays, then possibly surgery. Either way, Tress isn't going to be able to go over there. And she's about to have her first child. How can I take the joy and the love away from that moment for her? If I tell her, she'll go through the rest of the labour devastated and distraught. She'll be heartbroken. But if I don't tell her yet, then, yes, she'll be sad that

Max isn't with her, but at least she'll experience the joy of giving birth to her boy. I don't know for sure, Val. I really don't,' he admitted, 'but I honestly think this is what Max would have wanted me to do. He loved her. And despite whatever has happened here, I still believe that he would want her to have her time with her baby, to meet him before her world falls apart.'

Val gave a definitive sigh, as if she'd come to a conclusion, before speaking. 'I think you're right, Noah. Aw, Jesus, this is a tragedy and there's no good answer, but you can't risk upsetting Tress or the baby if it could harm them. And if all that lass is going to have to sustain her through the next weeks and months is the love for her son and the memory of bringing him into the world, then I think you're doing the right thing. Now tell me what we can do to help you. Can we call someone? Your parents? We'll stay with you for as long as you want us and we'll do anything we can. You just tell us.'

Nancy was agreeing. 'I was just saying the same thing to him on the way over here. Val, my heart is breaking for them all.' Noah felt her take his hand. 'And for you. What a good man you are, Noah Clark, and I'm so sorry this messed-up world has given you this.'

Noah could feel himself start to crumble again and he understood now what some of the parents of the children he treated would tell him. They often said that when they were being strong and holding it together for their kids, the thing that was the hardest to bear was sympathy. He'd watched mothers, fathers and grandparents sit stoically by their child through endless hours of chemo, through surgeries and tragic diagnoses, and he'd seen them laugh and joke and be strong for that child. But the minute their child wasn't there, and someone put their arms around them, the dams would open and they'd sob until there were no more tears.

He couldn't let that happen to him today.

'To be honest, I don't want you to call anyone,' he told her. 'Because if I have to tell my family, or anyone else, then that makes it real and I'm not ready for that. Anya's family are in New York, and obviously Max's parents are in Cyprus, so I'll go call them now and let them know what's happened. But it'll take time for them to get here, and I think the best thing I can do is spend that time taking care of Tress and the baby.'

'Are you sure? You don't want us to stay?'

Noah shook his head. 'Like Sally said, they only allow one person in the labour suite.'

Nancy saw the sense in what he was saying, but she had conditions. 'Right, well you call us every hour and keep us posted and we can be back here in twenty minutes if you need us, son.'

'I will, I promise.'

'And if you need us to make calls for you, we can do that too. Anything at all that will help you or Tress, just name it and it'll be done.'

Noah stepped forward and hugged them both.

'Right, people, well, it's that time.' Behind them, Sally had come out of the ward and was now all smiles, clearly lacking the ability to read the room. Or the corridor. 'I'm just waiting for the porter to come up and take her down to the labour suite.'

'That's okay, I can do that,' Noah volunteered. As a paediatric doctor, there were overlaps between his department and the maternity unit, so he knew the building and the staff well. In fact, Sally had been here when he first joined the hospital and she'd been a fount of information when he'd been just a young student doing his rotation on neo-natal. All the midwives in the department were excellent, but Sally was especially proficient and Noah was glad she would be with Tress today. He turned back to Val and Nancy. 'I've just got a couple of quick phone calls to make first, so if you ladies want to go say goodbye to Tress, I'll be back in five minutes.'

Nancy and Val nodded, both of them squeezing his hand on the way back into the ward.

'Can I use your staff area to make the calls?' he asked Sally.

'Of course you can. I hope one of them brings Mrs Walker's husband here. She's just been saying how she'd give anything to get him here. Have you got a way to track him down?'

Noah thought about saying nothing, but he might need Sally's support later, juggling phone calls and updates on Max and Anya, so he gave her the bullet points of the story, finishing off by saying that they'd decided not to share the information with Tress just yet.

Sally's eyes widened, full of compassion and concern. 'Oh, Noah, that's awful. For what it's worth, I think you're doing the right thing. You know as well as I do that there's added risk if the patient is distressed or in a state of high anxiety. We'll get her through this. I've got four other patients in varying stages of labour, but I'll spend as much time as I can with Tress and if there's anything you need, or if it all gets too much and you want to take a break, even for a few moments, please just buzz me.'

'I will, thank you. I'll just go make those calls.'

In the staffroom, he cleared his throat and took a deep breath, telling himself to stay calm. If he was hysterical, then both sets of parents were bound to feed off that and fear the worst and they weren't at that point. At least, not yet.

He called Anya's parents first, grateful that it was her father, Hank, who answered the phone and that her mum, Bonnie, wasn't there at the moment. Her dad said she was at church, which sounded about right. Her parents were people of faith, and her mother went to a service most mornings. Her dad was retired military, a thirty-year veteran of the US Air Force, and he took the news in military fashion. Noah could hear the pain in his voice although he kept it steady as he asked for the details, the facts, the potential outcome. Noah stuck to the basics. The car crash. The injuries. The treatment and when they'd have more news. They didn't need to hear any of the circumstances or be faced with speculation about the daughter they adored. What Hank needed to hear was that Noah would take care of her until they got there and beyond, that he'd do everything in his power to get her the best treatment, and that he'd be waiting for them when they landed. He assured Hank of all those things and told him how much he loved his girl before hanging up the phone.

Max's parents were a quicker call. It was early afternoon in Cyprus, and there was no answer at their home. They were undoubtedly at one of their usual haunts: the beach, the bar or the golf club. He left a message asking them to call him back as soon as possible, then hung up with a sinking feeling that they wouldn't bother. He second-guessed himself. Maybe he should have said that there had been an accident. He didn't want to scare them but he did want them to know this was important.

He called them back. 'Georgina, Colin, about my last message, I just want to stress how important this is. There's been an accident and Max was injured, but he's stable. Please call me back so that I can give you all the details.'

He'd tried. It was on them now.

Jobs done, he made his way back onto the ward and marvelled at Nancy and Val's capacity for maintaining positive, strong demeanours, and at their unfailing efforts to cheer Tress up with humour and laughs.

'And remember, you've to push not pull,' Val was telling her. 'It's the exact opposite of what you did for a bloke to get you preggers in the first place.'

'I'm leaving you at home next time, Val Murray,' Nancy chided her, as they both gave Tress final hugs and said their goodbyes.

When they were gone, Noah went to the head of Tress's bed, and unclicked the brakes with his feet.

'Right, my friend,' he said, with as much enthusiasm as possible. 'Let's go bring Walker junior into the family.'

19

NANCY

The two of them sat in the front seats of the Jeep Renegade that had brought them to the Glasgow Central Hospital car park a lifetime ago.

'Just give me a minute, Val,' Nancy whispered. 'I'm not ready to leave here yet.' The nausea was cutting her in two, her standard response to high-stress situations. And this was as high stress as it came.

Nancy closed her eyes for a moment, inhaled, exhaled, then started downloading all her thoughts, fears and worries to her pal in one great big rant.

'I can't believe any of what just happened. I mean, for the love of God, how could something so absolutely tragic happen to so many people on what was meant to be one of the happiest days of their lives? I'm heartbroken for Tress, Val. Heartbroken. And I'm heartsore for Max and Anya too. I'm trying not to judge because we don't know the full facts, so I can't even think about what was going on with them this morning, but I just pray that it isn't how it looks. If I was Noah...' She let that one drift off. 'Well, I don't know if I could act with as much grace as Noah Clark. That man is a rock, he really is. When all this is over, I'm going to go knock on Gilda Clark's door and tell her what an impressive man she raised. Although, I'm sure she knows that already. Are we doing the right thing, Val, not telling Tress? I know I asked you what you thought in there, but tell me the truth, out here, just the two of us.'

'I think we are,' Val replied, and Nancy could have hugged her for the reassurance that gave her. 'And even if we're not, then we did it out of love for her and for what we thought was best. I couldn't live with myself if we told her, and she got so upset it risked her or the baby's health. I'm no expert, but I'm just going with my heart and that's honestly what I would want someone to do for me.'

'Me too.' Nancy felt the nausea rolling back. It wasn't often that the heartbreak of never having children managed to rise past her pragmatic acceptance. A long time ago, she'd taught herself to deal with that pain by keeping it separate from the emotions she acknowledged in her everyday life. But today had been such an emotional day that the separation wasn't holding, and her emotions were flying everywhere. 'I'm going to go home, and I'm going to have a bath and then I'm going to get my comfies on and lie on the couch until I fall asleep. I'll keep the phone right by me in case Noah calls and he wants us to go back,' Nancy announced.

There was a silence that Nancy didn't even register, too wound up in the thought of getting home and washing the hospital off her. It felt like a week since she'd been sitting in her kitchen, roaring with laughter while Val and Angie permed her hair. It felt like days since she'd put this dress on to show it to the girls. And it felt like hours since she'd had a minute to think, to absorb everything that had happened today.

Eventually, she noticed that Val was just staring straight

ahead, wasn't speaking at all. An unusual enough event in itself, but the firm set of her jaw made it even more suspicious.

'What? Why have you got that face on? Are you disapproving of the bath or the comfies, because, let me tell you, they're both non-negotiable,' Nancy said, her teasing tone covering the fact that she was more than a little perplexed.

Eventually, Val turned her whole body so that she was facing her. 'What about the school reunion?'

Nancy was taken aback. 'What about it? No. Just no. I can't think of anything I want to do less than get a pair of heels on and go make small talk with folk we never particularly liked in the first place. Not to mention that a whole bloody load of our school pals have already popped their clogs, so tonight serves up a natty little reminder with our sausage rolls that we're all on the clock and ticking down to the moment we follow them and shuffle off this mortal coil.'

Her voice was rising with every word, getting stronger and more forceful and she couldn't stop it. Didn't want to. In fact, it felt bloody good to give some hell after the day she'd just had, and she knew Val would just give it right back.

Surprisingly, her pal was maintaining a far calmer demeanour.

'And what about Eddie? He's in this country for one night, and what? You're just not going to see him? You're going to miss your chance to find out if something could still be there between you?'

Nancy's emotions were still in full control, and nothing was stopping her. 'In the name of all that's holy, Val, don't you think the universe, or some other frigging power, is telling me that I shouldn't be going? Sometimes you just have to listen to the fates and accept that they're right.'

There, she'd said it. Case closed. End of story. Now time to end this conversation and go home so she could have a good cry in the bath.

Apparently, Val wasn't done. 'No, you don't. You don't have to accept anything,' she bit back, her rock-hard blonde bob sweeping from side to side as she, still perfectly calmly, shook her head.

'Och, Val...' Nancy was losing the will to argue. There was no point. She wasn't going to the bloody reunion and that was it.

The conversation was cut off by the incessant beep of a horn, and the two women turned around to see an irate bloke in a big fancy car – one of those Porsche Cayenne things that Rosie Daly from Myrtle Lane bought when she won the Postcode Lottery – pressing his horn at them and gesturing for them to hurry up and move their car out of the space.

Nancy glanced around her. The car park was busy, but there were plenty of spaces at the back. Clearly this bloke just wanted to park in the front row so he didn't need to walk his lazy arse too far to the door.

Nancy rolled her window down. 'Sorry, son, but we'll be a minute. There's more spaces over there.' She gestured to the back of the car park, thinking that was the matter closed.

But no. He threw his hands up in irritation and then had the damn cheek to press that frigging horn again, then roll his window down and gesture for them to move.

Her rage bubbled and she was about to throw herself out of the car when she saw that Val was ahead of her and already out of the other side and now she was the one in warrior mode.

'Son, I will take my shoe off and batter that car until the paint-work looks like the surface of the bloody moon if you do not reverse and stop blowing that horn at us. This is a hospital car park and you DO NOT know what other people are dealing with, but let me tell you that moving my motor so that you can get in here is now at the very bottom of my priority list and I'll sit here until a week on bloody Tuesday if it means you don't get the space. Now, and please take this in the spirit it was intended, just fuck yourself right off.'

With that, Nancy's ferocious, fricking fantastic pal climbed back into the car, took a breath and then turned back to Nancy, calm as you like, and said, 'Right, ma love, where were we?'

In the other car, one very red-faced, furious bloke slunk off, to a round of enthusiastic applause from three young nurses who'd alighted from a purple Vauxhall Mokka clutching Greggs bags, just in time to witness the whole thing. They then gave Nancy and Val cheers and unanimous thumbs up gestures as they passed the car.

The tears that Nancy had been holding back since she got into the car began to pour and Nancy had no idea whether they were from laughter or sadness or a combination of both. No, it was both. Definitely both.

'The surface of the moon?' she managed to splutter.

Val shrugged. 'Not my best work, but it was all I could come up with in the moment.'

That was the final straw that broke the back of the hysteria that Nancy was trying to contain. Her body was doubled over, and she was shaking and crying and getting out the rage, the worry, the fears, and Val was right there with her, tears tripping her too. Even through the red mist, Nancy knew that, for both of them, this was for everything that had happened today, for Tress and the baby, for Max and Anya, both lying in that hospital, for Noah whose life had just been torn apart. More than that it was for everything else too. For Val it was for Don, who was still here but slipping away with every hour that passed, and for Nancy it was for Peter, who was gone way too early, before they'd even had a chance to see out their retirement years on his sun lounger in

Palma bloody Nova. It was for every pain and heartache that these two women had dealt with and tucked away somewhere so that they could get back up and go on with their lives.

Nancy had no idea how long it took for them to pull it together, but when they finally had their breath back, it was Val who found her voice first.

'I think the fates are giving a different message today, Nancy, I really do. I think that they're saying that life is short and it can change in a heartbeat. I think they're saying that you never know the minute your whole world can be blown to smithereens. And I think they're saying that's why you have to grab every chance of happiness that you can find because you don't know when or if the next one will come along.'

Nancy took in the wisdom of the words, saw the sense behind them, and she was, not for the first time, consumed with gratitude that she had a pal like Val Murray in her life.

The silence hung for a few moments until both women instinctively knew that the words had sunk in, that the lesson had been learned. When Nancy spoke, every word was delivered with warmth and love and in exactly the way Val would expect.

'Did you read all that on another one of those cards today?'

Val nodded. 'God damn warrior, me.'

If anyone glanced in the front window of that bright pink Jeep Renegade, they'd have seen two women in their mature years, perfectly still, staring at each other, the only sign of life being the smiles on their faces.

'So, tell me,' Val prompted. 'Did you answer that message Eddie sent you earlier?

'Aw, bugger, I forgot all about it.'

Val shrugged. 'Understandable. It's been a bit of a day. But do it now. Tell him you're coming.'

'Has anyone ever told you you're way too bossy sometimes?'

Val's bob went from side to side again. 'Nope, they usually say I'm all sweetness and light.'

'I can see why.'

Nancy sighed, then reached over and took her pal's hand.

'You're right, Val. I know you are. Take me home so I can get changed for this shindig. For some reason, I've gone right off this frock, but I'll go. Let's show the fates that we're in bloody charge.'

20

MAX

Max didn't feel good. Didn't feel good at all. There was a pain in his head again and he wanted to shake it, to make it go away, but he couldn't make his neck move. Couldn't make anything move. Couldn't even open his eyes.

He was warm, though, and there were noises: machines whirring and bleeping and phones ringing in the background. Voices chatting to each other like he wasn't there. All he could do was listen.

'Hello, ICU. Can I help you? Yes, Mrs Baker, your mum is still stable and doing well. She got out of surgery a couple of hours ago, but she's come round, and her vitals are good. We're going to keep her here for tonight and then, all being well, we'll transfer her back up to the elderly ward in the morning. No, I'm afraid not. No visiting at all on this ward. But I'll let her know you called and that you'll be in tomorrow. No worries at all. You're very welcome. And, yes, of course you can call back tonight. I've just come on shift and I'll be here all night so I'd be happy to answer any more questions, but rest assured, we're taking good care of her.'

She sounded very caring, that nurse. Like Tress. The same soft, warm voice.

'Liv, can you just give me a hand over here for a moment, please.'

Wow, that sound was right by his head. Someone was touching him now, and he felt a tugging sensation in his face, around his nose and his mouth. Was there some kind of tube there? Was that what he could feel?

'I'm going off shift in five, so shall we just do the handover as we go round.'

'Sure,' the one that sounded like Tress replied, and the other one started speaking, lowering her voice so that it was barely above a whisper.

'Okay. Max Walker. Thirty-five. Brought in after an RTA this morning, extensive head trauma, swelling, bleed on the right occipital, neuro are on their way in to discuss options and make a decision on pathway. Should be here in the next twenty minutes or so. Stats stable, pulse and BP high, so keep an eye on that.'

'No problem. Anything else I should know?'

A sigh. 'You're never going to believe it, but his wife is over on Mat in labour with their son.'

A gasp. 'Oh no. Was she with him?'

'No. Don't know the details. Only know about that because this guy is a friend of Noah Clark down in Paeds and someone down there told Greg, the porter, in the canteen. Dr Clark is over with the wife now. Don't think she's got long to go.'

Oh fuck. Tress. The baby. He remembered now that he'd heard someone say that earlier. His son was on the way. He had to get to him. His brain tried to make his arms move, his legs move, tried to make his voice work, but nothing. Nothing. At. Fucking. All.

Panic was rising. What was wrong with him. And why couldn't he get to Tress?

Help me. Please, someone help me, he screamed, but only inside his head.

'Oh Jesus, that's awful. Wonder what happened. Do you think he found out she was in labour and he was racing to get here? That's like one of those really sad stories you see in a movie. Poor guy. He looks like a really nice man, too.'

'He does. Don't know how it happened, but it gets worse. Dr Clark and his wife were in the accident too. At least, I think that's what happened. Greg, the porter – honestly, he's like the hospital version of Twitter – he said Dr Clark and his wife and Mr Walker here all came in the ambulance together, so they must all have been involved. Apparently Dr Clark is fine, although the poor guy had to resuscitate his wife down in A&E.'

'No! That's awful.'

Max's head was screaming again. No! That wasn't right. Noah wasn't with them. Flashes of memory. Anya. She was next to him in the car. He was driving. Then a bang and they were upside down. Anya was hurt. Bleeding. Fuck, what had they done? What had they been thinking? Or not thinking? Why hadn't they stopped this before now? Why carry on? Why start in the fucking first place?

Noah knew. He would never forgive them. And Tress would find out too. And the baby...

More screaming in his head. More panic. More pain. He'd been a fucking idiot. He'd had everything he could ever want and he'd screwed it up. Why? What was wrong with him? Why hadn't he ended it with Anya as soon as he met Tress? Fool. Goddamn idiot.

Think, Max. Think of a way to fix this. There has to be a way.

'Anyway, we've to keep Cheska Ayton informed if there's any change. She was the admitting consultant.'

'That makes sense. She's pals with Dr Clark as well. They did a rotation on this ward at the same time a million years ago. When I was your age and hadn't got jaded and haggard yet.'

A buzzer interrupted their whispers and they drifted away for a while, before Max sensed that people were around him again.

Someone pulled up his eyelid, shone a light in there, closed it again. It was so strange, he could feel things, he could hear things, but he just couldn't move or respond. Someone had to help him. Had to get a message to Tress. *I'm sorry. I didn't mean it. Please, please forgive me. I'll do anything...*

There were all sorts of other movements and sounds and clicks and beeps and just when he thought it would never stop, a man spoke.

'Okay, ladies, gentlemen, let's go have a look at the scans and decide what we can do for Mr Walker.'

6 P.M. – 8 P.M.

21

TRESS

The labour suite sounded a lot grander than it actually was. Really, it was just a private room, with one bed, and a lot more space around it than the normal room. There was a lot more equipment too, and a table in the corner, surrounded by all sorts of pipes and tubes that Tress assumed were for the baby when it was born. There was a large exercise ball in another corner and a couple of comfy chairs too, although Tress had already established that the only position she could get comfortable in was kneeling on the floor, hanging over the arms of the chair, rather than actually sitting in it.

She'd contemplated a water birth, but she'd ruled that out almost immediately. Max had thought it was hilarious when she'd told him why. 'I can't swim. I fell in the pond at our local park when I was four and I've hated the water ever since. And swans. Don't like them either. One of them almost took my eye out.'

They'd been lying on the sofa and Max had roared with laughter and thrown his arms around her, squeezing her tight.

'I'd have saved you, Tress Walker. I'd have fought off those killer swans with my bare hands,' he'd teased her.

'I'm leaving you for Andy Garcia,' she'd told him, feigning irritation and turning back to the *Ocean's Eleven* movie on the TV. It was one of their favourites. They must have watched it a dozen times over the years. Max always said he loved the risk and danger of it all, while she just loved... well, Andy Garcia and George Clooney.

Although, right now, she loved Noah and her midwife, Sally, even more. At her six-month prenatal check-up, she'd run through her birth plan with the midwife. Ideally, a natural birth, but fully prepared to go with whatever the professionals felt she needed. And, given that she'd never experienced the pain of childbirth before, also fully prepared to change her mind and beg for an epidural if it all go too much.

She wasn't at that point yet – she'd only had to use gas and air so far – but she didn't know how much worse it was going to get. Her contractions were down to every twenty minutes and Sally was checking on her regularly, so she didn't feel panicked. And, besides, her personal doctor was with her.

'Is there anything I can do?' Noah asked her, his lovely face all concerned. This should feel really weird, being in such an intimate setting with a man that wasn't her partner, but the strange thing was that it didn't. Tress put it down to the fact that he was as close to Max as a brother, so therefore she'd always thought of him as family. And, also, there was something about him being a doctor that put her at ease and made her subconscious toss out any inhibitions she might have felt so far.

'I reckon I've got fifteen minutes or so until the next contraction, so if you could shove on some music, pass me a drink and track down my husband, that would be great.' It was supposed to be a joke, but the last few words unexpectedly caught in her throat and made it clear to both of them that it wasn't. She'd thought she was holding it together, staying positive and focused on the here and now. Her jaw clenched. Enough. She couldn't get distracted. Couldn't start fretting. How many things had she read about a mother's emotions transferring to the baby? And she'd also read somewhere about stress in labour potentially causing heartbeat changes and having an effect on the progression of the birth. She couldn't remember if it speeded it up or slowed it down, but she wasn't taking any chances.

'Look, let me pop out and get some drinks and make some calls and see if I can find him' There was a tightness around Noah's eyes and Tress wondered if he was worried about Anya. He'd told her that she was away at a conference in London today, the same one that Max had told her about, but he was having trouble getting hold of her too. 'Anya's secretary is bound to know something by now. She's like the oracle of all knowledge,' he added.

He was just about to pass her when she reached up and squeezed his hand. 'Thanks, Noah. I can't tell you how grateful I am that you're here.'

'Wouldn't miss it,' he said, and she could hear the emotion in his voice too. What a day. What a fricking day. She wasn't sure if she was going to hug Max Walker or give him the bollocking of his life when he got here.

Actually, she knew the answer to that already. Every iota of disappointment that she was holding on to right now would dissipate the minute she saw him with his son, because she knew how much Max loved him already.

Max discovering she was pregnant had been perhaps the most special moment of her life, even more than meeting him or the day that they got married. Although, it hadn't had the most romantic start, given that she'd spent the morning on the bathroom floor throwing up.

At first, she'd thought it was the prawn cocktail she'd had the night before, when they were out for dinner with Noah and Anya. It wasn't a special occasion, just their usual double date that they tried to have at least every couple of weeks, depending on Noah's shifts and whether Max and Anya were snowed under at work. That happened sometimes. Max had explained it to her and it made total sense. He headed up the finance department and Anya was in charge of sales and marketing, so when they were pitching for a major contract, both those departments had to come together and work out the most impressive pitch and price structure for the client, while maintaining the most beneficial terms for their own company. It was a delicate balance and sometimes it involved a tussle between the two departments because they had different priorities. She always knew when that had happened because Max and Anya would be a bit moody with each other when they met up and it would take a few days for them to get back to normal. She and Noah just stayed right out of it and left them to it.

Over the years, she'd tried to forge a deeper relationship with Anya, but she always got the impression – although she'd never vocalise it to anyone – that Anya wasn't interested in doing that and only saw Tress in the context of their foursome. She rarely accepted Tress's invitations to spend time alone, or have lunch, or even a glass of wine down at the bistro in the village, always citing work commitments. Tress had, rightly or wrongly, decided that it must be because Anya was a high-powered, gorgeous, career executive, while Tress ran a small business making sure the interiors of Weirbridge were as cosy as could be. Not exactly a lot in common there. That said, Tress had always reminded herself that

Anya was Noah's wife, and he was the loveliest guy ever, apart from her Max, so Anya must be a pretty special person too.

On the night of the dubious prawn cocktail, Anya and Max had clearly had a work disagreement because they were being frosty with each other. The two colleagues had barely spoken a word for the first hour or so of the dinner, so she and Noah had kept things going with village gossip (her), stories about new clients (her) and happy anecdotes about life on the ward that week (Noah).

Next morning, she'd woken up to the certain knowledge that she was about to throw up and had only just made it into the bathroom in time. Max had heard her and come in behind her, scratching his head, his boxers the only thing between him and full nudity.

'You okay, babe?' he'd asked, ignoring the obvious, that she was lying on the floor, her head pressed very unhygienically against the cold porcelain of the outer shell of the loo.

'Not great. Fricking prawns, I think. I'm never having them again.'

He'd nodded and gone off to get her water. While he was away, she'd managed to reach over to the cupboard under the sink and pull out the medicine basket that held all their pills and potions. That's when she saw them. The tampons she'd bought before her period last month. And they were still there.

No.

Not yet.

It couldn't be.

This was even worse than being off her favourite prawn cocktail for life.

'What's up? Apart from the obvious?' Max had asked when he'd come back, glass of water in hand, to see her staring at the wall, utterly disconsolate.

'I think I'm menopausal. I just realised I didn't get my period last month. For frick's sake. I'm barely forty-two. I thought I had years to go before the sweats and all that other horrible stuff.'

'Oh babe...' he'd begun sympathetically, 'that's...' He'd stopped. Frowned.

'I think you were supposed to keep going with the sympathy for a bit longer,' she'd tried to tease him.

'I would but... what if it's not the menopause?'

It was so obvious really, but by that time she'd gone almost four years without contraception, and she'd absolutely accepted that kids weren't in their future.

He'd raced to the supermarket and retuned in twenty minutes with five pregnancy kits. Tress had managed to shower and brush her teeth, but she still felt awful. It only took one test to confirm the news and when Max saw that line on the little window, he'd let out the biggest exclamation of 'Yassssss!' that she'd ever heard, then swung her around so ferociously that she'd had to lie her head against the loo again.

Naturally, the first person he'd called had been Noah.

Throughout her whole pregnancy, the two men had been in charge of procurement and construction, picking up everything she ordered for the nursery, decorating the room, building the cot, putting the pram together. Anya hadn't really been too involved, but Tress understood that. For some women it wasn't something that got them excited. Maybe when the baby was born it would bring them closer.

The noise of the labour suite door opening behind her distracted her from that thought. Still kneeling on the floor, hanging over the side of the chair, she stretched her neck around, wondering if it was Sally, back for another check, but nope, it was Noah. She much preferred that option.

Especially as she could see there was a new expression on his face.

'Did you find him? Is he here?' she gasped, hope pushing all calm focus right out of the way. Max had come back, she knew it. She knew there was nothing on earth that would stop him missing the birth of his boy.

'Not quite, but I know where they are,' he told her, and the two furrowed lines between his eyes told her that it wasn't the good news she was hoping for. Her spirits took a high dive off an already shaky cliff.

'I got a hold of Cara, Anya's assistant, and she's saying that Max's secretary made a mistake when she said he was off today. They went to London, just as they said and now they're on a flight back, but they couldn't get a direct one, so they've had to go via Dublin or something. I didn't get all the details. It's all been a bit of a rush, so I'm not sure exactly what's happened.'

Relief first. He was exactly where he'd said he'd be. She should never have doubted him. There were still questions, though.

'But why hasn't he called? I don't get it. When he got my messages, why didn't he call me?'

He paused for a second before he went on. 'That's the whole problem – neither of them got the messages. Apparently, there was an issue with the contract for those new phones that they were all given last week, and they've gone out of service. I don't know all the details, Tress, but all I know is that they're trying to get back and Max will come straight here.'

Sighing, Tress pushed herself up from the floor and eased her way over to the bed to sit on the edge of it. Noah sat on the chair and reached for her hand.

'Thing is, Tress, I'm not sure if he's going to make it here in time. So I think we just need to go with the probability that it'll just be me and you and if that changes then great, but if not, I'll be here.'

'Thank you. I can't tell you how glad I am that you're with me. I'm so grateful. And Max will be too.' Despite ordering her body and mind to stay positive, she could feel tears fall down her face. 'Bloody typical, isn't it really? The biggest day of our lives and he can't get to us.'

Noah looked pained as he leaned over and wiped the tears from her eyes then hugged her until the heaving sobs subsided. When she eventually let go, the look of utter devastation on his face was enough to give her a reality check.

Sniffing, she wiped the tears off her face with a towel that Sally had left lying on the bed, and pulled herself up straight, taking a deep breath and forcing herself to stop crying by pointing the obvious out aloud.

'Oh, would you look at the state of me. Noah, I'm so sorry.'

'You don't have to be sorry for anything.'

'Yes, I do,' she wailed. 'I'm sitting here crying and feeling sorry for myself when I haven't got the roughest deal in this whole big palaver.' Even if she wanted to stop, she couldn't, because she felt an irrepressible need to get a whole big rant out of her system.

'Max is probably absolutely frantic right now, petrified that he could miss the birth of his son. He must be going out of his mind! He'll be up in the cockpit of that plane trying to bribe the pilot with a hundred quid to put his foot down and get them here quicker. Meanwhile, you're stuck with an emotional wreck of a woman who has just put snot on your shoulder,' she nodded to the large wet stain on his scrubs, 'and who has done nothing but complain since you got here.'

'That's not true...'

'Well, from this side it feels like it is. The point is, at least I'm going to experience the birth of my child tonight. If he doesn't get here, Max might never know how that feels and that's heartbreaking. So...' She sniffed again, cleared her throat, and puffed out her cheeks as she exhaled. 'I need to stop feeling sorry for myself, and pull up my big girl paper maternity pants and make the most of this. And if, after all that, you are still willing to stay with me then I'd very much appreciate that, and so would your nephew,' she added, rubbing her huge belly.

Her boy moved inside her, as if he was agreeing with that speech, and the thought of that almost set the tears gushing again. It was a struggle, but she managed to stay snot-free.

'I think your boy probably already knows that I'm going nowhere,' Noah said, and for the first time all day, those little furrows between his eyes disappeared when he smiled.

'We're both really pleased to hear that because... because... because...' she was gasping for breath in between each repetition as the pain seized her and turned her stomach into a rock-hard spasm that was apparently shutting down her lungs now too.

Noah had both her hands and he put them on his shoulders, letting her offset the force of the pain by pushing against him, not even flinching when the volume of her scream must have blown out his ear drums.

'I've got you, Tress. I've got you. You can do this. That's it. Keep breathing. Push against me. Just keep pushing.'

She didn't even realise that Sally had come into the room until she was right next to her, rubbing her back as the pain finally let go and she could breathe again.

'Well done, Tress. Honestly, you're doing great.'

'I think Noah needs new ear drums.' Tress spluttered, holding on to her side while the muscles there loosened their grip.

'Och, he's fine. They'll grow back. The men definitely don't get the sympathy around here so just you keep any of that nonsense to yourself,' she joked. 'Dr Clark, I think there was a phone call for you out at the desk,' she said breezily. 'Right, Tress, lie back for me and let me have another check to see how you're doing. I think you might be getting close to meeting your boy.'

Tress couldn't help but smile. Enough of the sadness.

Tonight was about to be the best night of her life.

22

NOAH

Noah had lied to her. Straight to her face. Made up some stupid story about them being stuck on a flight and broken phones and... Fuck, he didn't know how he could live with himself after this. He wouldn't blame Tress one bit if she hated him and never forgave him, but it was the only thing he could think of to defer the stress and worry she was having about why Max wasn't here. And maybe he was wrong. There was a definite possibility that he was making a huge mistake, but there was no changing what was ahead of them right now – she was going to give birth soon, probably in the next couple of hours, and Max wasn't going to be here with her. His top priority was keeping Tress as calm as possible and telling her the truth would destroy her when she needed her strength the most.

Outside in the lobby, he pulled out his mobile. Sally's claim that there had been a phone call for him had been untrue. When he'd nipped out last time, he'd asked her to say that when she came back in to check on Tress, and to stay with her until he returned. It could be argued that including hospital staff in his lies was unethical, but he hadn't put Sally in the position of saying anything untrue to Tress. Besides, Sally's priority was Tress's welfare and wellbeing, and she was committed to taking care of her. Right now, keeping her calm, safe and positive were top of that criteria.

His first call was going to be to Cheska, the A&E consultant who had been one of his closest friends throughout their training. There were no other doctors he'd choose to take care of people he loved over Cheska Ayton and Richard Campbell, the two medics that had been waiting for them when the ambulance drew into the bay. They were friends, but they were also brilliant doctors, and if anyone could work some kind of miracle today, it was them. He just prayed that there were miracles to be had.

Anya would still be in theatre now, and it was killing him that he couldn't be by her side. He'd do anything to swap places with her. Anything at all. He'd loved her since the first day they met, and that had never changed, not even in the last few months when they'd been having problems, or last night when they were arguing. That felt like an age ago. His stomach clenched as he tried to remember his last words to her this morning.

'Anya, wait… I'm sorry. Can we talk? Five minutes…'

'No. I've got a flight to catch and I'm not going to miss it. I'm taking my car and I'll park it at the airport. We can talk when I get back.'

There had been no 'I love you', no 'I'll miss you'. He couldn't remember another time that she'd left without kissing him and exchanging sweet words.

This morning there had been none of that. Just a lie. *'I've got a flight to catch.'*

Why? What were they doing there? Now, in the silence of the corridor, the questions were back and so were the most obvious answers. Anya had lied to him. Max had lied to Tress. Were they having an affair? No matter how ridiculous that sounded, could it be true? No. It was incomprehensible. But… maybe.

All their lives, Max had been the guy who went after what he wanted, who never had enough, always needed more. A bigger adrenaline high. More excitement. The ultimate thrills. And, sure, if someone else had something, then he wanted it too. Was that it? Had he wanted Anya? Had he persuaded her to be with him?

No. Anya would never be unfaithful. But even as Noah was thinking it, he knew how persistent Max could be.

Fuck.

His forehead made contact with the wall, rested there. He closed his eyes and forced his brain to shut down the questions. Not now. The answers could come later. Right now, he just had to face every moment as it came, and do the right thing. He could only control his own actions, and in this moment, that meant doing what he'd come out here to do. He made his first call.

'Cheska, it's Noah. Any word?' Anya had been in theatre now for almost three hours and while he didn't expect there to be news yet, he had to keep checking, keep asking. Because if the worst... That thought stuck in his throat and then released itself in a tortured sob.

If Cheska heard it, she didn't say. 'Nothing yet, Noah, but that's okay. With the extent of Anya's injuries, I'd anticipate that it will be another couple of hours at least. I know cardiology were in with her, but orthopaedics and neuro were on standby too. The important thing is that she's still in there, still fighting.'

'What about Max?'

'He's had his scans and he was transferred to ICU. I'm still down in A&E, but last I heard they were waiting for neuro to discuss the images and put a plan together. I can call up to ICU and get an update if that helps?'

'No, no – I can do that. But thank you.' He knew how busy she'd be in A&E. They were critically short-staffed, and they'd been working obscene hours and running on empty for way too long.

'That's okay. How are you holding up?'

'I don't know that I am. I just lied to one of my best friends and I've no idea if I'm doing the right thing.'

'I don't know either, Noah,' she said softly. As interns, they'd spent endless nights in the halls, debating every kind of moral and medical dilemma, but this was never one that had come up. 'All I can tell you is that if it were me in that labour suite, I'd want you to do exactly what you're doing, because no matter how much I loved my partner, the person who would matter most to me is my child.'

It felt like all the air rushed out of his chest when she said that.

Two very pregnant women, walking along the hall of the labour suite, glanced over at him and he realised he must be an incongruous sight. A doctor in full scrubs leaning against the wall, on his phone, angst-ridden and close to tears.

'Thanks, Cheska. And if you hear anything, anything at all, can you text or call me? I'll have the phone on silent, but even if I can't speak, I'll call you right back.'

'Of course. Look, I have to go, we've got another incoming RTA, but you stay strong over there, okay?'

He appreciated her words, even if he didn't know that he could live up to her parting request. He closed his eyes. He could do this. Block everything out and take care of Tress. That was all he could do right now and he wasn't going to let her down.

He quickly dialled over to ICU and was just about to give up when the phone was finally answered. He recognised the voice as belonging to one of the nurses who'd been on the ward for years. 'Hi, Jenny, it's Noah Clark. I'm just calling for an update on a patient I believe you have in there: Max Walker.'

His heart was thudding out of his chest as he sent up a silent prayer. *Please don't give me bad news. Nothing bad. Please don't tell me anything that will make this absolute shitshow of a day any worse.*

'Hi, Dr Clark, I don't have anything at the moment. Neuro have been down and examined him, but they're still in conference. Do you want me to go interrupt them?'

He let out the breath that he'd been holding. 'No, it's fine. I'll call back. If there's any change to the patient, or if they decide to take him up to theatre, can you call me straight away please?'

'Of course.'

He thanked her and hung up. He could have waited, or had the scans sent over, or done one of a dozen other things, but the truth was, he just wanted to get back into the labour suite and be with Tress. He was a paediatrician, not an obstetrician, but he'd done a rotation on the maternity wards, and he was pretty sure that Tress didn't have long left to go. And nothing was more important right now than holding her hand when this baby was born.

He quickly checked his messages and picked up two voicemails. One from Anya's parents saying they'd managed to get a flight and were on their way to JFK airport as they spoke. That made him exhale with relief. Anya would want them there when she woke up.

The other was from Max's father, Colin, saying they were going to try to get home tomorrow, while his mum, Georgina, sobbed in the background, castigating Max's dad, shouting something about how they should have been here already, but Colin wouldn't agree to come home for the reunion. That one took a moment to click. Of course. Max's parents had been at school with Nancy. They'd obviously declined the invitation to come back for the party. Not surprising really. They didn't have the best reputation in the village and he couldn't imagine many people would be glad to see them. Everyone had heard the rumours about Colin and Georgina Walker. No boundaries. No monogamy in their marriage. And that meant they'd burned many bridges.

Had Max taken the same path? Had he just taken a blowtorch to their friendship? And had Noah been too trusting and blindly loyal to see it?

He realised that he wanted to talk to the one person whom he could trust to ask. His mum. But doing that would mean telling her everything that had happened and, much as he wanted to hear her voice, that was just being selfish. Tress needed him right now. No time for phone calls just to make him feel better.

He slipped his phone back into his pocket and then did a quick detour to the vending machine for more drinks and snacks. He'd eaten nothing all day, but he had no appetite. He just didn't want Tress wondering where he'd been all that time if he came back empty-handed.

Hands holding the juice bottles and chocolate, he pushed open the door with his shoulder and saw that she was back off the bed and kneeling on the mat again, this time her upper body supported by the huge ball.

'This is actually okay when you get the hang of it,' she said, rolling back and forward as she spoke. 'Sally showed me the best way to do it.'

'It's one of the many tips in my little book of exemplary childbirth,' Sally joked, and Noah was grateful for her positive energy.

'Yeah, well, here are my tips – eat when you can because you don't know when you'll have another chance. Pickled onion crisps or a Mars Bar?' he asked, holding up both.

'Noah Clark, you know how to impress a woman,' Tress grinned, and his spirits lifted a little. She was obviously going with her resolution from earlier and putting her worries aside to focus on staying positive and upbeat for the baby. He could definitely go with that.

He sat on the armchair next to where she was rolling and gave in to her request for the chocolate. She somehow managed to unwrap it and eat it while she was still in motion. She'd always been great at multitasking.

'Sally says we've to continue timing and she'll be back in half an hour. I reckon they're less than fifteen minutes apart now, but it's hard to tell the exact time when you're buckled over and screaming.' She said that with a smile that Noah returned. 'So, tell me,' she said between bites. 'What do I get for giving you all this experience that will one day come in exceptionally handy when you and Anya have children?'

Noah bit down on a pickled onion crisp while he contemplated his answer. This was so difficult. All he could think about was what was going on outside this room... *Enough. Focus*, he told himself. No matter how hard this was, he had to relax and block everything else out, otherwise Tress would pick up on his energy and start worrying again.

'Regular babysitting,' he offered. 'I'm thinking once a fortnight, alternating Fridays and Saturdays, and one week in the summer I'll take him away with us and teach him something new. Sandcastle construction. Swimming. Surfing.'

'You are not taking my child surfing,' she objected, laughing. 'Can you not teach him something a bit less dangerous for a toddler? I'm thinking Playdoh. Or maybe the merits of peeing standing up.'

'I can definitely do the first one. The second one depends on how many beers I've had.'

Okay, this was better. He was making her laugh, getting some dopamine going in there.

Tress was still rolling. 'I know I've said this before, but I just hope our wee guy has a friend that lasts a lifetime like you two.'

Noah's gut crunched tight when she said that, but he managed not to react as she went on.

'Max always says his life would have been totally different if he hadn't met you.'

There was no way he could cut this conversation off without it seeming odd, so he knew he had no option but to go with it.

'Yeah, both of our lives would have been, I guess. I don't remember a time when we weren't together, because we met on the first day of primary school. My mum used to say he was my brother from another mother. And she didn't love Georgina Walker, so I don't think she was necessarily very happy about that bit.' The memory made him smile. The truth was, his mother loved Max and maybe felt a little sorry for him. Noah's family had never had the big house and the flash parties that the Walkers had, but clichéd as it was, they had the kind of family that was just all about love and laughing. 'My mum just treated Max like one of us – and his bollockings were every bit as loud as the ones that she doled out to me and my siblings. She once pulled us all the way up the street by the backs of our jumpers because we got caught sneaking out of the house when he was sleeping over at ours.'

Tress was laughing again. 'What age were you?'

Noah shrugged. 'Maybe eight? Nine?'

'And where were you going? I presume it was at night-time?'

'Yep, pitch black. We were going to climb the fence into the park and play footie because we reckoned it would be brilliant to have the pitch all to ourselves.'

'No, no, no,' she was chiding him, playfully. 'Let me see if I can correct you there. I bet it was Max who had the idea to do that, and you knew you wouldn't be able to talk him out of it, so you

went along with him, even though you knew there were very definite flaws in the plan.'

'I'm not even going to ask how you know that.'

'Because he hasn't changed a bit,' she said, her smile a curious
mixture of happy and sad. 'It's one of the things that's always
scared me and thrilled me in equal measure about him. He's fear-
less. Exhilarating. And I've never met anyone who loves life more
or who's so obsessed with living it to the fullest. But sometimes...'

Noah knew exactly where she was going with this, but he
didn't stop her. If she was talking about Max, she wasn't worrying
about the next contraction and that had to be a good thing.

'... Sometimes it scares me. I think you and I probably have
similar natures. I'm more cautious. More thoughtful. But Max...
he just brings all the energy to the room and blasts ahead if he
thinks something's a great idea. I've never known anyone to live in
the moment the way he does. Sometimes I want to tell him to
slow down, to think something through. But that's not him. So
right at the start of our relationship, I had to make peace with the
fact that he'll always choose the good time, always take the risk,
always do what seems like the best idea right in that second. And
if that means that I wake up and find out he couldn't sleep and
has booked a weekend in Ibiza for us, leaving that morning, then
that's the terrible price I have to pay.'

It took everything Noah had to laugh at her rueful sarcasm
and go along with the joke. She wasn't wrong in her summary of
his best mate's personality. And that's what terrified him most,
because it let that thought back in, the one that was still waiting,
like the elephant in corner of his mind, for him to address since
he'd seen Max hanging in the upside-down driver's seat of his
wife's car and realised that all the inconsistencies he'd discovered
in his wife's plans led straight to that point. The lie about going to

London. The hotel booking in Loch Lomond. The king room. For two.

Was Anya one of those good times that Max chased after because he wanted to live in the moment?

Either way, Max and Anya had already paid a terrible price for their decisions.

And there was a really huge possibility that it was going to cost him and Tress everything too.

23

NANCY

Nancy had changed her mind about going to the reunion a dozen times, and that was just in between dropping her clothes to the floor and climbing into the bath.

All that she kept thinking about was poor Tress over at that hospital, and Noah, and the travesty of the accident with Anya and Max. If they'd let more people into the labour suite, then there was no way she'd even contemplate being anywhere other than by Tress's side. Compared to what was going on over there, her situation was so trite and frivolous.

Right at that moment, she was going to the reunion, but that might change by the time the bubbles from her Body Shop grapefruit bubble bath popped and disappeared. Val was right when she said that they had to grab on to every chance for happiness. Nancy knew it. But she also knew that she was absolutely terrified of all the potential outcomes the evening could bring. What if Eddie was horrified by the change in the girl he once knew? What if she was horrified by the change in him? What if they just didn't take to each other? Or, in some ways worse, what if they did? What if Nancy realised the minute she saw him that she should have picked him all those years ago? What if this life she'd lived with Peter, much as she'd loved him, had been a missed opportunity for finding love and fulfilment and, most of all, *a family,* with the person who'd been destined for her all along?

Bugger, she wasn't going. Nope, no way.

A bubble popped right in front of her face.

Okay, maybe she would.

That last question still lingered though, and as she closed her eyes and sank back into the warm water, she let the memory of the night she chose Peter play out in her mind.

She'd been sixteen. Weirbridge back then was different from now. Everything was different. Three channels on the TV. None of that technology nonsense, and if she wanted to speak to her pals she went to their houses, because her mother would have a fit if she dared to pick up the hallowed ornament that was only to be used in the case of absolute life-or-death situations. Now they were just called telephones.

On the afternoon of the school leavers' dance, Nancy was sitting out on the back step when Peter Jenkins from next door came over his fence and plonked himself down next to her. They'd been best pals for years, since they'd got past the stage where she thought all boys were pathetic and he thought football was way more important than girls. Actually, he still thought that, but he wasn't short of offers to change his mind. Half her pals fancied him rotten and there had been a whole load of teenage girls pitching up to sunbathe in their bikinis in her garden on the three sunny days they'd had that year. In fairness to Peter, he didn't even seem to notice them. He'd fire back the banter she aimed at him over the fence, but he didn't pay much heed to the others. That didn't stop Georgina Brown, who would later marry Colin Walker and become Max Walker's mother, right enough. Nancy and Georgina had never been particularly close, and that summer she had very real suspicions that Georgina's regular, uninvited visits to Nancy's garden had more to do with a fancy for Peter than a budding friendship. She had knockers that could be seen from space and even though she was going out with Peter's pal, Johnny Roberts, every time Peter appeared in the garden, she'd arch her back so much Nancy was worried she'd do herself a damage.

That afternoon, the skies had been overcast and all her pals were at home getting ready for the dance, so it was just her and Peter.

'All right?' His standard greeting.

'All right,' her standard reply. 'Except for the company,' she'd teased. Again, standard.

They'd chatted about irrelevant stuff for a while before they got round to the biggest event in the Weirbridge teenager's calendar. 'You going tonight?' he'd asked her, picking at a branch he'd rescued from the grass.

If she was being totally objective, which she never was, because to her, he was just a mate, she could see what her pals saw in Peter Jenkins. He was one of the only boys in their year that was already over six feet tall and if that Mick Jagger from the Rolling Stones had ever walked down Weirbridge High Street and donated his hair to the first bloke he saw, it was Peter. That's where the similarity to the singer stopped, though. Peter had a much more handsome face and green twinkly eyes. His football and his Saturday job helping pack potatoes at his uncle's farm had given him muscles too and made him much broader across the shoulders than most of the other lads.

In fact, the only one who was even more grown-up looking than Peter was her boyfriend, Eddie Mackie.

They'd been seeing each other for months and she was crazy for him. Besotted. She now understood all that love stuff that

David Cassidy and Donny Osmond had been singing about for years. He was absolutely, totally and definitely the love of her life. The first one, and she already knew that he was the only one that there would ever be. He'd asked her out at the village Christmas dance and they'd been going steady ever since.

'Yep. Got a new frock from Goldbergs. My ma is still raging at how much it cost. Says I've to pay it back at a pound a week when I get a job.'

'Take it you're going with that arse, Mackie?'

She'd smacked his bare forearm. 'What have I told you? Don't be talking about him like that. He's a good guy.'

'He's an arse.'

'He's a GOOD GUY!' she'd raised her voice, not through anger, but just to make her point. This was the way she and Peter communicated. He teased her and she threatened to do him an injury if he didn't shut his face.

'Nah. You'd be far better off going with me.'

Shocked, Nancy had raised one eyebrow. 'Peter Jenkins, are you saying that you want to take me to the dance?'

'Maybe. But only if it stops you going with that arse. It's my good deed for the day.'

Nancy had flicked back her long mane of red curls, laughing. 'Och, be honest. I'm irresistible. We both know it.'

For once, Peter wasn't laughing with her. 'Yeah, well, if you change your mind, I'll be there.'

That afternoon, Nancy hadn't given his offer a second thought. That was just the kind of banter that they had, and they both knew it meant nothing.

At seven o'clock, after a bollocking from her mother for using her priceless Mary Quant lipstick, Nancy had set off to meet her pals, Val and Shirley, to head to the school hall. There was a whole lot of giggling on the way there because Val was sporting a natty accessory. She'd let her boyfriend, Don Murray, give her a love bite, and she now had to go everywhere wearing a big woolly scarf so her mother didn't kill her.

'Totally worth it,' she'd said, causing another uproarious round of giggles.

When they'd got to the hall, they'd been stunned at the transformation. The school had somehow got hold of fancy lights and the whole room was lit red, with silver streamers on the walls.

The first thing Nancy did was scan the hall for Eddie. Yep, there he was. Over with a big gang of boys in the corner, just as she'd expected. It wasn't the done thing for couples to actually go to something like this together. Oh no. There was an unspoken format, passed down through the ages of the Scottish history of male/female teenage interactions. The guys all gathered together in the corners or over at the drinks table, while the girls ignored them and danced like they didn't care who was watching. Then, about halfway through the night, the blokes would gradually seek out their girlfriends, or vice versa, and they'd all pair off, the girls making sure not to leave a single pal alone. It was standard. And that night was no different, except...

When Nancy had exhausted herself dancing her platform boots off to 'Beg, Steal or Borrow' by The New Seekers, she'd gone off in search of Eddie Mackie and found him dry-humping Georgina Brown in the cloakroom.

'Bastard,' she'd hissed, and they'd at least had the decency to stop, but Nancy didn't care. She flew out of there, almost knocking over Georgina's boyfriend, Johnny Roberts, who was coming in the door. She just hoped he saw them and punched Eddie Mackie in the face.

Down the hallway, out the front door and into the street, she ran like she was being chased by something from a horror film. That's when Peter Jenkins had caught up with her.

'Nancy!' he'd yelled, right behind her.

She'd stopped, but mainly because her feet were killing her. If she'd had her running shoes on, she'd have gone for miles.

'What happened? You went out that door like your arse was on fire.'

For a moment, she didn't answer, just stood there, arms folded, seething.

He gave her a prompt. 'Eddie?'

Another pause, then her lid blew off like her mother's pressure cooker. 'In the fucking cloakroom. With Georgina fucking Brown.'

He didn't react, making her narrow her eyes.

'You knew?'

He'd kicked a stone on the ground before eventually conceding, 'I'd heard rumours.'

'So why didn't you tell me?' she'd yelled, aware enough to know that she was shouting at the wrong person.

'Would you have believed me?' he'd shot back.

'Aaaargh,' she'd screamed, before adding a more conciliatory, 'No.' That's when she heard the sound of approaching footsteps and turned to see Eddie Mackie racing towards her.

'Nancy!'

'You can get to...' Peter had spat, but Nancy had cut him off by putting her arm across his chest and nudging him back. 'I can fight my own battles, Peter Jenkins.'

'Nancy! Shit, I shouldn't have smoked those cigs,' Eddie had gasped, leaning forward and putting his hands on his thighs as he spoke.

To Nancy's shame, her first thought was that he was so damn handsome, she could barely stand it.

'Nancy, I'm sorry. It was stupid and I didn't mean it.'

His words snapped her back to reality and her fury immediately over-ruled her devotion. 'Didn't mean to be shoving yer tongue down Georgina Brown's throat? Did you think it was going somewhere else? Did it get lost?'

He was getting his breath back now. 'Naw, Nancy, it was just... Look, there's no excuse. I'm sorry. I made a mistake. But it was just once, and I swear it'll never happen again.'

Of course, she'd known he was probably lying. She also had a fair idea that it was probably killing Peter Jenkins to keep quiet.

Eddie had held out his hand. 'Come back with me. You know it's you I fancy.'

Peter had finally lost the battle of the silence.

'Don't do it, Nancy. I told you he was an arse. Come on home with me.'

It was the first time in her life that her feet were stuck to the ground and she honestly didn't know what to do. Was she really going to ditch Eddie, the boy she was head over heels for? The love of her life? Or was she going to go with Peter Jenkins, who she'd never thought of in that way, but who had asked her out and then come running to see if she was okay?

When she'd finally found her voice, it didn't even sound like her.

'I'm going home...' Eddie's face fell. 'On my own...' Peter's face fell. 'Because I don't need either of you.'

She'd turned and started walking, but she'd only got a few yards away when she'd stopped, turned back to them both. 'But, Peter, you can come with me if you fancy stopping for some chips on the way.'

And that was it. The moment she chose Peter Jenkins. That night, after a fish supper and a bottle of Vimto shared between them, he'd kissed her and they'd been together until the day he died.

At the time, she didn't even care that the whole village heard what had happened and were gossiping about it. In fact, it worked out for the best, because her mother felt so sorry for her, she never did make her pay her back for the dress. Although she had to be physically restrained from carrying out her threat to go round to Eddie Mackie's house and put a bin lid through his window. Maybe Eddie heard about the potential bin danger, because he left town not long after, and Georgina recovered from being dumped by Johnny Roberts by hooking up with some bloke from a nearby town who was two years older and drove a Ford Cortina.

Years later, Nancy and Peter had moved into their first house, and lo and fricking behold, Georgina Brown and her new husband, Colin Walker, had moved in next door. And she was still the same tart that she'd always been. Not that Nancy gave it a second thought. By then, it was all water under the bridge, and when that lovely wee rascal, Max, had come along, Nancy had felt weirdly protective over him. She'd once raked Georgina over the coals when she'd caught her out in the garden, snogging some bloke at their annual Christmas party. That woman had never changed, not even when she had a little one to look after.

But back to Eddie. Over the years, Nancy had occasionally wondered what would have happened if she'd chosen him that night, but there was no changing that.

Until maybe now.

A shiver and skin that was beginning to shrivel like a prune told her it was time to get out of the bath. She was going to the reunion. Nothing ventured, nothing gained. She wasn't going to let this pass her by and spend more years wondering what if. Eddie had been a silly boy back then, and it was daft to spend a lifetime punishing him for a mistake he'd made when he was sixteen years old. And besides, he'd gone out of his way to fly up to Scotland on his way back to Canada, just to see her tonight.

Wouldn't it be selfish to stand him up when he'd made that kind of effort?

Picking up her phone, she finally replied to Eddie.

Looking forward to seeing you too. Nx.

There. It was done.

Her hair was still sitting lovely from Val's blow dry earlier, so she just perked it up with a comb and put on some more spray. A bit of mascara and blusher and some lipstick too.

The feather dress was now lying in a heap on her bedroom floor, so she stepped over it and pulled out the frock she'd worn to Val's son Mark's wedding. It was a pale blush shift, chiffon sleeves, with a bit of embroidery around the neckline. Beautiful. Understated. Classy. That would do. The feathers could go in the wheelie bin tomorrow morning, and they'd chalk it up to a crime against fashion. And birds.

She pulled on her favourite wrap, a soft cream cashmere shawl that Peter had bought her for Christmas as a special treat the year before he died. It seemed right that she was wearing it tonight. She was taking a bit of him with her. She'd just make sure she hung it up in the cloakroom before she clapped eyes on Eddie in case Peter was watching from the heavens, saw what was going on and spontaneously combusted at the sight of Eddie Mackie.

Out the door, as Nancy headed to the same school hall that she'd gone to all those years before, she called the number that Noah had put into her phone. No answer. Damn. Maybe Tress had had the baby. Maybe Anya or Max had taken a turn for the worse. As she walked, the doubts came rushing back. What was she thinking going to a party when people she cared about were in trouble? She was about to retrace her steps home, change and go straight to the hospital, when her phone rang, a FaceTime call this time. As soon as she answered, she saw Noah and Tress's smiling faces.

'Sorry we missed your call there. Another contraction. Oh Nancy, you look so lovely,' Tress gushed. 'I was so worried that you wouldn't go.'

'I was a bit worried myself.' Nancy forced herself to sound jovial, although her heart was breaking for that poor girl who didn't know what was ahead of her. 'How are you doing, Tress?'

'I'm okay.' Nancy saw a flinch of something on her face that suggested she might not be telling the whole truth. 'Turns out Anya was going to the conference with Max and we think they are now on their way back, but they couldn't get a direct flight so it's taking a while. Just hoping he gets here soon. Contractions are coming quicker now, so not sure how much longer I've got. I'm fine, though. This lovely man here is taking care of me.'

Nancy could see every worry and ounce of pain in the smile Noah was forcing onto his face.

'Ouch. Need to go, Nancy,' Tress squirmed, another contraction coming. 'Have a great night and we want to hear all about it.'

The screen went black and Nancy shoved her phone in her purse, just as she got to the front door of the school. Both the primary school and the high school were on the same site and shared some facilities, including the dinner hall Nancy had worked in for thirty years. However, she was more used to going in the back door in her comfy shoes and work clothes, so this felt very different.

There was a table at the entrance, where a face she recognised sat handing out glasses of fizzy stuff to everyone who came in.

'Nancy! Ah, yer looking smashing. Wish I still had hips that size, doll. Fifteen years at the slimming club and I've put on four stone.' Doris from the baker's on the High Street cackled with hilarity as she handed Nancy a drink.

Laughing, Nancy gave her a quick hug of thanks and moved into the hall.

Her first reaction was a gasp.

Just like fifty years ago, the whole room was lit red. With silver streamers on the wall. And Eddie Mackie was standing in the corner.

As soon as their eyes met, he walked towards her, his gaze never wavering till the moment he was standing right in front of her.

Jesus, he'd barely changed. He was still trim, and somehow he'd managed to hang on to his head of hair, although it was grey now. And he was sporting a deep caramel tan that was a lovely contrast to his white shirt and navy suit.

Nancy could feel the butterflies raging up a storm in her stomach. 'It's been a long time, Eddie.'

The first love of her life, the one that she hadn't clapped eyes on for almost fifty years, held out his hand. 'It sure has, Nancy.' He sounded different, with a definite Canadian twang to his words. But he was still the same Eddie, who smiled with pearly white teeth as he added, 'But, darling, we're here now.'

24

MAX

How long had there been nothing but silence? Max couldn't even remember the last thing that he'd heard.

He remembered voices, questions, sounds, crashes, but nothing was in order. Anyway, that was all gone now. Now there was just silence. And memories. Earlier he couldn't put the pieces together, but now it was all a bit clearer and he remembered. He'd been with Anya. They'd gone to the hotel in Loch Lomond, their special place. They'd been there before. Once with Noah and Tress and then a few times just him and Anya.

Him and Anya.

It still felt strange to think that, because there never really was a him and Anya.

He knew it would be so difficult for other people to understand that, but it made sense to him. To them.

They were just a moment in time. They were fun. They were a way to turn a good night into a great night.

It was never meant to be more than that for either of them. Anya would never leave Noah because she didn't want to. She loved him. He would never leave Tress because he didn't want to. He loved her.

It was never supposed to hurt anyone, to affect anyone else, to break friendships or become more than it was. And it never would have done. He and Anya would have called it quits today as planned and they'd both have gone back to their lives, no harm done.

Of course, he wished now that he could roll back the clock and make different choices, because now that the mist was clearing he remembered hearing Noah's voice when he was in the car.

So Noah knew.

That was one of only two possibilities that he'd always been too much of a damn coward to even think about. Every time it had reared its head, he'd brushed it off. Of course Noah would never find out. Neither would Tress. It wasn't even worth thinking about because it could never happen.

Now it had, and Max knew that no one would believe him when he said that Noah was the only person, other than Tress, whom he'd ever truly loved.

What people would never understand was that his affair with Anya was a totally separate thing. It had nothing to do with how he felt about Noah. In his mind, it wasn't risking a friendship, because the worst was never going to happen. To him, it was jumping out of a plane and not being the least bit scared, because he didn't fear the landing would go wrong, he just wanted to enjoy the thrills between the sky and the ground.

That was his relationship with Anya – the thrills between the sky and the ground.

And he'd just realised that they'd crashed on landing.

He just had to make Noah forgive him because he couldn't

contemplate a life without him. Or without Tress. They weren't meant to live their lives anywhere but by each other's sides.

He had so many plans for their future, for all the things that they were going to do together. Him. His boy. Noah. Max had planned it all. They'd have holidays together and they'd teach their kids to do all the things that they'd learned when they were growing up. They'd spend weekends together. Days at football pitches and basketball courts cheering their kids on. They would cross all the milestones together: birthdays, Christmases, first days at school and last days before they went off to college. They would always be what he and Noah had been since the day they'd met: they'd be family.

And they'd have Tress and Anya by their sides too. He'd never worried for a second that him and Anya would struggle to maintain their friendship. They'd both known what this was. Both agreed to start it. Both loved it while it was happening, apart from a couple of bumps in the road, caused by her guilt or his lack of it. When that had happened, they'd be cool with each other for a few days. If Noah or Tress noticed, they'd blame the frostiness on a work disagreement and then they'd both shrug it off and resume life in their own little secret world. The most important thing, though, was that they'd both agreed to end it and forget it ever happened. It was time. They both knew it. They just hadn't made it all the way over the finish line.

Now, Noah knew. Max had to persuade Noah to forgive him and to forgive Anya too. It wasn't her fault. She was a good person and she loved Noah as much as he loved Tress. She had never doubted that she wanted to grow old with the man she'd married, even when it seemed like their timing was off. Anya wanted kids when Noah was working night and day as a junior doctor. Then Noah wanted kids when Anya found the career of her dreams. It was just timing, and their affair was never meant to be a deal-breaker for her marriage, never meant to be an option for something more.

From the very day they'd met back in college, when she'd blown off Max's charm and gone for the good guy, she'd loved Noah. Max was just a dive through the clouds. On the outside, he knew no one would understand that, or believe it, but it was true. None of this was on Anya. If he hadn't tempted her into something that he saw as so frivolous, this would never have happened. It was his fault and he could admit that. Just as he could admit that some of his desire for her came from jealousy. Noah and Anya had found each other, had met the person that they wanted to spend their lives with, and underneath all the wild crazy relationships that he'd entertained himself with over the years, there was part of him that wanted that too. Maybe in the beginning he'd thought being with Anya would feel like that, just for a moment. It never did.

He only understood that feeling when he met Tress. That's when the affair with Anya should have ended, but they'd both given into temptation to keep it going because they still worked together, travelled together, had so many opportunities and it felt so good.

Now he wished he'd had the sense back then to give up sky diving and realised that no matter how free you felt when you were falling, the landing could still end everything.

He should have given it up when he finally had a partner it would hurt to lose. Tress was his soul mate. Why had he risked that?

And why hadn't he seen that the other partner he couldn't bear to lose had been there all along.

It was Noah.

And if Tress had found out now too...

No. He couldn't even think about that. Couldn't contemplate

what that could mean. No matter how furious Noah might be with him, he wouldn't tell Tress their secret.

Max was going to make this right for them all.

He would.

When he got out of here.

He just wished he knew where here was.

He didn't like this. He just wanted to get up and go to Tress.

A memory from earlier resurfaced. Someone had said she was in the maternity wing giving birth. Was that right? Or had he imagined that? Fuck, he was so confused. He didn't know what was real and what was in his head. He had forgotten where he was and why he was there again. Thoughts were coming, then disappearing.

All this silence was giving him too much time to think, too many questions to ask. Too many uncertainties to ponder.

And right now, he had many.

He wasn't sure if he was asleep or awake.

If he was drunk or sober.

If all this was real or a dream.

He wasn't sure if he was alive or dead.

8 P.M. – 10 P.M.

25

TRESS

Tress's head fell to one side after the most ferocious contraction so far, resting just inches from Noah's. He was right by her side, where he'd been for the last hour as the contractions had got more frequent, more intense, more painful, more urgent. Tress didn't think she'd ever be able to make this up to him. Or look him in the eye, now that he'd seen bits of her that were not supposed to be viewed by your husband's best friend. He'd taken every single moment in his stride, never wavered and never once acted like he was doing this because he felt he had no other choice. Tress had always thought that he was one of the good guys, now she knew he was more than that; he was one of the best.

'Noah, can you do something for me please?' she asked, as he pushed her hair back off her face to stop it sticking. 'Can you take a picture please?'

If he thought it was an odd request at a time like this, he didn't show it, as he fished his phone out of the pocket of his scrubs and held it up to put her in the frame.

'No, I want you to take a selfie of the both of us. I want the baby to always be able to look back and know that he had people who loved him right from the moment he entered the world. We can photoshop Max in later if he feels like he's been excluded,' she added. It was meant to be a joke, but Tress wouldn't be surprised if Max insisted. He'd want to be a part of this moment, even if it was after the event and required the help of technology.

She'd come to terms with him not getting here for the birth a couple of hours ago, and since she'd done that, her worry and stress levels had gone down, and her optimism had risen. It was all going to be fine. Max might miss this day, but he was going to be there for every day of their child's life from now on and that was what counted.

Noah dipped his head in next to hers and took the photo, then resumed duties when another contraction came sweeping in. She'd managed to get this far without an epidural, but only because by the time she'd cracked and asked for one, it was too late. When the contractions were every five minutes, Sally had examined her again and saw that she was fully dilated.

'Oh Noah, I don't care in the least today, but I've got a strong feeling that I'll wake up tomorrow and be utterly mortified that you've been privy to several conversations about my vagina today.'

He'd grinned the kind of grin that Tress was sure had half the women and men in this hospital hopelessly besotted with him. 'I hate to be the guy that points this out in a completely dickhead way, but I'm a doctor. This is just work for me.'

'I'm an interior designer. Doesn't mean I want to see what my clients get up to in the beds I pick for their houses.'

The contractions were even closer together now, every two minutes or so. She was going to meet her boy soon. Her boy! And all she wanted was him here safe. Right in this moment, nothing else – not even a delayed husband – mattered.

'Okay, Tress,' Sally said, coming towards the bed wearing full protective clothing, a face mask and gloves. 'Everything is straightforward, and Dr Greyson is working on a complicated birth with another patient, so it's just going to be you, me and Dr Clark.'

Tress was actually relieved. She wanted Sally in charge of getting her son here safely. In the last few hours, she'd become completely comfortable and confident in Sally's cool, calm manner, but appreciated her sense of humour too. Besides, the only doctor she needed to get her through this was Noah.

Sally was positioned between her legs now. 'It's going to be time to push soon. I'm just going to wait for the right moment and then we'll get to work. Are you ready for that?' Sally had the grace to ask her, even though Tress was well aware that she didn't have a say in the matter. This baby was coming out whether she was ready or not.

Still, she nodded, then rested her sweat-soaked head back against the bed. Noah was at her side, gripping her hand, and Tress had already made him promise that no matter what, he'd stay up at this end of the action, not for modesty, but so that she could feel the support he gave her with every word he said.

Sally was still talking. 'When the next contraction comes, I want you to push, really hard, for as long as you can.'

Noah's fingers were wrapped in hers. 'He's almost here. You can do this, Tress. I'm right here.'

She was barely aware of what she was saying, but she could hear her voice murmuring, 'Keep talking to me, Noah. Keep telling it's going to be okay.'

'It's going to be—'

She cut him off with a strangled yell as the next contraction came, and the pain tore through her, as she pushed so hard, she honestly thought she was going to pass out.

'Okay, Tress, that was fantastic. You're doing so well,' Sally soothed her. 'On the next contraction, you just need to do that all over again. Are you ready?'

Biting her lip, Tress nodded, while Noah held a cool cloth to her forehead. 'Almost there, Tress. You've got this.'

She was about to disagree, when another pain made her scream and push so ferociously, she felt that her insides were being ripped apart.

They did the same thing three more times, and just when she thought that she couldn't take another single second of the pain, she felt a massive release, and then she held her breath until...

He cried. Her baby cried. And so did Tress.

Noah cut the cord and Sally wrapped a towel around the baby's back and lifted him straight up on to Tress's chest, so that they were skin to skin, and she could see his face, and his fingers and toes, as sobs of relief made her tremble.

'We did it, Noah,' she whispered, watching the tears fall from her friend's eyes, as he gazed at the beautiful, perfect little person taking his first stretch in the world. She could already see that her son had Max's fair hair and his almond-shaped eyes, and maybe her nose and her chin. 'Hey, little one, I'm your mamma,' she whispered, stroking his cheek. 'And I know your daddy is so sorry that he's not here yet, but any minute he'll come charging in that door and you'll see how amazing he is.'

A tear from Noah's cheek splashed onto the baby's head and Tress smiled as she brushed it away.

'But you need to know that your Uncle Noah is here, and he is amazing. He's been here for you all night and he's going to be the one who'll help you to be a really smart doctor just like him. Oh, and he's married to Auntie Anya, and she's going to love you so much too.' Her sobs had turned to a smile that she could not stop as she continued to share her world with him. 'Oh, and you missed Auntie Val and Auntie Nancy, but I know that they'll be back soon and you'd better prepare yourself for some serious loving from those two. And just in case you ever need to feel that someone else is taking care of you, your grandma, Julie, is up in heaven and she'll be watching you every day of your life. So you see, little one, we might not be many, your family here, but you already have all our hearts.'

'All of them,' Noah echoed, and Tress grinned at him.

'Noah, he's beautiful.'

'He is. And that was the most incredible thing I've ever experienced. I'm so glad I was here to share this.'

Tress's gaze went back to her son, and she had the overwhelming feeling that she wouldn't stop staring at him for a long time to come. 'We are too.'

The whole time they'd been talking to her son, Sally had still been working on her. 'Tress, you've done so well. The afterbirth is out and I'm just going to pop in a couple of stitches.'

Tress and Noah just stared at the baby's face until Sally was done and came up to their end of the bed.

She leaned over, so that she could see the little one's face. 'I've delivered a lot of babies, but you might be the best one yet,' she said, with unmistakable affection.

'You say that to every baby, don't you?' Tress teased.

Sally nodded, laughing. 'I certainly do. It's important to start boosting their egos and building their confidence as soon as possible. I like to think I kick that process off for them. Let me know when you can bear to be parted for just a few moments so that I can get him cleaned up and weighed and checked over.'

Noah wasn't keen on letting him go yet. 'Maybe when he's about five.'

'See, I told you he loved you,' Tress whispered to her son.

Sally was busy writing a tag for the baby. 'Okay, baby Walker, born ninth of February 2023 at 8.17 p.m. Have you got a name for this handsome one yet, or are you still thinking about it?'

Tress felt a jolt of sadness as Sally's question brought home to her that this wasn't how she had imagined the next few moments playing out. She and Max had talked about it endlessly from the moment they'd known they were having a boy. It was his suggestion and there was never going to be any other option. Or any argument from Tress.

'I thought Max would be here and I know he wanted to say this,' Tress began, glancing up to see that Noah was still staring at his nephew, transfixed on his beautiful face. 'But, well, he isn't,' Tress laughed, 'so I'm just going to steal his thunder. This...' The arm that wasn't supporting her son reached over so that she could take Noah's hand. 'This is Noah Max Walker. And we really hope that's okay with you.'

Sally was the first to react. 'Oh, that's beautiful.'

'But...' Noah stumbled over his words, and Tress thought that was the first time she'd ever seen him do that. She hoped it wasn't because he didn't want another Noah in their family. Maybe he preferred to be the only one. 'Tress, that's incredible, and I'd be so honoured. But don't you want to wait and talk to Max or even just think about it for a while? You might look at him over the next few days and decide you want to call him something else. I promise I won't be offended.'

'No. He's been Noah to us since the day we found out I was having a boy, and Max told me what he'd like him to be called.'

Tress remembered every word of the discussion. 'We're not doing all that traditional stuff and calling him after me,' he'd declared. They were sitting on a rug on the grass at the park next to the health centre, having just left the scan that had revealed she was carrying a boy.

'You're right,' Tress had agreed. 'I was thinking Humphrey.

Maybe Cedric,' she'd teased, giggling in the sunshine. In all honesty, she didn't care what he was called, she was just so thrilled to be lying there imagining a little boy who looked exactly like Max, running around the garden in the rain.

Max had gently stroked her belly. 'What if we called him Noah?'

She'd mulled it over for a few moments before saying it out loud. 'Noah Walker. I like that. No, wait a minute, Noah Max Walker. Yep, that's it.'

And that's what it had been ever since.

'He said that there was no one he'd rather this little guy takes after,' Tress told Noah, who, somehow, looked distraught, and Tress didn't understand why. Maybe he was still shell-shocked, but this was a happy time. The worst bit was over and they'd all got through it safely and in one piece. Time to celebrate and to inject a bit of laughter. 'Face it, Noah, the man loves you and now Noah Max Walker does too. And after the shift that you've put in today, and everything you've done for us, my husband is going to love you even more.'

Tress wondered if he'd been at the gas and air, because despite this being one of the most special moments of her life, he looked so sad.

'I just hope that's true,' he sighed, his voice so heartbreakingly tortured that she barely recognised it. 'Tress, there's something I need to tell you.'

26

NOAH

The way she was staring up at him, with completely innocent expectation, almost broke him. Noah hadn't planned to tell her straight away. He'd hoped to give her more time with her son, but the fear that they may not have that time to spare had been exacerbated after his phone buzzed and a message came in from Cheska. Two words. Max. Urgent.

His heart thudded. All he could think was that meant one of a few things, none of them good. Maybe Max was being taken up to theatre imminently. Maybe they needed a decision. Or maybe...

No, Noah refused to think the worst. That wasn't happening. Not today.

Sally had heard what he'd just said. *'Tress, there's something I need to tell you.'* The ultimate professional that she was, she'd taken that as a cue to step forward. 'Let me take little Noah and get him all cleaned up now,' she prompted gently.

Tress nodded and, with another kiss to his perfect forehead, reluctantly handed him over. Noah couldn't help thinking that on any other day, in any other world, the last couple of hours would have been up there with the most special in his life. He'd seen many babies being born, but this had been something else: the emotion, the joy, the explosion in his heart when the little guy appeared. And Tress... she had blown him away with her strength and the sheer force of her determination to have the baby born into love and peace and happiness, despite all the emotions she must be feeling with Max not being here. Max... it was time to tell her.

Sally retreated to the corner of the room, giving them their privacy.

Noah's heart was thudding, he was sweating, and he wasn't sure he could get the words out. How could he do this to her? How?

He inhaled, shoring up every bit of strength and courage that he had for the conversation that he knew was going to be, without doubt, the most difficult one of his life. Nothing else came close to the turmoil he was feeling right now. All he wanted to do was to keep them in this little bubble of bliss, to let Tress have this night with her baby, but the time for lies was over. Hands trembling, stomach churning, he stayed right by her side as he tried to find the words.

'What do you need to tell me?' she asked, cheerily at first, then with a dawning realisation. He watched as her expression went from quizzical to concerned to fear in seconds. Her words choked back to a whisper. 'Noah, you look like someone has died. Tell me. What's happened?'

Tell her. Just say it. Stay calm. Don't get emotional. Just. Say. It. This was standing on the top of a hundred foot cliff, ready to fall, knowing your body was going to be washed up on the rocks down below.

'Tress, I had to lie to you and I'm so sorry. I just hope that you'll be able to forgive me.' His words were coming out in a rush, falling over each other, each one as desperate as he was to escape from what was happening right here and now. He knew if he led with 'there's been an accident' that she'd hear nothing else afterwards. One of the worst parts of his job was to deliver bad news to parents, to children, to colleagues and he was trained for it, but this was different. This time his heart was breaking too.

'Forgive you? What for?' The fear on her face, the tremble on the lips that had been kissing her child just seconds ago, almost unhinged him and he felt a tear running down his cheek.

The words continued to rush out and he couldn't stop, because he knew if he did, he'd crumble and that wasn't what Tress needed right now. She needed him to be strong. To tell her the truth. All of it. 'Max didn't go to London, Tress. He was in a car accident, and he's been hurt. When I came to see you today, I wasn't working on my ward. I'd just brought him in. I wanted to tell you then, but your labour had just escalated, and they were working on him, assessing his injuries, so there was nothing you could have done. He's over in the ICU in the hospital right now and they're making decisions on how they're going to treat him. I was too worried about you and the baby to tell you before, but you need to know now.'

More emotions, each one of them flickering like a ticker tape across her face. At first incomprehension, then horror, then panic. Then came desperation. 'But he's okay, isn't he? He's going to be fine?'

His heart was shattered and the shards were ripping his chest so it hurt to breathe, but he kept going. 'Tress, I promise you from now on everything that I tell you will be the truth. And the truth is that right now I don't know. I haven't checked in with them since before the baby was born. I need to go call them.'

'Check in. Check in right now, Noah.'

'Okay, I'll be right back...'

'No. Call them now. Here. I want to know.'

This wasn't how he wanted to do it, he'd rather establish what was happening first, then tell her in the best way possible, frame it in a way that cushioned the blow. But this wasn't his show. He wasn't in charge. He'd protected and concealed all day, but this was Tress's life, Tress's husband, and he need to let her take the lead and do this in whatever way she needed to.

He called Cheska's number, his heart pounding in time with the ring of the phone, worst-case scenarios shooting through every corner of his mind, taking prisoners of every positive thought.

'Dr Ayton's phone.' Not Cheska. Someone else's voice. His memory identified it. Bernadette. One of the charge nurses in A&E.

'Bernadette, it's Noah Clark. Is Dr Ayton there?'

'I'm sorry, Dr Clark, she's dealing with a trauma right now...'

Shit. Tress was sitting on the bed right next to him, staring straight ahead, as if some kind of numb trance was shutting her body down one cell at a time.

'But she said if you called then to ask you to come to ICU immediately.'

'Okay, thank you.' He hung up. 'Tress, I'm going to go—'

'No. Not without me. I'm coming too.'

'Tress, you can't...'

'How long has my husband been in this hospital today?' she demanded in a voice that Noah had never heard before. Angry. Insistent.

No lies. Truth from now on. That's what he'd promised her. 'Since about three o'clock.'

His eyes flicked up to the clock in the corner of the room, just above where Sally was wrapping the baby – he still couldn't call the little one Noah, not yet, not after everything that had happened today – and placing him in a Perspex crib, ready to wheel back over to them.

'Almost six hours, Noah, and I had no idea. Maybe he needed me. What if he's been calling me? Does he even know I'm here?'

Oh, fuck, no lies. No lies.

Noah nodded. 'He knows. At least I think he does. I think he got your message and was coming here when he was in the accident. But his injuries are serious, Tress. As far as I know, he hasn't been awake since he got here. When I found him at the scene...'

Something clicked with her when he said that, and she flinched. 'Wait a minute, what scene?'

'The accident, Tress.' He'd said that before, but he knew the mind was so selective when taking in bad news. And that was before you considered the after-effects of the gas and air, the birth, the stress, the hormones. He was surprised she wasn't curled up in a ball right now.

'The car crash?' Her traumatised mind was trying to remember, to connect it all and put it back together. 'But why were you there? Were you with him when the car crashed? Did you go to the airport?'

He just wanted to hug her. To go. To get good news and to come back to her and tell her it was all going to be fine. But as that thought registered, he knew that even if Max recovered, there was going to be no healing some of the wounds that had been inflicted today. And, right now, leaving Tress like this, not even an hour after she'd given birth, wasn't an option. Over at ICU, Max had the best people taking care of him and that wouldn't change whether Noah raced over there now or in the minutes it would take to make Tress okay with him leaving her.

No lies. 'He didn't go to the airport, Tress. He went to a hotel in Loch Lomond.'

'The conference was moved?'

Oh, Christ, make this stop. His brain begged for mercy, silently pleaded for her to stop asking for stabs of information that would make her bleed. He had to tell her, though. No more secrets. He owed her that.

'There was no conference, Tress. He wasn't working. All I've managed to put together is that he left the hotel almost straight after arriving. That's why I think maybe he found out you were in labour. He was driving too fast...'

That registered. Another flinch.

'But he didn't have his car today. He left in a taxi.'

He had to say it. There was no other way. No more drip feeding. It was only exacerbating the pain, twisting the knife.

'He was driving Anya's car. He was with Anya, Tress. I don't know why. I honestly don't. I found the hotel reservation on her computer this morning and I went to find out where she was. I didn't know she was with Max. But when I got there, the accident had already happened. All I could do was help them.'

'Noah, none of this is making sense. Does it make sense to you?'

Not in any world.

'No. It doesn't make any sense to me.' He sighed, rubbing the back of his neck with his hand to try to stop it snapping with the stress of this. 'I have more questions than answers and the only people that can explain it all are over in the hospital right now.'

'Anya? She's hurt too?'

'Yes. She's in surgery.'

He wondered if Tress was going to go straight to the worst assumption and he braced himself for rage, but it didn't come. In the barrage of information, her mind hadn't connected those dots yet, but he knew it would.

'Oh Noah, all this time you've been here with me and Anya is over there hurt? I'm so sorry.'

Even now, when she was still trying to process the horror of what had just happened to her, she was considering his feelings. Max Walker didn't deserve this woman. She was the opposite of Max in so many ways: calm, selfless, considerate. And now that he knew Max had lied to them both, honest was on that list too.

'She's been in surgery the whole time, so there was nothing I could do. And there's nowhere else I could have been today but here with you and him...' His eyes flicked over to the baby in the corner. Tress's went there too, and for the first time since he'd started talking, she began to cry silent tears.

'Tell me exactly how badly they are hurt, Noah.'

'Anya has significant injuries, broken bones. Her heart stopped in the ambulance...' Tress gasped, so he quickly elaborated. 'But we got her back and, like I said, they took her into surgery. I haven't heard anything since.'

'Oh, Noah, I'm so sorry,' she said again. She reached for his hand, as if she wanted to comfort him, but he took it to give her support for what he knew he was going to have to tell her next.

'And Max?' she asked fearfully.

'Less obvious injuries, didn't see any broken bones...'

'That's good, isn't it? So he'll be okay?'

No lies. It had become his mantra. He couldn't change it now. 'But he had a massive head trauma, possibly internal bleeding too. That's all I know, Tress, I swear. I need to go and find out, but you can't come with me. Let Sally stay here with you...' He glanced over at Sally, who nodded her agreement. 'And I'll get back as soon as I can.'

Her fingers, still clenched tightly around his, showed her hesitation.

Sally registered it too, and she would have Noah's gratitude for ever for the way that she stepped in. She pushed the baby across to Tress's side and gently lifted him out of the crib and handed him to his mum. 'Let's you and me stay here and take care of this Noah,' she said softly. 'He'll be hungry soon so he'll need his mamma.'

Tress's hand immediately slipped out of his and reached for her sleeping son. She pulled him close to her chest, placed her lips on his forehead, closed her eyes, as if making some kind of silent pact with her child.

Noah was itching to run but waited until she was ready to let him go. It only took a few seconds, before she lifted her gaze and her eyes locked on his.

'Go find my husband, Noah. And I don't care what he's done, or how badly injured he is, you just tell him to get up and get over here. Tell him to find a way. You tell him that his son needs him. And so do I.'

Noah leaned down and kissed the top of her head, the same way that he did every time he came into their house, every time he was leaving, every time he said goodbye. This time felt different. 'I'll be back as soon as I can, I promise.'

He was at the door, his hand pulling the handle down, when she spoke again, in a rushed outburst that he could hear came from sheer desperation.

'And Noah...'

He turned back. Tress. Her baby. She should be euphoric, but instead she'd been ravaged by the consequences of actions that were not hers, and that pain was in every shadow and curve of her face. It was a snapshot that he didn't think he would ever erase from his mind.

'No matter what, don't let him die. Promise me.'

He didn't speak, just nodded and, with a sad smile, slipped out, overwhelmingly aware that it would be cruelty to offer a promise that he couldn't keep.

27

NANCY

This was the night that Nancy had thought about for months, that she'd agonised over, that she'd dreamt about and that had thrilled her to the very core as she'd counted down the days.

Now she was here, and Eddie Mackie was spinning her around the dance floor, his hand on the small of her back and all she could think was...

'Eddie Mackie, if you don't take your hand off the top of my arse, I'll use your fingers to make ma mince for tomorrow night's dinner.'

'You all right over there, Nancy?' Dora from the baker's chimed in, from her new, eagle-eyed resting place on a seat beside the bar. From her disapproving, suspicious expression, Nancy saw that Dora had a long memory too. Before there was Diana, Charles and Camilla, there was the Weirbridge love triangle of her, Eddie Mackie and Georgina Brown. But somehow, in recent weeks, Nancy had overlooked the fact that she'd come off on the wrong side of that one and given this eejit the benefit of the doubt. What the hell had she been thinking?

The sixty-six-year-old Eddie was a bit of a silver fox right enough, and aye, he still had the moves and had put in an impressive shift to The Beatles' 'A Hard Day's Night', but, oh sweet Barbara Cartland, he still talked absolute, unadulterated, smarmy pish, which was exacerbated by the seventeen-year-old Eddie's relentless drive to get into her knickers.

Nancy was about to ask Dora if she had a spare barge pole.

The man had barely let up. For a start, he'd been all 'darling' this and 'darling' that, which had set Nancy's overfamiliarity aversion racing. She hadn't seen him for fifty years and he spoke to her like they'd been together all that time and she'd been wafting about in kaftans serving him up daily martinis. 'Darling, shall we have another drink? It's not Chablis, but we can slum it for one night,' he'd preened after they'd downed the first glass of vino. Christ on a bike. This was the boy that would get steaming on a Saturday night with a bottle of Woodpecker cider he'd raided from his ma's drinks cupboard.

She'd tried to make the best of a bad lot by just keeping him on the dance floor so that she didn't have to listen to any of his nonsense – the dancing only being an acceptable option because it came with the added bonus of burning off a few hundred calories an hour and she'd skipped her water aerobics down at the local swimming pool today – but now it was wearing thin.

She still couldn't believe that she'd got a perm for this. What a fricking waste of £12.99 and all that time and effort.

And, oh holy lech, he was now feeling her up and thinking she'd be fine with it. She wondered which A&E he'd be taken to if he tried that again.

This was definitely a man who was way too used to getting whatever he wanted and whose ego was as inflated as the bank balance he'd seen fit to mention at least half a dozen times already. A millionaire, apparently. Nancy wondered if that was pounds, dollars, or convictions for having the gropiest hands in the free world. And yep, she'd just made that word up, but it was the only one that summed up his wandering paws.

The worst thing was, he wasn't even taking her rebuffs seriously.

'Ah, Nancy, you always were a card,' was his answer to her threat of minced Eddie for dinner. 'Shall we have a wander and go get some fresh air?'

Listening to him now, Nancy weighed up her options for answering that question.

No, she didn't want or need fresh air. What she wanted was to go home, pull her pyjamas on, pour a wee glass of Prosecco and shove on the latest episode of *Shetland*.

At the same time, though, at least a wander around might mean she'd manage to get a chat with some of the other old friends here. There were a good forty or fifty people, and while she knew the ones who still lived in the village, she was struggling to put names to some of the faces that she didn't recognise. Who knew so many of the class of 1973 were still alive and kicking? It was the only little nugget of consolation in what had been, so far, an experience that was up there with the eye-wateringly painful smear test given by a student doctor in 1987.

'I suppose. Let me just nip out to the Ladies'. I'll be back soon. Hopefully about the same time as your flight back to Canada.'

Every word was meant, but there he was guffawing again, like this was all some great big tease and he was in on the joke. It clearly took some amount of arrogance not to realise that he *was* the joke.

Out she went to the foyer of the school, and into the Ladies', strategically placed between the cloakroom and the front door, so that in the old days, when they came into school they could sign in and hang their jackets up so it looked like they were still on the premises. They'd then sneak back out the door and congregate in the lane up the side of the chip shop, where they'd embark on the serious, high-brow activities of gossiping and smoking Embassy Regal. It was a wonder any of them left school with functioning lungs.

They'd had some laughs, though. If anything, Nancy had real sympathy for the teenagers today. Aye, they had all the expensive bags and make-up that cost the same as a pair of shoes, but they didn't have the privacy to make their mistakes in their own time. If there had been video evidence or social media stories about half the stuff her and Val had got up to back in the day, they'd have been... what was it they called it now? Cancelled. Yep, they'd have been cancelled and run out of the village.

Although, she was now a sixty-six-year-old woman and social media had still somehow managed to get her into a sticky situation. If it hadn't been for bloody Facebook, Eddie Mackie would never have been able to track her down.

That was it, she decided at she came out of the cubicle in the loos, she was going home. She was going to tell him to keep his mucky paws to himself and bugger off back to Winnipeg. That was if the Canadians didn't have an immigration block on the old lech.

A thought struck her and she pulled her phone out of her bag to check if she'd missed anything. Nope, nothing. Still no word from Noah or Tress about the baby, but it was early yet. And with Max and Anya... She shuddered, thinking about the bloody devastation of it all, but she just had to hope that no news was good news. What a day it had been. Thank God she'd had Val with her, because she didn't know if she could have dealt with all that on her own. She'd give anything for her pal to be here with her tonight too, but she understood Val's reasons. It must be heartbreaking to watch the man you loved disappear but still see his face every day.

Nancy felt a lump forming in her throat at the thought of that, followed by a ferocious pang of longing for her Peter. It was an almost all-consuming, physical need to touch him, for those big arms of his to wrap around her and to feel him kissing the top of her head, then murmuring his usual, 'I don't half love you, Nancy Jenkins.' Jeez, how she missed him. What had she been thinking even contemplating having any kind of flirtation with another man? Maybe she'd had the best one out there for a reason – better to have an incredible love that was gone, than to have a mediocre one that lasted a lifetime. Nancy realised she was blinking back tears. Och, today had left her an emotional wreck. In fact... change of plan. Forget that new episode of *Shetland*. As soon as she'd sacked Eddie off, she was going to stop at the house and pick up a bottle of wine, then head on over to Val's and keep her company for a couple of hours. Don was usually in his bed by eight o'clock and the two of them could sit up and watch George Clooney movies until their hearts were content.

Right. Time to go. Enough wallowing. It wasn't going to get her anywhere. She washed and dried her hands and then dabbed on a bit of lippy – these were dire straits, but she still had standards. When she was done, she caught herself in the mirror. There she was. Sixty-six years old. A lifetime there, looking back at her. For a second, she imagined she was looking at her sixteen-year-old self. What would she say? She smiled.

'Nancy, one day you'll be right back here. You'll be in yer swansong years, and it'll show on yer face. And let me tell you, my darling, you'll be older, but you'll be no bloody wiser.'

The thought made her lippy crease as she broke into a chuckle. She was about to leave, when she remembered something else and peeked back in the mirror.

'Oh, and Nancy, you're going to end up with that handsome big Peter Jenkins from next door. Tell him to wear a hat every time he goes *out in the sun, or you'll lose him way too soon.'* That thought brought the tears back and she blinked furiously again. Not now, Nancy. Hold it together, love.

She left the toilets, and was about to go searching for Eddie to bid him a fondless farewell, when her gaze caught the cloakroom door and she stopped, suddenly conflicted about where to go. Disco. Cloakroom. Disco. Cloakroom. Sod it. Why was she bothering to spend her time saying goodbye to Eddie, when she could just nip into the cloakroom, grab her shawl and make a swift exit. In fact, come to think of it, the thought of seeing that smarmy face again made her want to drop to her knees and commando-crawl to the exit.

Cagily looking left and right like a pantomime villain, she scanned the foyer. No sign of him. Brilliant. Operation Yes Yer Chucked Ya Perv was a go.

Into the cloakroom, she made for the rails on the left-hand side where she'd left the shawl that her lovely Peter had bought her all those years ago. She just prayed that the shawl wasn't some lightning portal from Peter to her, because he'd be sitting on a cloud, laughing his bits off at the nonsense she'd got herself into tonight.

'I thought you might have the same idea as me.' The voice came from behind her, and she didn't even need to turn around. Although, she did it anyway. There he was. Eddie. Lounging up against an old pommel horse someone had shifted from the gym, like he was James Dean on the edge of some swanky car.

'You mean get yer jacket and make a swift exit without saying goodbye?' she said tartly.

He guffawed for long enough to make Nancy's teeth rattle. She couldn't take any more.

'Eddie, how many times have you been married?'

'Four, sweetheart.' He said that like it was an achievement.

'Aye, well, I'm not going to be number five. I'd rather chew off ma ring finger.'

That threw him and for the first time tonight she saw a crack in his façade. She was too weary to be the one to glue it back together again, but she didn't want to leave on bad terms.

'Look, I'm sorry, but this isn't for me. When you got back in touch, I think I was just taken with the excitement of it all. Maybe for a minute there it made me feel young again. Like we were still teenagers and there were so many adventures and possibilities in front of us. But the truth is, Eddie, we're not. I'm a sixty-six-year-old woman and I should have known better than to think I could still have the same feelings I had for you when we were sixteen. We're different people now.'

He was rooted to the spot, mouth clamped shut, expression startled and definitely not responding, so Nancy did that calm, mature thing she always did when she was in an awkward spot and carried on spouting out words like her life depended on it.

'The truth is that I'm a different woman because I had the absolute privilege of being married to my Peter for over forty-five years. That man set a standard that I don't think any other bloke could ever match up to. So I'm going to spare you the effort, Eddie, and bid you goodbye. I hope you find the woman that you're looking for, but it isn't me.'

Only when he cleared his throat did she notice that a steady flush of red had been rising up his neck. 'Don't you flatter yourself, darling. I knew that the minute I clapped eyes on you.'

Oooooh, so now he had found his voice, and it was the one of a twisted old bastard. And there had been her, Nancy chided herself, trying to play nice. She should have known better.

'Yup, that went both ways. You know, it's such a shame that Georgina Brown isn't here and you could do yer best to actually shag her this time. She once told me she got halfway there and realised you had the cock of a springer spaniel. Have a good night, Eddie.'

With that, and an irresistible urge to giggle, Nancy Jenkins made for the door.

It was only when she got there that she saw another bloke was standing just inside it and must have heard every word. She strutted right by him, went through the door, and it was then that she heard him shout.

'Nancy!'

Ah great. No doubt one of Eddie Mackie's wingmen ready to dole out a second round of irritation. She really couldn't be doing with this, but she'd never walked away from a challenge.

'Make it good, love,' she warned him, dryly. 'Because you'll only get one shot.'

He was still walking towards her, and Nancy began to experience twinges of recognition somewhere in her mental floppy disc that was marked 1970s. Not as tall as Peter, and not a single hair on his head, but with those blue eyes and that cheeky smile he was wearing it well.

'Johnny Roberts,' he went on, clearly thinking he had to fill in the blanks. 'I was Peter's mate, until—'

'Until you joined the Army and we never heard from you again,' she finished, incredulous and downright delighted.

'Yeah, well didn't fancy coming back to Weirbridge after Georgina Brown got with that tosser behind my back. Couldn't walk down the street without someone talking about it.'

It was all unfolding like a movie now. Of course. He'd been Georgina's boyfriend. And the night Nancy had caught Eddie and Georgina at it in the cloakroom, Johnny had been right behind her and saw the same thing at the same time. Poor bloke. He'd always been such a decent fella too. Never one of the loud cocky ones, but handsome enough to pull off the strong, silent brooding type. Her Peter had counted him as a good pal back then.

'It's smashing to see you, Johnny.'

'You too. From what I heard in there, you've not changed a bit.' His eyes twinkled when he laughed and that made Nancy grin.

'Yeah, sorry you had to hear that. Why were you in there anyway? Revisiting the scene of the crime?'

Dora was back at the front desk and she shouted the answer to that question. 'Naw, Nancy, I sent him in. Saw you go in there and knew that Eddie Mackie was already there. I'm in charge of crime prevention and I thought you'd have banjoed him by now.'

At that moment, Eddie slunk out of the cloakroom and marched out the door, staring straight in front of him the whole time, ignoring them all. Dora's roaring cackle turned her cheeks red.

When he stopped laughing, Johnny took over the conversation again. 'I see you've got your shawl there, so you were probably leaving, but... don't suppose you fancy coming back in for a dance?'

Nancy couldn't even think about it. The day had been too long, too tiring and she just wanted to get over to Val's, pour a glass of wine, plonk herself down on the couch and take her bra off. 'Thanks, Johnny, but I'm just heading over to see my pal, Va—'

The word got lost, as, right at that moment, holding hands, Val and Don were walking in the door right in front of her, both of them decked out in their very best glad rags.

Nancy could have cried. In fact, the tears were suddenly blinding her. 'Val! I thought you said...'

Val reached over with her free hand and hugged her. 'I know what I said. But I gave you that big speech about living for the day and getting every bit of happiness out of life that we can. After all that sadness today, I decided it was time to listen to my own advice.'

Nancy blinked back the tears, let her pal go and hugged Don. 'Hello, lovely. I'm so glad you came.'

From his stilted response, she knew that Don, a man she'd known most of her life, didn't recognise her. Some days he did, some days he didn't. She didn't mind one bit either way. Especially when his eyes narrowed on the man standing behind her.

'Johnny Roberts!' he exclaimed, like this was the best thing that had ever happened to him. 'Are you home on leave from the Army, pal?"

To his credit, Johnny sussed out what was happening straight away. 'Aye, Don. Just came back for a few days to see you.'

Don shook his hand with gleeful enthusiasm. 'Well, we'd better get inside and make the most of it. Val, ask the DJ to get a bit of Tom Jones on.'

Val looked at her, then over at Johnny.

'What do you reckon then? You two coming for a dance?

28

MAX

Awake.

He was moving. He wasn't sure why. When he'd woken back up, he'd tried to open his eyes, tried to speak, to move, but still nothing. It was like he was frozen in ice, yet he didn't feel cold. He could still hear the voices, though. They were talking about him, something about injuries and trauma and MRIs and reports and... He was only picking up snippets, so he couldn't follow it all. Eventually he'd heard a man's voice, familiar, not Noah, but someone else he'd heard earlier, say, 'Everyone agree?'

There were lots of murmurs, until someone else spoke clearly again. 'Okay, I'll arrange to get him moved straight away.'

He'd drifted off again, and only now wakened with the movement of being wheeled somewhere. And more voices. Right next to him. He could hear them loud and clear.

'Is this the guy?' one of them said. 'The one from the crash?'

'Yes.' Still moving.

'God, what a tragedy.'

'Why, what did you hear?'

'His wife is over in maternity, having their kid.'

'Shut up!'

'Right, in here. Careful. Here we go. To your left. Back a bit. Okay, that's good. Stop there.'

There were loads of clicks and jolts and then he wasn't moving any more.

Sleep.

Awake.

Another voice. 'Max, it's me. Noah.'

Noah! He wanted to lift his hand and high-five him, maybe a fist bump, or even a hug.

There was a long pause, then Noah started speaking. He sounded sad. Upset. What happened, mate? Max wanted to ask him, but still he couldn't speak. Fuck.

'You know, I've no idea if you can hear me or not. I've always told my patients' families to speak to the people they love when they're unconscious, because maybe they are listening, so I'm going to go with that, because I've got some stuff I need to say.' A pause, then a hint of a laugh. 'That's a first. Me talking and you listening. Don't think that's happened too many times in our lives. Pretty devastated that it's taken a coma to get us here. But listen, I've had a talk to the team here and, Max, and I need to be honest with you, it's not good.'

A strange sound. A sob. No. Noah never cried. He was a doctor. Always calm. Always knew what to say and do. Always the one to fix everything. Always strong.

Another one. Definitely a sob this time. Oh fuck, what's wrong? What's up, buddy?

'So I need to tell you a few things, just in case this doesn't go well today and you go to a place where you need to be at peace with the things you've done down here. Max, I don't know the whole story yet because Anya is still in surgery. I just checked on her, but there's no news yet. You almost killed her today, do you know that, Max? You were driving, you were speeding, and you almost killed my wife.

'I've tried all day to find an innocent answer to why you were at a hotel with her, but sometimes the most obvious reason is the right one. So here's what I think... I think you were seeing each other. And I don't know how I can even say those words because before today I'd have told anyone who said that how fucking ridiculous it would be.

'But, hey, ridiculous was your thing sometimes, wasn't it? The stupid, reckless shit was always the stuff you loved most. But that's the thing. I don't think you loved Anya. As a friend, sure, but not the 'in love' kind of love. And that makes me wonder why you did the things I think you did. Why the fuck would you sleep with my wife, Max? How could you do that to me?

'Maybe it was a challenge. Maybe you never got past the fact that you saw her first, but she wanted me. Or was it that you just couldn't stand that something was all mine and you had to take it? Or was it just a bit of fun and you didn't give a toss about the consequences? Because the consequences are pretty fucking huge, pal.'

Max felt a pain start in his chest as the facts slipped back into place in his aching head. He'd been having an affair with Anya. Yes, he remembered that now. And Noah knew. Shit. Oh no. No. No. No. This was never meant to happen. He was never meant to find out. This was supposed to be over before anyone knew anything about it. They were done, him and Anya.

Forgive me, Noah. We can get past this, mate. Just let me explain. Let me tell you how it was. It sounded fucking obvious now, but we didn't mean to hurt you and I'm so, so sorry. Come on, man. Don't be mad at me. It's one blip in a lifetime. We can get over it. Can't we?

Max knew Noah wasn't hearing the conversation in his head, because his friend had already started speaking again.

'You've hurt Tress, Max. She is the most incredible thing that ever happened to you, and this will break her heart. I think it already has. Because you know where she is? Could you hear what I told you earlier? Or did you get her message and that's why you were speeding in that car? Panicking that you'd been caught out?

'Let me tell you anyway – she's over in the maternity wing of this hospital and I had to lie to her all day and tell her you were coming back to her. And you know what? She believed every word because she loves you more than life and she thinks you are the best fucking guy on the planet. I think we both know now that isn't true.'

Another sob. Sometimes he sounded angry and sometimes sad. So hard to keep up.

'And the only reason I left her to come and see you now is because she's not in labour any more. Because, yeah, that was the other consequence of this, Max. You missed the birth of your baby.

'You've got a boy, Max, and man, he's the most beautiful thing I've ever seen. You missed him. Tress had to bring him into this world without you and I need to tell you she was amazing. You don't deserve her, you really don't. And you don't deserve him either.'

The pain in Max's chest was cancelled by the thud of his heart and he wanted to scream, to laugh, to punch the air. His boy was here. He was a dad. How fucking cool was that? He needed to get up from here and go see him.

Someone. Anyone. Help me. Come on, get me up. Let's go. Let's go see my boy.

A movement. A hand on top of his. Noah was holding his hand.

'So here's what I have to say to you, buddy. All my life you've been my best mate, and I have loved you every day of it. I wouldn't go back and change a single thing about our lives until now, because we made each other better. I know that. I'd have done anything for you, and I know you felt the same. We both proved it a million times. I don't know how this is going to end, but if it's not good, then I need you to know that I love you still. Because to lose that would make me look back and regret so much and I don't want to do that.'

Max felt something on the side of his face. Water. A tear? He didn't know if it came from him or Noah or both.

'But here's the thing… And if you were awake now, I know you'd call me a sanctimonious prick, but I don't give a crap because you need to hear about the rest of the consequences.

'Tress would never lie, so if he asks, then your son will know that you weren't there on the day he was born. And the truth always comes out. That kid is going to grow up and one day he'll learn that his father wasn't there because he was screwing his best friend's wife. Tress, or me, is going to have to explain just how someone could do something so fucking terrible. Your kid is going to have to think about that, and find a way to deal with it. We all will. All because you made the choice to take something that wasn't yours.

'So, pal, if you go somewhere today, and you have to have made peace with the things you've done and the people you've hurt, know this. I don't forgive you. I never will. There's no peace because you took that away. And that's on you.'

All Max could hear now was the screaming, and he knew it was inside his head.

10 P.M. – MIDNIGHT

29

TRESS

Tress couldn't speak. Couldn't cry. All she could do was stare at her boy and feel the warmth of his body against hers as he fed from her. Sally had helped him latch on and now the midwife was sitting at the table in the corner, just a reassuring presence in the room. Tress knew that she had finished her shift an hour ago, but she was still there, and Tress couldn't put into words how grateful she was that she wasn't alone while she waited for news on how Max was doing.

She'd heard nothing since Noah had left her to go and find out what was happening. How long ago was that? Five minutes? Twenty-five? An hour? She didn't want to look at the clock because that would bring some reality into the moment, and she wasn't ready for that, but she forced herself to do it. Just after ten o'clock. Her son had been in the world for almost two hours now, and already his whole life had been shaken up.

Tress felt her mind go somewhere dark, so she brought it back to her boy and shut down every other thought, every doubt, every question she had. Now wasn't the time. She didn't want to pass her fears, her anxieties, her worries on to her son, so she had to stay calm, had to lock all that away and give him nothing but love and care. This wasn't about her any more. It wasn't about Max. It was about the baby. And her son needed her to be strong.

That's why, when the door opened, she didn't jump or scream, just raised her eyes and watched as Noah came in, and refused to think the worst when she saw the utter misery on his face.

He spoke first. 'Hey, he's feeding,' he said, barely louder than a whisper and with a sad smile.

Tress waited, as her fears rushed back and this time even her son couldn't help her to shut them down.

'How is he? Noah, please tell me he's okay. I beg you.'

Tears falling now, she instinctively held her hand above her son's head to protect him from them.

'Tress, I'm so sorry,' he said softly. 'He's...'

Noah stopped, the words refusing to come out, and that's when she knew this was bad. This was as bad as it got. She watched as Noah cleared his throat, swallowed, took a breath, then finally managed to look at her again.

'He's not okay. He's sustained massive damage to his brain. They brought in a team of the best surgeons to operate, but when they saw his scans, they realised that there was nothing they could do. They've moved him to a private room and they've made him comfortable.'

A low, guttural moan, like the anguished wail of a wounded animal, filled her head, but she kept it there, too scared to let her son hear, determined not to bring pain into his life so soon.

She somehow managed to breathe out the words, 'How long does he have?'

Noah shrugged softly. 'We don't know. Hours, not days.'

'I want to see him.'

At first, she thought Noah was going to argue again, but he just nodded slowly and she saw understanding in his eyes. 'I think you should too. I've spoken to the team at the other end, and I told them I'd bring you over.'

'And I want to take his son.'

He began to object. 'Tress, I don't think —'

This time, her voice had found its strength and it was quiet and it was calm, but it was not going to be denied. 'Noah, I want to take his son and I need you to make that happen.'

This time, he didn't resist.

'Sally, I'll need your help,' he told the midwife and for the first time Tress saw the glistening of tears in her eyes.

The next few moments were a blur as Sally took the baby, then helped Tress dress in the other set of pyjamas that she'd brought in with her. Slippers were pulled on to her feet, a blanket wrapped around her, and they both supported her as she forced herself out of the bed and into the wheelchair by her side. Noah was back in the clear plastic crib, swaddled and sleeping, his face so peaceful Tress had to reach over and touch it. She needed his strength. His peace. And he needed her to be strong for him.

Noah moved behind her and she felt him place his hands on the handles of the wheelchair. 'You ready?'

'I'm ready,' she lied. Of course she wasn't ready. Her heart was breaking, she was more terrified than she'd ever felt in her life. She wanted to scream, to cry, to crumble, but that wouldn't help her boy. He was the most important thing now. She had to protect him. To hold it together for him.

Wordlessly, he signalled to Sally to go ahead of them. Sally pushed the crib through the door she'd wedged open only a few minutes before and they followed her.

'We need to take the lift down to the basement,' Noah told her. 'The main hospital is in a separate building, but there's a corridor in the basement that connects the two. It's safer than taking you both outside.'

Tress felt another wave of gratitude that he was here, especially when his wife was hurt too. 'How's Anya? I should have asked. I'm sorry.'

'Still in theatre. No update.' He was hoarse now.

Tress reached for his hand, squeezed it. 'What's happened to us?' She still couldn't take it in. It was like none of it was real. Like some parallel existence.

'I don't know, Tress.'

He was broken. She was broken. Max was... Nope, she shut that down again. Couldn't go there. No feeling. No emotions. Strong for her boy. And the only way she could do that was to stare straight ahead and stop thinking about what was behind her, what was in front of her, and the horrors that were waiting at the edge of her field of vision, desperate to spread across and turn her world to darkness.

No what ifs.

No fears.

No recriminations.

Not yet.

After alighting from the lift, they went through the corridor, passing porters pushing stretchers, nurses eating crisps on their breaks as they walked and chatted with their colleagues. They all turned to see the incongruous sight – a mum and baby being rushed through the staff service corridor. She made eye contact with no one.

At the next lift, a man in a boiler suit was alighting when they arrived and held the door open for them. Sally pushed the baby in first and Tress followed, Noah pushing her wheelchair in a semicircle so that they were facing the doors, ready to get out when they opened.

'You okay, Tress?' he asked gently.

Still staring straight ahead, she reached behind her to the

handle of the chair and found his hand again, then wordlessly
pulled it onto her shoulder, giving him her answer. She could do
this. So could he. And they would do it together.

When the doors pinged open, she saw the darkness for the
first time through the windows in the lobby. The labour suite had
been four walls, no glass, so time had meant nothing, the setting
of the sun forgotten. Now she saw that this day, both the best and
worst of her life, was almost over.

They turned left and began along another corridor, the
people and walls and lights all a blur until they stopped at two
locked double doors. Noah reached forward with his pass and
they clicked open. Two nurses were at a desk to their right and
both of them jumped up, one coming round the table to join
them.

Still Tress stared straight ahead, unable to bear the pity that
she knew would be written clearly on their faces.

'Room seven, Dr Clark,' the nurse told Noah, then walked
ahead, Sally and the baby behind her, Tress and Noah at the rear.

About twenty metres along the corridor, the nurse stopped to
open a white door with a small glass panel running down the
right-hand side of the top half.

This was where he was. The wave of fear almost felled Tress,
and she buckled forward, making Sally spin around, and Noah
fall to her side.

'Tress, you don't have to do this. We can go back and then wait
until you're ready. We'll do whatever you want.'

She wanted to run. To hide. To be anywhere but here. But
those weren't options. She had to see him, had to introduce him
to the one person in the world who might be able to bring him
back. If there was any hope at all, any chance of a miracle, then it
would be because Max found a way to come back for their son.

Drawing herself back up, she exhaled, steeled herself. 'No, I'm ready.'

Noah squeezed her shoulder, then waited as the nurse held the door open to let them by.

It was a private room, only one bed, and it took Tress a couple of seconds before she could fully turn to look at the man to her left, lying under the crisp white sheet, hooked up to a machine at his side. When she finally did, she expected to be faced with a horrific sight, but no. Lying in that bed was her husband, the man who had left her this morning, kissed her goodbye and told her how much he adored her. The man who had stroked her stomach as he told his son he'd be back soon. The man that she loved with every piece of her heart and soul. The man who didn't have a bruise or a cut on his face. The tubes and monitors and the bandage on his head were the only clues that he hadn't just fallen asleep and would wake up any moment and flash that irrepressible grin that greeted her every morning.

The nurse retreated and Sally pushed the crib past them, to the space under the window next to a blue armchair, then leaned down to hug her. 'I'm going to go now and give you some time,' she said quietly.

'Thank so much for everything, Sally. I don't even have the words...'

'No words are needed. I'm going to have a cup of tea in the staffroom along the corridor, so just let me know when you need me.' With that, she was gone.

Noah pushed Tress over to the side of the bed. 'Do you want me to stay or leave?' he asked her. 'I can wait outside.'

Tress didn't even consider her answer. 'No. Please stay.'

With a wordless nod, he crossed to the chair in the corner of the room by the crib and the window. There, but almost invisible.

Slowly, Tress turned her head to her husband, and now that she was closer, she could see the rise and fall of his chest.

This man was her heart and soul and all she wanted to do right now was to touch him, to let him know she was here, because if she did that, he would come back to her, she knew he would.

She reached over, took his hand, felt its warmth.

'Max, it's me. I brought someone to meet you.'

Noah jumped up and pushed the crib over as close to the bed as it was possible to go.

Still holding it gently, she lifted Max's hand over and placed it in the crib, touching the cheek of the child he'd loved before he'd even met him.

'This is your son,' she whispered. 'I need you to come back for him, Max. I need you to fight and to do whatever you can to get back to us, because we need you here. Your son needs you here. Please, Max, come back. Don't leave us.' She felt one solitary tear slip out and brushed it away. Max had to know she was being strong for him, for them all.

They sat like that as the seconds on the wall clicked round to minutes, time and time again, until there was a gentle knock on the door, and the nurse who'd guided them in earlier opened it.

'I'm so sorry to disturb you, but, Dr Clark, we've been asked to tell you that your wife is out of surgery and has just arrived on the ward.'

Noah jumped up from the chair, then stopped. 'Tress?'

The answer to the unasked question was never in doubt. 'You need to go to her,' she told him.

When the door closed behind him, Tress took her husband's hand, the one still in the crib, touching her boy. She then put her other hand on her son's back, so that they were all connected. The three of them. A circle.

'Can you feel his heartbeat, Max? I've told him that he's going to be called Noah, just like we planned.' Her gaze went to her sleeping son. 'Noah, this is your daddy.' Rivers of tears were falling down her cheeks now. 'We made you together, and he loves you so, so much. I don't know what's going to happen, but I know that you're going to be the most amazing little boy, because this is your daddy.'

She turned back to her husband, this man who had given her more than she could ever have dared to dream for.

'We love you, Max,' she whispered.

That's when the pulsating line on the monitor behind his head stopped beating.

30

NOAH

Noah paused before he entered Anya's room, exhaled, steeled himself not to react no matter what he saw or felt when he went in there. He thought again of how his job demanded that he stay calm when his patient was scared, stay strong when they needed reassurance, mend them when they were suffering. Until today, he'd never had to do that for someone he loved.

Dr Richard Campbell, his old friend who'd been down in A&E when they'd got to the hospital a lifetime ago, had been waiting at the entrance to the ward, ready to brief him when he got there. As always, he got straight to the point. 'Mixed results, Noah,' he'd said, straight off. 'We treated the facial lacerations and nothing there is worrying us. There were no surprises for orthopaedics either – broken right wrist, and four breaks in left finger joints. No significant head trauma either. But the internal bleeding was considerable. Her spleen was irreparable, so we had to remove it. That's the worst of it. You know how it goes from here. Time. Rest. I think she'll make a full recovery, at least physically. She seems to have full recall up to the point of impact. Since she came round in recovery, she's been pretty distressed and asking for you constantly.'

Noah had sighed, partly with relief. It could have been so much worse. 'Has anyone told her about Max?'

Richard had shaken his head. 'No. We've withheld all information. I think that one is for you, mate. And, Noah, I'm sorry this has happened to you both. Goes without saying that if there's anything at all Liv and I can do, we're here for you.'

Richard's wife, Liv, was a charge nurse on the palliative care ward and one of life's fundamentally good people. It struck him that until today, he would have put Anya in that category too. Now... He couldn't go there. Not yet. He had to speak to her first, give her the benefit of the doubt, hear what she had to say. After fifteen years of loving her, being loved by her, he owed her that.

Richard had reached over and hugged him, and for a moment Noah had just wanted to stay there, to feel the human touch, to put off whatever was going to come next.

'Thanks, mate,' he'd murmured, letting Richard go. 'I appreciate that.'

Richard had nodded. 'I'll be around if you need me.'

When Noah entered the room, Anya's eyes were closed, and he was glad that she wouldn't see the jolt of devastation that surely showed in his face before he took a breath and pushed it back down. It wasn't the injuries – those were on the surface, and he knew the swelling and the lacerations would heal. He knew the bandages would come off and she'd look just like Anya again, and any scars that remained would never dimmish how beautiful she was to him. What shocked him was how he felt. There was no resentment. No judgement. No demands in his mind for explanations. Only raw, visceral love and devastation that he'd almost lost her today, as well as overwhelming relief that he hadn't. Right now, he didn't care about any of the doubts or the lies. All he cared about was that she was here.

'Noah.' A whisper.

He flew to her side, to the chair by her bed. 'Hey, you,' he said tenderly, touching the side of her cheek that was unblemished by the accident. 'You had me worried there for a moment.'

The tears were already slipping from her swollen, bruised eyes.

'Noah, I'm so sorry. I don't know what to say, to explain...' A choke cut her off and he jumped in.

'Anya, don't. Please. It doesn't matter. I don't care. You're here and that's it. That's everything.'

He meant every word. And, yes, he felt the weight of the double standard; why he held such resentment towards Max, yet none to this beautiful woman he'd married. Their actions were somehow on a different level in his mind. Anya had lied to him, perhaps risked their marriage, their love. But Max had hurt more than Tress's heart – he'd gambled with their friendship, with Anya's life, and with his child's future.

'It does matter. I need to tell you I'm sorry.' Her voice was thick with sadness. 'I lied to you. I was with Max.'

Okay, if she needed to do this now, he could go with it. He had to.

'I know. I found you. In the car. After the crash.'

She emitted a low, desperate groan. 'Oh my God, Noah, that was you.' It was a statement, not a question. 'One of the nurses told me that a doctor had found us. That we were lucky. That he had pulled me from the car and then saved my life. That was you.'

'That was me.' When the drugs wore off, she'd probably think to ask how he'd come to be there, but right now, that wasn't registering.

'We were rushing back. He got a message. About the baby. From Tress.' Her sentences were stilted, her voice barely more than a croak. The drugs. The anaesthetic. The intubation. The pain. But he could see that she was determined to keep talking, to say what she needed to say. 'Tell me. The baby...'

'Born a couple of hours ago. He's fine. So is Tress. He's beautiful, Anya. The most gorgeous little guy I've ever seen.'

More tears slid from her eyes, but with two bandaged hands she couldn't wipe them away, so Noah reached over and brushed them from her cheeks.

'And did Max get back? Was he there to meet his son?'

Her question booted him in the centre of the chest, winding him, before conflicting thoughts piled on to the crush against his windpipe.

The first thought: she was asking about Max. She didn't know. He would have to break the news to her.

The second thought: also, she was asking about Max. The guy he was pretty sure she'd been having an affair with. The guy she'd told lies for. She'd betrayed his trust for. And now, he was still the person on her mind?

Noah had never been an angry man. It just wasn't in his nature. Losing his temper would mean he'd run out of rational ways to defuse or deal with a problem. But now he was struggling to contain the raging fury that was sucking out his soul. Every moment that passed was delivering another layer of pain to this reality. Now that he had her back, could see her, talk to her, knew that she was going to make it, the fear of losing her was giving way to the truth that maybe he already had. Maybe he'd lost her to Max. And the seeds of that betrayal were growing into triffids of devastation and fury that were slowly choking him.

He cleared his throat.

The effort to stay calm, to deliver his words with kindness and honesty, was killing him, but this was another of so many life-defining moments today, and when he looked back, he didn't want to be ashamed of how he'd reacted. He had to lead with kindness, and let anything else come later.

'No, Anya, he wasn't there. Babe, Max was hurt in the accident. Really badly. He's upstairs in another room, and Tress and the baby are with him now.'

A howl burst from her throat, the action making her wince with the pain of the movement. 'Oh God, what have we done? What have we done to us all?'

The quiet beep of the heart monitor behind her started to increase, and Noah knew her blood pressure would be rising too.

'Anya, please, take a breath. I'm here. I've got you. Don't worry about what's happened, just think about now. This moment. Me and you. And breathe, Anya. Just slow breaths. Nothing else matters.'

'But, Noah, you don't understand. I was with Max. With him. We were...' she paused.

He suddenly realised that he couldn't stand to hear her say it. Of course, he'd known all along. In his gut and in his heart, he'd known that there wasn't some million-to-one explanation, that the room with the king-size bed had been for his best friend and his wife. He'd told Max how he felt about it. He'd vented his fury and his disgust with the guy he'd shared his whole life with. But he realised that if Anya had denied it, if she'd come up with some bullshit story, some completely improbable nonsense that would be utterly ridiculous to anyone else, he'd have chosen to believe her. He'd have gone all in. Because, right now, feeling like a fool for buying some stupid story would be a whole lot better than facing up to the catastrophic pain of knowing that two of the people he loved the most had sacrificed him for their own enjoyment.

She sighed. 'We were together. In every way that was wrong.'

There was silence, until he found the strength to speak again.

'I know that too.'

'I'm so sorry, Noah. We didn't mean to—'

Fuck, he couldn't stand this.

'I know,' he cut her off, still keeping his voice low and calm, every part of him screaming inside for her to stop talking, stop saying it, stop making it true.

Anya's mind was on the opposite track, desperate to confess, to clear her conscience. 'Today was supposed to be the last time. We were... saying goodbye. Not for life, just for the part of it that was only me and him. We were so stupid. But we had no idea...'

Another sob, another gulp. The monitor behind her sped up again and Noah had a flashback to the ambulance, to pressing on his dead wife's chest, desperately trying to push her life back into her, to make her heart beat again and bring her back to him.

'Anya, please... we can't do this now. You need to stay calm. You need to breathe. You need to sleep.'

'No, I need to talk to you,' she countered desperately. 'Noah, I need you to understand. This was never about us, or because I didn't love you.'

No more. He couldn't bear it. Make. It. Stop.

'Babe, talking about it right now isn't helping you. Your body has been through so much today and for now all that matters is that you rest. Everything else will still be here tomorrow. Or next week. Or whenever the time is right.'

'I just need to know if you can forgive me.'

The question stunned him. Shocked him silent. And the answer was... he didn't know. The last twenty-four hours had been the most demanding, devastating, confusing of his life and that was going to take time to process. He'd told Max that he would never forgive him. That he knew for sure. But could he find some way accept and recover from Anya's betrayal? That was for later, but for now he made a split decision. He was prepared to lie to protect her heart, to let her find the peace she was going to need to recover.

He inhaled... took a breath... ready to give her an answer that he knew might not be true. 'Anya, I—'

A knock on the door interrupted him.

It opened slightly, enough for Noah to see Richard waiting there. At first, Noah assumed his friend was here to check on Anya, but Richard's hesitation told him otherwise.

'Noah, can I have a word?'

His heart sank. Richard didn't want to speak in front of Anya, so what did that mean? New results that were causing concern?

'Sure.'

He began to rise, when Anya said, 'No. Don't go. Whatever it is, I want to know. Don't hide anything from me, please,' she begged.

Noah hesitated, conflicted. Whatever it was, they would deal with it, and what Anya didn't need right now was the worry that something was being kept from her. Until this morning, he'd have sworn that there were no secrets in their lives. Now he realised there were already way too many.

He nodded, motioning to his friend to acquiesce to Anya's wishes.

Accepting their decision, Richard came into the room, and stopped at the end of the bed. Now that he was closer, Noah could see the tension in his friend's shoulders and the sorrowful expression. Shit, this was bad.

'The ward upstairs has been trying to get a hold of you...'

Fuck. He'd switched his phone on to silent when he'd been in Max's room with Tress and the baby.

'I'm really sorry to say that Max Walker died a few minutes ago.'

Noah's head dropped, the force of the blow so hard that it felt almost physical.

And the woman in the bed beside him screamed.

31

NANCY

The February night air made clouds with their breath as the four of them left the school, and headed for Val and Don's house. It had been Don who'd invited Johnny back for a nightcap, but there had been no argument from Nancy. She had laughed more, danced more, and enjoyed herself more in the last few hours than she'd done since... since... well, since her Peter was still here.

She let that thought go. She wasn't going to spoil this lovely night with sadness. There had been too much of that already today.

Val and Don were walking a few of steps in front of her and Johnny and Nancy could hear them singing away, Don doing his old party piece, crooning 'Love Me Tender' to Val.

Nancy kept her voice low, so only she and Johnny could hear. 'You were great with Don tonight.'

Johnny shrugged off the compliment. 'I'm just glad I got to see him. We were good pals back in the day. How long has he been unwell?'

'Few years. It's been hard for Val, but she's some woman, she really is,' Nancy said fondly, deploying the ultimate Glaswegian words of admiration and affection. These days, she heard the young ones calling each other princess, or queen, or goddess. But to Nancy and Val and their ilk, 'Yer some wummin' would always be the biggest compliment.

Johnny nodded. 'That's how my Brenda went too. Alzheimer's. It was a hard time, and I don't think I was always the best at dealing with it. Especially at the start. But after we got some support and help, and our kids pitched in to help, well, it got better. And no matter how rough it got, I wouldn't take away any of it because, to me, she was still my Brenda.'

The sadness in his voice made Nancy's heart go out to him. 'That's what Val says too. How long...?'

She let the question hang there, knowing he'd catch it.

'She passed three years ago. First year was tough, I'm not going to deny it. She was the life force in our family. All my years in the Army, she was the one that held our family together, who pretty much brought our two boys up single-handed. She was the organiser, and even after I retired, I left her to it because that's what she enjoyed doing. When she was gone... to be honest, I didn't know where to start. Took me a while to find my way, to fill my time. I'd never have come to something like this two years ago, but now... I'm getting used to going out by myself and I'm getting on with it.' He smiled, changed the tone, 'And if it meant I got to watch you putting Eddie Mackie in his place, I'd be out every night of the week.'

They were chuckling when Nancy detected a sound and suddenly stopped.

'Val! Freeze!'

In front of them, Val and Don stopped and turned back to find out what was going on.

Nancy held up her handbag. 'Val, my phone just buzzed and I

think it's the text thingy. I can't look. Honest to God, I can't. I need you to do it.'

Worry furrowed Val's brow as she let go of Don's hand and took two steps back towards them.

As Johnny and Don watched on, Val opened the bag and cautiously, slowly, took out the phone, handling it like it was high-grade plutonium and she was a bomb-disposal expert that wanted to make it home for her dinner that night.

'The password is... IHATEFECKINGPHONES with a four at the end,' Nancy said, before adding in Johnny's direction, 'It's ma lucky number.'

Val didn't comment as she took a week and a half to type that in, then stabbed at the screen a few more times with her thumbs, then...

'Oh Nancy!' She promptly lifted her eyes and burst into tears too.

Nancy couldn't stand it – she grabbed the phone, turned it round and... burst into tears.

Don and Johnny were wide-eyed with surprise and concern, so Val took the handset back and consulted the message again, preparing to read it to them. 'Jesus, Nancy, that text came in ages ago. Half past eight. You must have had no signal in the school. Anyway, it says... "Baby boy born at 8.17 p.m. Both mum and baby doing great. Thank you so much for today. No news yet on others. Will keep you posted. Noah."'

Nancy exhaled, took her hand off her heart, then threw her arms around Val. The two women squeezed each other, silently sharing their joy, relief, dread, fear, worry and everything else in the melting pot of emotions this moment had brought to them both. 'Och, Val, how amazing is that? I was bloody terrified there.'

'Who's Noah?' Don asked, confusion clear.

Val smiled at him as she took his hand. 'Noah Clark, Don.

Remember Gilda's boy? Don't worry, my love, it's been a long time since you've seen him. Anyway, let's get you home, you handsome big thing.'

Don beamed as Val reached up and kissed his cheek and Nancy had to swallow. They'd melt your heart, those two.

They all started walking again, their cheer now insulating them against the cool of the night.

'So, can I ask you, just so I know for any future encounters,' Johnny began.

Nancy knew from his tone that he was messing with her, but decided she liked it.

'Do you always have your phone answered like that? Or do you sometimes just pick it up and do it yourself?'

She punched his arm playfully. 'Depends if my assistant is available.' They kept on walking, as she tried to explain. 'You wouldn't believe the day we've had. It's a long story. We'd be back here for the fifty-fifth reunion by the time I was done telling you, and God knows if we'll make it to then...'

'Bloody hell, Nancy, you really need to stop with the cheery optimism,' Val teased, over her shoulder. 'Maybe stick to something more upbeat like, oh, I don't know... bunions. That's it. Tell Johnny all about yer bunions.'

She was hooting with laughter, and much as Nancy tried to purse her lips and ignore her, she crumbled into giggles in a heartbeat.

'I actually find bunions really attractive. Got a bit of a feet thing,' Johnny said solemnly.

That stopped the two women in their tracks.

'You're joking...' Nancy gasped, appalled.

Johnny kept a straight face for about three seconds, then cracked, his laughter the loudest of them all. 'Of course I am. Get to a chiropodist pronto and get the bunions sorted.'

The four of them were still chuckling when they turned into Don and Val's path. Their son, Mark, must have been watching out for them, because he opened the front door before they'd even knocked.

'What kind of time do you call this?' He feigned outrage. 'And, Val Murray, you'd better not have been smoking down behind the school sheds.'

It was like every Friday and Saturday night of Nancy and Val's teenage years, except now it was Val's son castigating them instead of whatever set of parents caught them first.

'I'll leave you all to it,' he said, laughing. 'I'm half way through a Fast and Furious movie and haven't had this much peace to watch a film since the wee one was born.'

Val hugged him, before he escaped back to their living room, then she led the way as the rest of them piled into the kitchen, a smashing big room with matt white units and a huge old oak table in the middle. The things that table had seen. It had been their meeting point for years and the laughs they'd had, the tears they'd shed, and the medicinal cups of tea they'd drank there had got them through everything they'd ever had to deal with.

Val went to her posh display unit in the corner and retrieved her best glasses, then over to the fridge for beers for the men, before finally liberating their favourite bottle of vodka from the top shelf. It was the expensive stuff, that Grey Goose, and it was Val and Nancy's secret stash, the one they kept just for the rare, lovely occasions that they managed to get a wee hour to themselves on a weekend night.

Nancy got the lemonade out of the fridge, and in a couple of minutes they were sorted. Drinks. Great company. And... Don had been over by the sideboard, and now they realised why. The sounds of 'Crocodile Rock' blasted from the speakers on the CD player on top of it. That was them away again, dancing in the kitchen, singing their hearts out as they twisted and turned.

They went through some Elton, a bit of the Beatles, and they woke up the street with a raucous accompaniment to the opening bars of Lulu's 'Shout'. Ah, it was magnificent. Bloody brilliant. The perfect end to the night.

'In the name of the holy Drifters, I'll need to sit down before I fall down,' Nancy announced, after nearly pulling a muscle belting out 'Saturday Night At The Movies'. 'I haven't moved this much since I did a sprint round Marks and Spencer on the last day of the sale.'

'Four skirts, two bras, three sets of knickers and a pulled hamstring,' Val informed the group, invading her friend's privacy, but Nancy couldn't stop laughing enough to care.

They plonked themselves back down at the table, and Val gestured to Don and Johnny, over at the sideboard talking about the other old lads they used to know.

'Look at that,' Val said, eyes glistening. 'Yesterday he didn't know what the CD player was for. And last Sunday, he didn't recognise our Mark. Yet for now it's all back. It's a bastard this thing. I've loved every minute of tonight and the thing is, when that happens, it gives you hope. Makes your heart soar. And you think… maybe he can hang on to whatever he's got tonight. But then tomorrow, it'll probably all be gone again.'

Nancy let her speak, didn't try to cajole her or to tell her it was going to be okay. She'd learned that when Peter was ill. People thought they were doing her a kindness when they said things like, 'Ah, he'll be fine – they can work miracles these days,' or 'If there's anyone who can beat this, it's Pete.' She wanted to tell them that didn't help, but she always bit her tongue because they meant well. In reality, all it did was dismiss and brush off what

Peter was feeling, what she was dealing with, the tornado the
illness had swept through their happy lives.

Val had never treated her that way. She just made her tea and
gave her time and friendship while she listened to her vent, or
rage, or laugh, or cry, or just talk.

And now, whenever she needed her, that's what Nancy did for
Val too.

Val shook off the momentary sadness, and raised her glass.
'But hey, fifty years after Eddie Mackie dry-humped Georgina
Brown in the cloakroom, we're still here and you put him right in
his place. I'll drink to that forever.'

'To dry-humping,' Nancy cheered, with a riotous cackle.

Mark had the misfortune to walk into the kitchen at exactly
that moment, although he didn't even bat an eyelid when he said,
'Please tell me I never need to hear the story behind that toast,
Aunt Nancy.'

Nancy had a twinkle in her eye as she winked. 'If you pour me
another wee vodka and lemonade, I'll make sure it never reaches
your ears.'

'Thanks, you're a saint,' Mark quipped.

'Saint Nancy of The Blessed Vodka,' Val added, smudging her
blue eyeliner as she wiped away tears of laughter.

'Nearly forgot what I came in for,' Mark said, as he handed
Nancy's handbag to her. 'You left your bag on the hall table and it
was ringing.'

Val and Nancy froze and looked at each other, both thinking
at exactly the same moment that a call at this time of night was
never good.

Val tried to rationalise it. 'It might be Tress, phoning to tell us
about the baby,' she said, her desperate hope almost palpable.

Nancy dug the phone out and checked the screen.

One missed call – Noah Clark.

One new message – Noah Clark.

A few clicks and she opened the message, and then closed her eyes as she slowly turned the phone to show Val.

Max died. Please come.

The two of them put their drinks down at the same time, both immediately snapping back to completely sober.

'Mark, son, can you stay here and look after your dad?' Val asked.

'Of course, Mum. You okay?'

Val's voice was trembling. 'Max Walker is gone and...'

For once, she couldn't find the words, so Nancy found them for her. 'Oh, that poor lass and that wee bairn.'

Mark went straight to the practicalities. 'What do you need me to do?'

'Call a taxi for us, please, son. Me and Nancy just need to get to the hospital.'

32

MAX

Max Walker.

Son of Colin and Georgina Walker.

Husband to Tress. Father to Noah Max Walker.

Time of death: 11.28 p.m.

9 February 2023.

Age 35.

R.I.P.

MIDNIGHT – 8 A.M.

33

TRESS

Tress wasn't sure how long she'd sat with him. After Max's heart had stopped, there had been a riot of people and machines and sounds and voices, and Sally had rushed back to help her move Noah outside the door, where Tress had put her hands over her baby's ears, protected him, unable to leave in case they somehow brought Max back to them.

They didn't. His brain was damaged, but it was his heart that had given up first.

They'd been allowed back into the room after hope was lost, when everyone had left, except one nurse who'd tended to Max, tenderly disconnecting machines, removing tubes, before pulling the sheet up to his neck and leaving them be.

Still Tress had refused to leave, unwilling to waste a moment that she could be with him. It was only when Sally came back again a little while later and spoke in a voice that was barely above a whisper, that she finally listened.

'Tress? I'm so sorry. I can't imagine the pain you're feeling, but I'd like to take you back over to the maternity ward and take care of you and the baby there.'

As if he'd heard the words, her son stirred, his beautiful face contorting into a frown that was backed up by a tiny yelp of acknowledgement, then immediately settled again and went back to sleep. Tress's hand hadn't left his tiny fingers since his father had passed.

Another piece of Tress's heart chipped off.

'Just two more minutes, please?' Tress whispered back to Sally, who retreated silently, leaving them alone again.

It was still impossible to comprehend where she was, and how much her life had changed in one day. She was a mum now. But no longer a wife. She knew she had to say goodbye but couldn't bear to do it. She wasn't ready. Not now. Not tomorrow. Maybe not ever.

But even as she was thinking that, her gaze fell on her son, and she felt the shift again, the one that had been slowly changing all day. Just as she knew she had to stay calm for him when she was in labour, now she knew she had to be strong for him in his life.

If only Max had felt the same.

She dismissed that thought. No. Not yet. She could fall apart later, she could rage and she could curse him for being so stupid, but she couldn't do it now. She had her son to take care of, so she had to let Max go.

Moving the sheet that covered her husband, she gently placed her hand on his shoulder. 'Max Walker,' she said softly, 'I love you with every bit of my heart. No matter what, that will never change. I will love you and so will your son. And we'll have the best life, because that's what you wanted for us, and that's what he deserves.'

Tress heard a movement behind her and turned to see Noah, his face ashen, eyes bloodshot. He came to her, knelt by her side, put his arms around her.

'I'm sorry, Tress. I'm sorry I wasn't here for you.'

Her tears merged with his as the two of them clung to each other. 'But you were. You were here. You've been here all along.'

She loosened her grip, letting him move back a little, giving him space to see his friend, to say his own goodbye. For Noah, who rested his hand on Max's, it was silent, and she understood that. They had always had that unspoken telepathy, never needed to talk everything out. This wouldn't be any different.

They sat for a few moments until Noah was done and he exhaled, took his hand away, ended his final touch.

Even in her grief, Tress could see that he looked ten years older than he did yesterday, his sadness almost visible as it oozed from every new crease in his face.

'When you're ready to go, I'll take you back over. Sally is outside too, to help us.'

Tress paused, knowing that there was something else she needed to ask him, questions to be answered before she could leave. A few more seconds would change nothing.

'How is Anya?'

Noah shrugged sadly. 'Lots of injuries, but they should heal. It'll just take time, but I think she's going to be okay.'

'Did you speak to her?'

'Yes.'

She had to ask him. She had to know, and she had to know here, because then she could leave it with Max and she could take her son and never have to talk about it again, never let its stain shadow his life.

'Were they having an affair, Noah? You said no more lies,' she added, just to remind him that she didn't want to be protected from the truth.

His pause told her the answer before his words.

'Yes. But not a serious one. They were ending it this morning.

Calling a halt because Max wanted to spend every moment with you and your son.'

'For how long?'

'I don't know. Does it matter?'

Tress shook her head. 'No.' To her, it didn't matter if it was once or for a million years. It was the same thing. It was a betrayal.

'They weren't in love, Tress. I know that doesn't make it any easier.'

'I think it might make it worse.'

Noah didn't argue. 'I know.'

They sat in silence for a few more moments, while she worked it all through the blur of her mind. When she was ready, she spoke. Not to the man beside her, but to the one in front of her.

'I forgive you, Max. If you can hear me, I want you to know that. I've always believed that my mum was up there, watching over me, taking care of me. I always thought she brought me you. I need you to know that I forgive you, so that you can watch over your boy without facing the guilt of what you've done. And I forgive you because if I don't, it'll cloud every day for the rest of my life, and he deserves so much more than that. Goodbye, my love. And thank you for our son.'

Slowly, gingerly, she stretched back and spoke to Noah.

'Okay, I'm ready to go now. Thank you for being honest with me about their affair. But, Noah...'

He was crouched down, his eyes level with hers.

'I'm leaving it here. I don't ever want to talk about it again.'

'Then we won't.'

Noah went to the door, gestured to Sally to come back in, then gave the midwife space to take the crib out first, before coming back for Tress's wheelchair.

At the door, Tress didn't look back. She'd said everything she needed to say. Maybe tomorrow she would think of more, but not now. She was done. She'd read somewhere that forgiveness wasn't something you did for other people, it was something you did for yourself to let you move on. Somehow, there was a release in that feeling. Tomorrow, or maybe next week, or perhaps next month, she would reflect and she would grieve. But she wasn't going to do it now, because right at this moment, the only person that truly mattered was the newborn babe in the crib in front of her.

They went back down in the lift, then along the service corridor into the maternity block, then into the other lift. This time, they ascended to the fourth floor, back to the ward that she'd first been admitted to when she was Tress Walker, Max Walker's wife, ready to have his child. Now she was a widow and a single mum.

Sally took her along to a room with only one bed in it. 'We thought this might be better for you, Tress, but if you'd rather be among other people, I can move you back to the main ward.'

'No, this is fine. Thank you, Sally. You've done so much...'

'Not at all. I was glad I could be here for you. For you both. I'll be back in tomorrow, so I'll pop back and see you then.'

Tress remembered that this nurse was supposed to finish her shift hours ago, and yet she hadn't. She'd stayed because she wanted to take care of them and the gratitude Tress felt caught in her throat as she spoke. 'Thank you.'

'You're so welcome.' Sally hugged her, then cast a tender glance at the baby, before saying goodbye to Noah.

Just as she left, another nurse popped her head in the door. 'Hello, Dr Clark. Mrs Walker.'

The name jolted her, and Tress wanted to correct her. She wasn't Mrs Walker any more. That was yesterday. 'Please call me Tress,' she said, in as friendly a tone as she could manage.

'I will,' the nurse agreed. 'And I'm Sita. Has the baby latched on and fed yet?'

'Yes, earlier. He's been sleeping ever since. Should I wake him?'

Sita popped over to the crib and smiled as she checked out her newest patient. 'No, not at all, but when he wakes, I'll help lift him over to you. Are you sore? Do you need pain medication?'

Tress had a jolt of realisation. This was what if felt like to be a new mum. This was normal. To this lovely nurse, she wasn't the wife who was trying to find her husband, or the widow whose husband had just died. She was just the woman who had given birth a few hours ago. She was a new mum. That was it. That was her title. And that little bit of normality was like a tiny flower pushing through the mud of the pain that had ravaged her today. 'No, thank you. I'm fine.'

'And what about something to eat? Sally said you didn't have anything in the labour suite. How about some tea and toast?'

It was the simplest thing, the very basic of care. Food. Drink. Yet to Tress it was so much more than that. It was someone else caring for her at the end of a day that had come close to breaking her. Since the baby was born, she hadn't given a thought to her own body, to the pain, or to what it needed to get through the coming hours and days, but other people were here and they wanted to help her. Her whole life, she'd been independent, strong, capable of looking after herself, but now she was going to let other people care for her.

'I'd appreciate that very much.'

'No problem. I'll be right back with them. Final question, I promise. Would you like me to help you get into bed?'

Tress glanced up at Noah, and a silent conversation passed between them.

'Thanks, Sita, but I can do that,' he told her, reading Tress's mind perfectly.

When the door closed behind the nurse, Tress began to put her weight on the arms of the wheelchair, and Noah scooped his arm under hers to support her. Now she was registering twinges of pain from the birth, but nothing she couldn't handle.

Noah pulled back the sheet, then let her shift her body on to the mattress, before covering her back up again.

'Noah, I feel like no matter how many times I've said thank you to you today, it will never be enough.'

He pushed the chair out of the way. 'No, it'll always be too many. There's no need, Tress. I'm just so relieved that you're not upset with me for lying. I hope I did the right thing.'

His earnest expression told her he'd been worrying about that, and yet another piece chipped off her heart. Other than their son, this friend was the kindest gift her husband had ever given her. 'You did the right thing, I promise. I know you did it to protect me and this little boy. I'm just so sorry, because it must have been excruciating.'

Stretching over, he checked on the baby, then sat on the pale blue chair next to her bed.

She reached for his hand. 'Noah, I'm fine. And I mean this from a place of love and gratitude for everything you've done today, but you can go. Go back to Anya and take care of her. If I need anything, Sita has got my back.'

'No, I'd rather stay h—'

Another knock at the door, then a waft of perfume and two faces full of love and concern and worry filled the doorway, both speechless for the first moment since the beginning of time.

Tress filled the silence, mustering all her strength to smile. 'Hello, ladies. I think this little guy would like to meet his aunties.'

34

NOAH

'You awright down there, pal?

Noah raised his head and saw a guy, maybe in his twenties, eyeing him with curiosity as he swayed in front of him. Noah got the picture straight away. Black eye, swollen shut. Dressing over a wound on his head. Shirt ripped and jeans caked in mud. When he was a junior doctor, he'd done a rotation and countless bank shifts on A&E and he knew that this was just a Thursday night evictee, probably brought in after a fight in the city centre, checked over, patched up and sent on his way. And he didn't seem to be in the least perturbed by any of it.

'I'm fine, mate, but cheers for asking.'

'Aye, no bother.' Then, obviously thinking his altruism had bought him some karmic credit, he added, 'Don't suppose you've got a fag, have ye?'

Despite the absolute clusterfuck shitshow of the day, Noah couldn't help but give a rueful smile at the ridiculousness of the moment. 'Don't smoke. Those things will kill you.'

He could see that Rocky Balboa was about to get arsy, so he

salvaged the situation by pulling a tenner out of the pocket of his scrubs and offering it over.

One battered man now flipped straight from arsy to elated. 'Ya dancer. Cheers, pal. No' a bad night's work,' Rocky quipped before whistling off down the road.

It didn't escape Noah that he must appear to be such a shambles that a mangled, battered drunk had checked on him. If he were being objective, he could see there were red flags. He was sitting on the ground, leaning against the outside wall of the A&E block. Rumpled scrubs. His head on his knees. One of his shoes was off, because it had escaped him, flown off when he was kicking the shit out of the wheelie bin in the alley beside the building. He'd booted it with everything he had, roaring at some refuse injustice, time and time again until the exertion was too much, and he'd dropped to the ground, exhausted, desperate to catch his breath.

He had no idea how long he'd been there. He just knew that it wasn't yet long enough. He needed air. Needed time to think. To process what had happened today.

Max was dead. His closest friend for a lifetime.

If someone had told him yesterday that this was coming, he'd have fallen apart, devastated, inconsolable.

If someone told him yesterday that his wife would come close to dying, he'd have stopped her driving, held her close to him, protected her with every bone in his body, taken the impact of the blow to save her.

If someone had told him yesterday that he'd discover his wife was having an affair, the knowledge of that would have slayed him. And he had no idea how he would have reacted because it was such an outlandish thought to him. Not Anya. Absolutely not Anya. And yet... yes. Anya.

The same Anya had screamed when she'd heard that her

lover was dead, roared so loudly that two nurses and Dr Campbell had raced to her. They'd tried to persuade her to take a sedative, but she'd refused, almost as if she needed to inflict the pain of this on herself. Noah had held her, shushed her, let her cry until there were no more tears and she found her voice again. 'You need to go see him. Help Tress,' she had implored. It had taken all the magnanimity he possessed not to say that he wished she'd thought about Tress before now. But no. Still not the time for recriminations. Instead, he'd left her with Richard, and did as she asked. He'd gone to Tress and the baby and he'd stayed with them until Val and Nancy had arrived. Then he'd come outside and assaulted a wheelie bin, raging at the world.

Now, exhausted, all he could feel was... nothing. The anger that had consumed him earlier had left him and all he could see was the futility of it all. The absolute pointlessness of a life that was lost for all the wrong reasons. Of the two marriages broken in the wreckage of that car.

There was nowhere he wanted to go right now. Not home. Not back inside. He knew Tress had to have that time with Val and Nancy. She needed to detach from looking at the face of the man whose wife had slept with her husband. He wondered if she'd ever manage to look at him without feeling that pain and he wouldn't blame her if she didn't, or if she pulled away from him, no longer able to bear the association with the most devastating day of her life.

His family aside, had he just lost everything and everyone else that he loved?

He inhaled the cold night air into his lungs and saw that he was shivering. He hadn't even felt it until that moment, but it forced him to stand, to make a move, to retrieve his shoe from a puddle at the side of the skip.

Anya. It was the only place he could go.

He stopped at the nursing station in her ward, and saw that a different nurse was on duty, one that he knew well. June had been there since he had started his training, had covered for his mistakes when he was working on her ward, and encouraged him to keep going, all the while throwing cheek in his direction. She was a rough, tough, endlessly entertaining protector to every junior nurse and doctor that came through here and he'd never been so glad to see her.

'I heard what happened. How are you holding up, son?'

'How do I look?' he asked wearily.

'Like you've been kicking the shit out of the bins out the back. I heard about that too. It's all over the canteen, just so you know. Och, I'm heart bloody sore for you, Noah. I'd hug you, but I've got a horrible feeling that would make you cry and I'm shite with the emotional stuff.'

They both knew that wasn't true, that this was her way of connecting, of letting him know she was there for him.

'How's Anya?'

June tried to hide it, but the flinch of disapproval that twisted the smoking lines around her mouth and made her purse her lips for just a split second gave it away.

'She was awake when I last checked about fifteen minutes ago. When I came on shift she was still distraught, after the news about your... friend, but she's calmer now.' The pursed lips made another fleeting appearance. 'She's still refusing to take a sedative. Said she wanted to be awake when you came back. I'm glad you did.'

He caught the inference. June might not have come back to see a cheating spouse and wouldn't have judged him if he'd made the same choice.

'Thanks, June. I am too.' He gave her a grateful smile, then crossed to Anya's door, paused, inhaled, steeled himself to do this.

There was only a dim light in the console behind Anya's bed, but she was sitting up, staring at the door, as if she hadn't moved since he'd left.

No hellos. No platitudes. Before he could utter a sound, she blurted, 'He's really dead?'

Keeping his voice steady and soft, he told her what she needed to know. 'He is.'

Her tears were silent, raining down from her bruised, swollen eyes onto her hospital gown.

'Oh, God, Noah. What have I done?'

Noah felt a flash of anger. Why was she absolving Max, taking sole responsibility for his behaviour, for his crimes? It was as if he still had some kind of hold over her, and that threatened to sweep away all the calm that he'd managed to fight for when he was outside.

'It wasn't just you.'

She lifted her face to meet his eyes. 'I know that. But in all the years that we knew him, Max was faithful to no one, not even Tress, and he loved her so much. Yet, he still betrayed her. I think that's just who he was, and I don't know if he was ever better than that. But I was. I'm not that person.' She caught the irony of what she'd just said. 'Although... now I guess we both know that I am that person.'

His emotions were all over the place, swinging from anger, to fear, to sorrow, to love. The pain that was in every word that she spoke made him want to go to her, to hold her, to tell her that he'd fix this.

'I know I've got no right to ask this, but how is Tress?'

'Heartbroken. Sad. Confused. Devastated. She's with the baby and Val and Nancy are there too, so they're taking care of her.'

She closed her eyes, spoke almost to herself. 'And they'll hate me too.'

He didn't argue. 'Your parents are on the way. They'll be here in the morning.'

'Have you told them?'

'About why you were there? And who you were with? No. And I won't. That's up to you, Anya. Look...' he began, as he moved from the end of her bed round to the side. 'I'm not your enemy here. I've got no idea where we go or how we move on from this, but I'll never be the person who tries to punish you for what's happened. I just need to know why. Were we not enough?'

Her eyes closed, and he waited in silence until she opened them again, ready to speak.

'Max used to say we were skydiving,' she began, nothing but sorrow in her words.

'Skydiving?' Noah didn't understand.

'Yes. That up there, in the plane, there was just excitement and thrilling anticipation and the adrenaline rush of the danger that was about to come. And on the ground, there was the relief and gratitude of knowing you were safe, that you'd made it, that everything was the way it was supposed to be. And him and I... we were the middle. We were the dive. The short, crazy moments of excitement that gave you a high and made you feel invincible, like you were amazing, that you could do anything. You and Tress, you were our ground, our sure thing that we could count on, our safety, and I never took that for granted, Noah. What I did with Max... it wasn't love, I swear. The problem was, the thrill of the dive was addictive. And every time we landed, I'd feel that safety with you for a while, but then—'

'Why couldn't you have found that high with me? Why couldn't you tell me you needed something more than what we had?'

Her eyes locked on his. 'Because I didn't know until it

happened that first time and then it was too late. I was in. Addicted.'

Anger, guilt, self-recrimination, devastation – a maelstrom of desperate emotions fought for supremacy. He settled on hopelessness. 'I had no idea. I thought we had everything we needed. Maybe if I'd paid more attention—'

'No!' she cut him dead. 'None of this is on you, Noah. It's all on me. This was my midlife crisis, my rebellion against normality. We'd been together for fifteen years, since the day I started university, and I wouldn't trade a single day, because I was happy. But you wanted to start our family, like we'd agreed, and I was panicking because I didn't think I was ready. And I love my job, but it's so demanding and I felt so much pressure to make sure I was brilliant at it. I know that these sound like excuses, but I'm just trying to explain where my mind was. My whole life had been safe and my future has been mapped out since we met: great job, a husband I adored, children that I would love, the end. And that sounds perfect – it *was* perfect – but a while ago I realised that I'd never taken a risk in my life, never touched the fire just for the thrill of it. Max was the thrill. And I was ready to say goodbye to it. We both were. We really thought we could just return to our lives, that no one would ever know. No harm done.'

Was it crazy that so many things she was saying made sense? He understood now why she'd pushed back against starting a family, why she was still challenging herself in her job. She wasn't ready to settle down to the life that was all planned out in front of her. Maybe he should have tried to understand instead of pushing her, but how could he have known that when, until this morning, she'd never actually said that she wanted anything different? Even as he was thinking that though, another part of his brain was throwing up arguments. Why couldn't she have told him? Why do something that could wreck their marriage? Why not work through it together? Why choose to hurt him? Why Max? And since when?

'How long were you seeing him?'

Tress had asked him that earlier and he'd had no answer. Now, he had to know, but he could see from her crestfallen expression and the new tears that she didn't want to tell him. Somewhere in his soul, the blood froze and sent a violent chill around his body.

'Don't ask me, Noah,' she begged.

He shrugged. 'I already did.'

Her lids closed, as if she couldn't watch his reaction. 'Since my first day at Bralatech.'

Holy. Fuck. He tried to calculate that shocking sum in his head.

'Since before he met Tress? What the fuck was wrong with you?'

As soon as he'd said it, he caught his breath and clamped his mouth shut, reminding himself that this wasn't the time. Today was the day she'd died in that ambulance. He wasn't going to be responsible for stopping her heart a second time, even if she'd split his in two.

There was silence. A long, empty void.

'I can't expect you to understand, I know that. But what we were doing had nothing to do with you or Tress. Max loved her. Wanted to spend the rest of his life with her. We talked about ending it when he met her, but it kept coming back to the way we thought about it. A thrill. A wild ride. Nothing that was ever supposed to interfere with our lives at home.'

Something was bugging him. 'So why stop now then? You said you were calling it off this morning?'

'The baby. That was his new thrill, his new all-consuming obsession. He didn't need me any more and in some ways that was almost a relief. You don't need to believe me, but over the last few months the guilt has been killing me.'

The cloud of dejection around her was almost making him feel sorry for her. This was his wife. The woman he adored. She was part of him. Until this morning, she'd been his world. What was he supposed to do with this? How was he supposed to react?

'Noah...' she interrupted his internal struggle. 'I know I've got no right to say this, but I asked you earlier if you could ever see a time when you could forgive me and you didn't answer.'

He dropped his head, the question echoing in his brain, and thought about Tress, about the things she'd said to Max about leaving the pain with him because if she hung on to it, then it would continue to hurt her, to steal her life from her. Maybe he could find a way to do that too, to take Anya home but to leave the pain here, in this room, and close the door behind it.

Anya wasn't Max. At her core, she was a good person, someone who cared and who loved and who had never hurt anyone, until now. Was he just meant to cut her off, to judge her on one huge mistake? Was that what love was?

'I don't know, Anya. Maybe not today or tomorrow, but I'll try to forgive you. I just don't know if you'll ever be able to forgive yourself.'

35

NANCY

It was the daylight beaming through the crack in the blinds that woke Nancy. That and the feeling that someone had taken a baseball bat to her bones in the middle of the night. She stretched up, trying to get her spine to realign into something approaching a straight line and groaned as the aches gave her a resounding V-sign and told her she deserved it for sleeping in a chair that was probably an instrument of torture in medieval times. Not that she would rather have been anywhere else but here last night.

She managed to wedge one eye open and saw that Val was still in the identical chair at the other side of the bed. That lovely nurse, Sita, had found the extra chair for them when it became clear that they weren't going anywhere. Nancy had a feeling that having two visitors kipping overnight on the maternity ward was against a few hospital policies, but it seemed that half the hospital had an affection for Noah Clark, and he'd managed to pull the strings to make it happen. It was just as well, really. Val had been making murmurs about chaining herself to the sink if they tried to budge her.

The baby stirred and Nancy slipped her finger into the palm

of his balled-up hand, then watched him for a few moments as he wriggled, then settled again. He'd been up a couple of times during the night, but Tress had managed to feed him, and he'd dozed off again, no bother.

'You okay there, Nancy?' Val whispered, startling her.

Nancy nodded, trying to work out how to get her finger back out of the boy's clenched fist without waking him. She was going to have to have a lot more practice at this baby stuff, but she was up for the challenge. Since the moment she'd set eyes on this beautiful wee soul, she'd felt a responsibility, a love, a real longing to help take care of him whenever and wherever Tress needed her. This was as close to having a little one to love as she'd ever been, and she was ready to be whatever Tress and her boy needed her to be.

Eventually, gradually, she seamlessly retrieved her finger, and sat back up straight, earning another round of complaints from the muscles in her back. She was going to need a week with a chiropractor after this.

Nancy kept her voice down, so as not to wake a sleeping Tress. 'Ma bones are aching, Val. I'm telling myself it's the chairs, but I think it might have more to do with doing the Locomotion after three vodkas last night. If you hear of any hip replacements going, can you give me a shout.'

'No chance. I'll be keeping that for myself.' Val pushed herself up, shook off the cobwebs. 'Did I miss anything last night? Tress had drifted off before I fell asleep. That must have been about 3 o'clock. What time is it now?'

Nancy glanced up at the clock. 'Just after seven.'

'Bugger, I'd better check my phone.'

Nancy could see the flash of panic in her pal's eyes, and she understood it. She'd cared for Don, day in and day out, for years now, and it wouldn't be easy to just cut off that worry for his wellbeing, even though she knew Mark had stayed over and was perfectly capable of taking care of Don by himself.

Val pulled her phone out of her bag and went through the usual palaver of seven presses, three frowns, a 'bloody hell' and a 'bollocks', before she finally got to where she was going. 'It's a text from Mark,' she announced.

'Everything okay?' Nancy asked, praying that nothing had gone wrong on the one night that Val hadn't been home. If it had, Nancy knew she would never leave Don's side again for the rest of their lives.

Val's shoulders relaxed a little. 'Aye, it's all fine. He says his dad is still in bed because he stayed up till 3 a.m. playing cards with Johnny. Is that not brilliant?' Val beamed. 'What a lovely man that is.' She went back to reading the text. 'And wait till you hear this. Mark says Johnny stayed the night too, because he wanted to see how you were when you got back.'

Val finished that with a wink and a grin, and Nancy responded with her very best frown of derision. Although... She wasn't going to admit it out loud, but there had been a couple of times last night that she'd found herself with another wee flurry of butterflies in the stomach when Johnny was talking to her. Not Eddie Mackie butterflies. Those ones all died of smarm intoxication. No, these were real life, in the flesh, loving his chat, enjoying his company, butterflies.

In the early hours of this morning, when she'd been the only one still awake, she'd got to thinking how maybe it wasn't a coincidence that he was there and that they hit it off. Him and Peter had been pals for years and they'd always had each other's backs. Maybe this was Peter asking his friend to step in for him one last time. And if that's what it was, she was grateful, because whether she ever saw Johnny again or not, last night had reminded her what it felt like to live again, to go out there and be bold and take a chance. If that's what Peter was trying to tell her, she'd heard him loud and clear.

Over on the bed, Tress stirred. Nancy and Val glanced at each other, and Nancy knew that they were both thinking the same thing. What had happened to that poor woman yesterday had been the stuff of nightmares.

When they'd first arrived, Tress had talked them through everything, telling them exactly what had happened, right up to the point where she'd said goodbye to her husband and told him she was leaving his sins with him. The serenity and strength in that lassie had been incredible, but a few times, she'd succumbed to the pain, and Val and Nancy had held her, tried to take that pain for her. They'd tried to lift her up when the grief crushed her, and then they'd listened in admiration as she told them how she was going to move on from here.

'I'm only telling you everything because I need you to understand what we went through, but I won't be sharing this story again with anyone,' she'd said, her eyes fixed on the face of the child lying in the crib by her side.

'Sometimes it's good to talk, though,' Val had said gently, 'And you know we're always here to listen.'

The baby must have heard that, because he chose that moment to wake up for a feed. With some help from Val, who had breastfed both her two, Tress had managed it.

When they'd eventually fallen asleep, it was still dark, and now it was almost daylight and Tress was about to start a brand new day, the first morning of her life as a mother. It broke Nancy's heart that it was Tress's first morning as a widow too.

In the bed, Tress pushed herself upright, frowning.

'It really happened? Max is...' She cut herself off, refusing or unable to say the word. Instead, her gaze settled on her baby, eyes swimming with new unshed tears. 'He's here. And you are too. Thanks for staying.'

'We wouldn't be anywhere else,' Nancy reassured her.

Just at that, the door opened and Noah came in, holding a cardboard tray with four coffees. Tress had said time and time again last night that she wanted a happy environment for every day of her boy's life, so, of course, Nancy went right in with both feet.

'Noah, I swear I'm going to take you home and keep you there,' she quipped, then immediately second-guessed herself. What was she like? A time like this and there she was making daft jokes. 'Val, tape my gob up,' she mumbled to her chum, who just shook her head in resignation. 'Don't have a roll of tape big enough, doll.'

It was a slight consolation that Val was just as bad on the foot and mouth, bad joke front. It was clearly a generational flaw. Something to do with the water in the seventies.

Noah dished out the coffees, then checked in on the sleeping baby. 'How has this wee one been?'

'Perfect,' Val told him. 'How are you doing, son?'

'I'm okay.' Noah definitely looked better than he did the night before. He'd obviously showered and put on a fresh set of scrubs, although his eyes were still red-rimmed and bloodshot. Nancy's heart ached for him. She wanted to ask him how Anya was, but for once she bit her tongue, in case the question upset Tress. What was the done thing here? There were layers of complications in this situation that she couldn't even begin to navigate. So many questions. How would Tress deal with Anya? How would Noah feel about his wife now? Would he end up stuck in the middle of turmoil between his dead friend's wife and his own wife if he forgave her adultery? Or had too much happened for there to be any going back for any of them? Nancy's head was sore just thinking about it. And that was before they even began to factor in the whispers and the gossip and the rumours that would fly around the village like a bonfire night rocket. Well, she decided, her and Val would shut those down pronto and no one would dare cross them, not if they didn't want their own muck exposed. Nancy Jenkins knew everything about everyone in that village and she wasn't afraid to use it if anyone caused so much as a glimmer of pain to this lass.

'Noah, how is Anya?' For a horrible second, Nancy worried that she'd spat that out, unable to keep her gob under control, but no, it was Tress. And in this situation, Nancy decided, Tress was a better woman than her for caring how her husband's mistress was.

'She's as good as she can be,' Noah reported. 'Physically, she'll heal. The pain meds are helping. But mentally... To be honest, she's devastated about what she's done and everything that it's caused. I know people will say she deserves that, so I'm not asking for sympathy for her, just telling you how she is. Her parents will be arriving soon, so I think that will help. They're a good family and they'll be a support to her. I think she'll need it.'

'How do you feel about it?' Tress asked him.

'Numb. Confused. Changes by the minute. My head is all over the place, so I don't want to make any decisions about the future...' They all had a fair idea what he meant by that. 'I'm just trying to do practical stuff to keep it together. Tress, there's a few things I need to talk to you about, is that okay?'

'Go on,' she said, giving him permission, her hand over the side of the baby's crib now, resting lightly on her son's back. Nancy had the feeling this babe was going to be her source of strength and her comfort blanket in the days to come.

'Max's parents are arriving later today and there will be decisions that need to be made about his... funeral.'

Tress closed her eyes, shuddered.

'I can deal with all of that if you want me to?' he offered.

The gratitude on Tress's face was palpable. 'Are you sure, Noah?'

'Of course.'

Gilda Clark's door was definitely getting knocked, Nancy reminded herself, because this man was a credit to her.

'Okay...' He took a deep breath, struggling with the words. 'I'm going to pick them up at the airport – no matter what, their son has died, so I want to take care of them. I know they'll ask me questions, so I need to know what you want me to tell them. About Max. About Anya. About the baby. About everything.'

Christ, this was like a knife through the heart. The horrors that this young pair were dealing with.

Nancy watched as Tress processed the question, thought through the answer, all the while staring at her son.

'Tell them that their son was a good man. That he was in a car accident with our friend. Tell them nothing of the affair. They don't need to know that. Then tell them they have a beautiful grandson that would love to meet them.'

'Are you sure?'

'I'm sure. My child is short on family. If they want to be a part of his life, and to love him, then I'll take it.'

The three of them pondered that for a minute, before Nancy couldn't hold her tongue any longer.

'Tress, that wee one is lucky to have you. And you know that Val and I... well, you can feel free to tell us to bugger off if we're too much...'

'That's been said about us once or twice before,' Val conceded, making Tress smile.

'But we're here for you. And for the wee one. And for you too, Noah. For as long as you'll have us.'

Tress's eyes grew misty again. 'You know, I grew up with a single mum and she wasn't perfect, but she made me feel loved every single day. Her life wasn't easy, but she never gave up and her friends were a big part of that. Then I look at everything you two have been through and you're still standing and that makes me think I can do it. I can't speak for Noah, but if there's a space for me and my boy at your kitchen tables, then we'd like to accept, as often as you'll have us.'

The room was bathed in light now and it felt like something new. A new future. A new family. A new baby. A new someone to love.

'Today and every day, ma darlin',' Nancy told her, the emotion, the sadness, the happiness, the gratitude, catching in her throat. 'Today and every day.'

EPILOGUE
EIGHT MONTHS LATER

The queues at Glasgow Airport were long, but the ones for October holiday destinations were the worst. Noah pulled the wheeled suitcase to the line for the flight to London Heathrow and saw that there were only a dozen or so people in front of them.

'No second thoughts?' he asked the woman by his side.

With tenderness, Anya shook her head. 'No second thoughts.'

They'd tried to fathom a way ahead for their marriage, but when they were finally sure about how they felt, they'd both realised that there was no going back for either of them. There was no trust and there were too many shadows. Every time he felt the aching chasm left by the death of his best friend, it would come with pain, then anger, followed right up by the sting of betrayal. And every time he felt the aching chasm in his marriage, the same sequence of emotions would play out.

There was no getting away from the total devastation that their selfishness had caused in his life, in Tress's, and in the baby's world too. That little boy was only ten days old when his mum had cradled him close to her at his father's funeral. It had been a private ceremony. Just Tress, Max's parents, Noah's immediate family and, of course, Nancy and Val too. Anya had still been in hospital, so that had avoided a difficult decision for them all. Remarkably, the rumour mill in the hospital and the village had never really got going. All anyone really knew was that Max and Anya had worked together and had been in a crash while racing back for the birth of Max's baby. The sympathy had quashed any inkling of gossip before it even started.

The effects closer to home were so much more difficult to navigate, though.

On a good day, Noah had stuck by his vow to try to forgive Anya, but on a bad day, the resentments were still there. And one of the worst aspects of that was watching her suffer too. Her physical injuries had healed, leaving only some small scars on one side of her face that were easily covered by her hair, now that she'd grown it out longer. But in the weeks and months after the crash, her mental scars had refused to heal. The guilt ate at her, the shame consumed her. Everywhere she went there was a reminder of Max, of Tress, of Noah, of the times they'd shared as two couples and four inseparable friends.

The final straw had been when she'd quit her job, too tired of the looks she got when she entered a room. While the Weirbridge and Glasgow Central Hospital rumour mills had remained relatively silent, the Bralatech scandal drums had battered out a steady beat. Only a month after returning to work in April, she'd resigned, too mortified by the rumours that had spread about her and Max. Secretaries gossiped. Both their partners had called that day looking for them. Both of them had been on a day off that their partners didn't know about. They were in a car crash together. It didn't take a genius to come to the obvious conclusion.

The distance between their separate rooms had spread to separate lives. For the first couple of months, Anya had locked herself away and Noah had worked round the clock, and when he wasn't at the hospital, he was with Tress and the baby, delivering on his promise to be the best uncle he could be. It wasn't hard. The love he felt for this tiny person was huge and there was nowhere he'd rather be than lying on Tress's couch, with the wee guy on his chest, while they watched a movie, sang songs, chatted...

That became his happy place. Anywhere but home.

In June, Anya had moved out, telling him that they needed some separation if they were ever going to have a chance to start afresh. Deep inside, Noah was pretty sure they both knew she wouldn't return. 'Live your own life, no rules, no conditions,' she'd told him. 'And I'll do the same. Let's see where we are when I get back.'

She'd gone to stay with her mum's sister in St Andrews and their contact had dwindled until she'd called him one morning in early August.

'There's no way to fix this for either of us, is there, Noah?' she'd asked, the sadness in her voice telling him she already knew the answer. And so did he. In another world, a one-night stand might have been forgivable. Maybe even a brief fling. But this was so much more. He couldn't imagine ever laughing with her again. Couldn't even think what it would be like to make love to her, knowing the last person she slept with could have been Max. Couldn't rid himself of the trauma of that first sight of them, half dead, hanging in that car.

'No, I don't think so,' he'd told her honestly.

Later that day, she'd called again to say she'd spoken to her parents. She'd told them the whole truth and they had urged her to move back to the USA, to build a life without the constant reminders.

Over the next few weeks, they'd filed for divorce: no recriminations, no squabbles, just a sad but inevitable goodbye. She'd arranged for her Scottish life to be shipped to the USA ahead of her, and now she was leaving. He'd volunteered to bring her to the airport and the timing had been perfect because...

'Noah, that's us.' Anya nudged him in the ribs.

He'd been so lost in his thoughts that he hadn't realised that they'd shuffled to the front of the queue.

'Where is your final destination, madam?'

'New York.'

Anya was going home. She was going to live with her parents until she found a new job that inspired her. Fresh start. New life. With lessons learned. That predictable life that she'd thought was in front of her, now burnt to the ground by the flames from the crash.

It was time. And it was the right thing for them both.

The guy behind the check-in desk took her passport, checked in her luggage, then handed the passport and boarding card over.

Noah folded his arms around her, holding her tight for one last time.

'You go have an extraordinary life, Noah Clark,' she whispered into his ear. 'Because you will always be the very best person I've ever known.'

'I will. And you be happy, Anya. Wherever that takes you.'

Goodbyes said, they both pulled back, wiping tears from their faces.

Anya took the handle of her carry-on case and nodded to a place further along the terminal. 'You'd better go. They're waiting for you.'

And with that, she was gone.

Noah waited until she was out of sight, then headed to the people who were waiting for him. Val and Don. Nancy and Johnny. Tress and her son. And the doctor who had volunteered to come along for the ride, to help Val take care of Don. It was pure coincidence that Anya had booked her flight for the same day that baby Noah's big, extended, chaotic family were leaving for a two-week holiday to Paphos. While they were there, Max's parents had promised to make the journey from nearby Limassol to visit them, and Noah hoped they'd make good on that.

'Noah Clark, will you move that gorgeous body of yours a bit faster please?'

Nancy Jenkins was in no mood to be kept waiting. There was a bar upstairs, and a whole lot of shops, so there was a glass of sangria and a new pair of sunspecs waiting for her. And Johnny Roberts was going to be by her side the whole time. Not that he'd left it very often in the last eight months. When she'd got home from the hospital the day after the crash, he'd been there and she'd remembered how lovely it was to share your life with someone who cared.

At first, it was a friendship, but they'd been kidding themselves. Two weeks after they'd met, he'd kissed her for the first time and they'd slow-danced in her garden to the sounds of 'You To Me Are Everything' by The Real Thing. Over the next few weeks, she'd met his family and seen how much he was loved. He was a good man, Johnny Roberts. And she knew that Peter Jenkins would approve.

'Nancy! For the love of all that is holy, would you snap out of it. You've slipped into yer own wee trance there and we need to get moving if I'm going to get ma lip balm out of Boots. It's that coconut one. Makes me feel all exotic.'

'Eh, who put you in charge, Val Murray? You know, you're getting even bossier in your old age. If I decide to form an army and invade the hotel pool to get rid of all those bastards that put their towels on deckchairs at six in the morning, I'm putting you in charge.'

'I'd sort that lot out before breakfast. Literally.' Val's chuckles were contagious and Nancy felt her heart swell as she watched Val and Don share the joke. There was no denying that, on the whole, his condition was getting worse. The seesaw of good days and bad days was tipping down at the side that made Val fret. But having Johnny around was a big help. For some reason, and it was a mystery to them all, Don still saw Johnny as his pal from his teenage years in Weirbridge and related to him like they'd never been apart. It was a sweet reprieve for Val, and it gave her some time back. And for that they were grateful.

'Nancy, if my boy's first word is the swear one that you just used, I'll be round at your house with an official complaint,' Tress quipped, grinning. 'Honestly, I'm going to have to buy him a set of headphones to block you two out. You're meant to be a good influence, not have him swearing and drinking vodka and lemonade before he goes to school.' Tress leant down and put her hands into the pram. 'Cover your ears, son. I've no idea who those people are, but I'll ditch them before you can talk.'

Tress knew that they were all well aware that she was joking. Val and Nancy had become the mothers she no longer had, the grandmothers her son would cherish and the friends she could always count on. Especially in the beginning. There were some days that she didn't want to get out of bed, that she thought the pain would crush her. She would never understand why Max did what he did, but when Noah gave him Anya's explanation, ridiculous as it was, the whole skydiving analogy at least let her believe that it wasn't about love. In a weird way, that helped restore the faith she'd lost in her own judgement. How could she have loved a man who was cheating? How could she not have seen that? The truth was, no-one with a trusting heart would have seen it. Not her. Not Noah. It had taken her a while to accept that, but she'd got there, with the help of the incredible care and support that Noah had given her every single day.

Many other things had helped too. They'd never been great parents to Max, but his mum and dad had actually stepped up when it came to their grandson. They'd been back twice since the funeral to visit baby Noah and this holiday had been their idea. Max's dad had also taken care of all the paperwork and insurance policies and it had been a huge relief to discover that Max's company provided life insurance, enough that she was able to pay off their mortgage, set aside funds for Noah's future, and in the meantime, she had enough to live a comfortable life until she was ready to go back to work. In fact, as financial director, the life insurance perk had been one that Max had set up for all the employees, proof that he could be thoughtful when he really tried.

But, of course, the greatest source of strength and solace over the last eight months, the reason she had clawed her way out of the depths of devastation that Max had caused, had been her son, Noah.

He was Max's double. Fair hair. Green eyes. With a crazy sense of adventure that already had him crawling around like a puppy doing zoomies. He laughed easily, rarely cried, and loved nothing more than to snuggle into his mama. She adored every second of being his mum and no matter how low Tress fell, that picked her up every time.

He'd been a tonic for Val and Nancy too, but those women had brought so much more than just love for her son to Tress's life. Her friends had helped her see that even after the worst had happened, there could still be happiness. Val's face still lit up when Don walked into a room. Nancy and Johnny were like teenagers in love. And Noah... well, he was slowly but surely coming round to the thought of a new relationship too.

Doctor Cheska Ayton had entered all their lives and changed them for the better. She'd become the friend that Tress treasured, a dancing partner for Nancy when Johnny's knees were playing up, and it was nothing short of miraculous that she was balancing her role in A&E with a research project on the treatment of dementia. That expertise had made her an invaluable support for Val, and she'd come along on this holiday to share the load. At least, that was part of the reason. The other was that she was utterly and totally besotted with Noah Clark and had been since they'd trained together. Not that they'd acted on it yet, though. They'd both shared their feelings with each other, but they'd agreed to wait, because Noah Clark was too much of a good guy to start a new relationship while his wife was still in this country. Tress wholeheartedly approved, because she wanted everyone to have that all-consuming, glorious love that she felt every time she looked at the new male in her life.

Her son, Noah Walker. The love of her life. And yes, she'd kept his name.

At first, Noah had feared that giving the baby his moniker would forever associate him with the accident in Tress's mind. It didn't. Having Noah as his name only conjured up thoughts of kindness, of love, of loyalty and of the goodness of a man who'd become like a brother to her.

It was his original middle name that she'd dropped. There was no longer a 'Max' in there. Max would always be his father, but she wasn't giving her son the name of someone who had jeopardised their happiness. And if that was harsh, it came nowhere close to what Max had done, so she felt no remorse.

'Right, troops, are we ready?'

Nancy led the way, charging on like a speed walker, for the others to follow.

They were quite a sight. Two older couples, two younger women, one man and a baby, and only two of them linked by genetics. It was an unusual family, but it was the one that they'd picked for themselves. And not one of them would have it any other way.

MORE FROM SHARI LOW

We hope you enjoyed reading *One Day With You*. If you did, please leave a review.

If you'd like to gift a copy, this book is also available as an ebook, digital audio download and audiobook CD.

Sign up to Shari Low's mailing list for news, competitions and updates on future books.

http://bit.ly/ShariLowNewsletter

Explore more from Shari Low.

ABOUT THE AUTHOR

Shari Low is the #1 bestselling author of over 20 novels, including *My One Month Marriage* and *One Day In Summer,* and a collection of parenthood memories called *Because Mummy Said So.* She lives near Glasgow.

Visit Shari's website: www.sharilow.com

Follow Shari on social media:

f facebook.com/sharilowbooks

y twitter.com/sharilow

instagram.com/sharilowbooks

BB bookbub.com/authors/shari-low

Boldwood

Boldwood Books is an award-winning fiction
publishing company seeking out the best
stories from around the world.

Find out more at www.boldwoodbooks.com

Join our reader community for brilliant books,
competitions and offers!

Follow us

@BoldwoodBooks

@BookandTonic

Sign up to our weekly
deals newsletter

https://bit.ly/BoldwoodBNewsletter

Made in the USA
Middletown, DE
02 July 2024

56767128R00172